MULTICULTURAL COMMUNICATION and POPULAR CULTURE

Racial and Ethnic Images in Star Trek

Marquita L. Byrd

San Jose State University

To My Best Friend For Life!!!
Love Marquita
1998

The McGraw-Hill Companies, Inc.
Primis Custom Publishing

New York St. Louis San Francisco Auckland Bogotá Caracas Lisbon London Madrid Mexico Milan Montreal New Delhi Paris San Juan Singapore Sydney Tokyo Toronto

McGraw-Hill

A Division of The McGraw-Hill Companies

MULTICULTURAL COMMUNICATION and **POPULAR CULTURE**

Racial and Ethnic Images in Star Trek

McGraw-Hill's Primis Custom Publishing consists of products that are produced from camera-ready copy. Peer review, class testing, and accuracy are primarily the responsibility of the author(s).

1 2 3 4 5 6 7 8 9 0 BKM BKM 9 0 9 8

ISBN 0-07-011924-4

Editor: Todd Bull
Cover Design: Mary Good
Printer/Binder: Book-Mart Press, Inc.

Dedication

This book is dedicated to
astronauts and cosmonauts of colour
around the world

Special recognition to five
outstanding astronauts of colour

Arnoldo Tamayo Mendez,Cuban
World's First Black Astronaut
USSR Soyuz 38 1980

Airforce Lt. Col. Guion S. Bluford
First African American Astronaut
Mission Specialist
1983 space shuttle flight

Dr. May Jemison
Medical Doctor
First Black Woman Astronaut
The only "real astronaut" to ever
appear on Star Trek

Airforce Lt. Col. Ellison Onizuka
First Japanese American Astronaut
Died 1986 on
US space shuttle Challenger

Dr. Ellen Ocha
First Hispanic Woman to
Travel in outer space

Brief Table of Contents

Author's Note
Acknowledgments
Chapter 1 Introduction 3-30
Chapter 2 Black Screen Images 31-56
Chapter 3 Blacks in the Original Series 57-72
Chapter 4 Blacks in the Next Generation 73-85
Chapter 5 Blacks in Deep Space Nine and Voyager 86-102
Chapter 6 Blacks as Aliens 103-123
Chapter 7 Asian Images in Trek 124-160
Chapter 8 Native American Images in Trek 161-189
Chapter 9 Latino/Hispanic/Chicano Images in Trek 190-212
Chapter 10 Racial and Ethnic Images on Screen 213-235

Extended Table of Contents

Author's Note x

Acknowledgments xii

Chapter 1:Introduction 3-30
Multicultural Communication 4
Popular Culture 4
Nature of Race and Ethnicity 5
Racial and Ethnic Categories in U.S. 12
The Nature of Star Trek 20
Star Trek as Mythology 21
Star Trek as Rhetorical Vision 23
Conclusion 28
References 29

Chapter 2:Black Screen Images 31-56
Exigencies 32
Traditional Black Mythic Images 33
Professional Black Mythic Characters 38
The Guises 42
Standard Themes 44
Standard Contexts 46
Binary Relationships 46
Relationship of Blacks to Whites 47
Black Characters on TV Today 48
Conclusion 51
Movie Review :*First Contact* 56
References 57

Chapter 3:Blacks in The Original Series 57-72
Character Sketches 58
Uhura: Where No Black Has Gone Before 59
Daystrom: The Villain 62
Masters: The Engineer 63

Boma: The Voice of the Chorus	**64**
Commodore Stone: Administrator	**65**
M'Benga: The Doctor	**66**
Trek books, Cartoons, and Films	**67**
Conclusion	**69**
References	**70**
Chapter 4: Blacks in *The Next Generation*	72-85
Character Skethces	**72**
Geordi: The Tinker	**74**
Worf: The Warrior	**76**
Guinan : The Sage	**78**
Martin Benbeck: The Moral Voice	**81**
Tryla Scott: The Captain	**83**
Conclusion	**83**
Movie Review: *The Fifth Element*	**86**
References	**87**
Chapter 5: Blacks in *Deep Space Nine* & *Voyager*	87-102
Character Sketches	**87**
The Wormhole	**89**
Sisko: The Captain	**90**
Kassidy Yates: Freedom Fighter	**95**
Worf: More Than A Warrior	**97**
Tuvok: Black Vulcan	**99**
Conclusion	**102**
References	**103**
Chapter 6: Blacks as Aliens	103-123
Klingons: The Black Bucks	**104**
Romulans: The Darker Cousins	**107**
Ligonians: Tribal Blacks	**109**
Tamarians:Metaphoric Speakers	**111**
Jem'Hadar: The Slaves	**114**
The Dominion as Allegory	**118**
Conclusion	**120**
References	**121**

Chapter 7: Asian Images	**24- 160**
Exigencies	**125**
Myths about Asians	**127**
Taxonomy of Characters	**127**
Stereotypes of Pacific Islanders	**134**
Professional Asian Women	**135**
Professional Asian Men	**136**
Standard Themes	**137**
Standard Contexts	**140**
The Original Series: *Star Trek*	
Sulu: Professional Asian	**140**
Khan Noonien Singh: Villain	**142**
Elaan: Dragon Lady	**145**
Gov. Cory: Administrator	**149**
The Omega Glory	**150**
The Next Generation	
Alyssa Ogawa: Nurse	**153**
Chang: Administrator	**152**
Jim Shimoda: Engineer	**154**
Cross Overs: The Next Generation	
to *Deep Space 9*	
Keiko O'Brien: Professional Asian	**154**
Molly O'Brien	**156**
Voyager	
Harry Kim: Professional Asian	**156**
Conclusion	**157**
References	**158**
Chapter 8: Native American Images	**161-189**
The Myth	**162**
Exigencies	**164**
Myths that Bind	**165**
Taxonomy of Characters	**166**
Standard Themes	**172**
Standard Contexts	**173**
The Original Series	
The Paradise Syndrome	**174**
The Next Generation	
Journey's End	**177**

Voyager
Character Sketches 179
Chakotay 181
The *Voyager* Story 181
Conclusion 186
References 187

Chapter 9: Latino Images 190-212
Latinos: The "Invisible" Minority 191
Exigencies 193
Standard Themes 194
Standard Contexts 195
Taxonomy of Characters 196
Latinos on TV 202
Current Latino(a) Actors 203
Latinos on Star Trek
The Original Series
Commodore Mendez 204
Rodriquez 205
Rodriquez 205
Sanchez 205
The Next Generation
Torres 206
Solis 206
Flores 206
Juarez 206
Lopez 206
Mendez 206
Mendoza 206
Quinteros 207
Deep Space 9
Kai Opaka 207
Enrique Muñez 208
Voyager
B'lanna Torres 209
Conclusion 210
References 211

Chapter 10: Theory of Racial and Ethnic Images 213-235

The Nature of Theory 214
The Theory of Racial and Ethnic Images on Screen 215
Exigencies 216
Taxonomy of Characters 219
The New Professionals 226
The Guises 227
Standard Themes 228
Standard Contexts 229
Binary Relationships 230
White Actors Playing Characters of Colour 231
People of Colour and the White Community 232
Impact of Images 233
Conclusion 233
References 234
Movie Review: Independence Day 236
Movie Review: Cinderella 238

Figures

Figure 1 Page 49 TV Show and Occupation of Black Head of Household or Lead Male Character
Figure 2 Page 50 TV Show and Occupation of Lead Black Female or Black Female Supporting Role
Figure 3 Page 133 Asian Stereotypes and Their Origins
Figure 4 Page 135 TV Stereotypes of Pacific Islanders

Author's Note

Confessions of A Black Trekker

Hello! My name is Marquita Byrd...and I am...I am a Trekker. I have three strikes against me. I am African American, I am female and I am a Trekker! I've been humiliated by some of my best friends. I have been subjected to derisive laughter from family members. On the job I have been the object of ridicule: some hint that I may be missing a nacelle engine. I am alienated from others in the Black community because they point, whisper and shake their heads as I walk by wearing my Bajoran earring.

The last straw is when I admit to them that I've been...I've been attending Trek conventions. It's true. It was at the conventions that I began to suspect how off the beaten track I was as an African American. I have never seen more than ten blacks at conventions numbering anywhere between 500-1,000 at cities in the south, Midwest and on the west-coast.

I attended my first convention in 1982 at the Houston Astrodome. That led to others where I attended workshops on how to be a Klingon and I shamelessly bought paraphernalia in the Orion trading room. I have seen all of the original crew except Nimoy. I have attended lectures by Jonathan Frakes (Wil Riker), Michael Dorn (Worf), Terry Farrell (Dax), Nana Visitor(Kira), George Takei(Sulu), Nichelle Nichols (Uhuru), DeForest Kelly(Dr. McCoy), and several others from the show. Once, Marina Sirtis (Counselor Troi) spoke to me in the convention hall after a lecture. She wanted to know if I realized that I looked like Marsha Warfield.

My relatives have become enablers. My oldest son has his own Trek uniform, which he wears on Halloween. My youngest is allowed to play with my six-inch replica of Worf, but he knows that the transporter I got for my birthday is strictly off limits! When the children are good I allow them to push the buttons on my hand held communicator. They both buy Trek figures for me as gifts on special occasions. Once for Christmas my dad gave me a tape of conversational Klingon.

My social life is in ruins because of my Trekoholism. The last time I ran a personals ad it read as follows:

> Open hailing frequencies. This is Lt.Uhura. I have gone where no woman has gone before searching for Geordi or Sisko, but to no avail. So far I have not encountered intelligent life forms. Seeking someone to enjoy planet side R&R with on Ligon I.If interested please reply by subspace frequency. Live long and prosper.

As you might have guessed no one replied. There was one bright note though, I won a lunch for two for writing the best ad for the week.

Being a Trekker has even begun to effect my work. I announced in class the other day that I was searching for a special issue of Barbie and Ken in Trek uniforms. Any student having information leading to the where about and purchase of such items would receive a reward. It is rumored on campus that to truly understand my lectures, especially in multicultural communication, a student must know Trek lore and be able to explain what the IDIC symbol stands for (Infinite Diversity in Infinite Combinations).

According to my calculations I spent about 630 hours attending classes and studying to complete the B.S., M.A. and Ph.D. in Education and Speech & Dramatic Arts over a ten-year period. I estimate that over the past 21 years I have spent 1,326 hours, 720 more spent reading sixty or more Trek novels. I'm glad I'm now finally able to combine Trek with my scholarship and teaching. I figure I ought to get something out of those 2,000 plus hours spent Trekking.

I have been pregnant with this book for 21 years and in actual labor for a year. The fact that you are reading it means that I have finally given birth--what a relief! The birth is just in time to mark the 32st anniversary of Star Trek.

It is tough being a Black female Trekker. But some of us (people of colour) must look to the stars and teach our children to dream about and prepare for space travel. Otherwise, if humankind ever kicks this dust ball for destinations unknown there may be only people of European descent on those ships. Before Roddenberry and Trek that's how it was.

Acknowledgments

Michael Crain has been my principal Trek buddy. He and I should own stock in Ma Bell paying for the time we've spent on the phone from Missouri to California talking through episodes. I would like to thank Michael for engaging in those critical sessions. I would also like to acknowledge Sterling Harwood and SDiane Bogus, academic colleagues and Trek buddies, who not only spent time with me discussing the shows, but also reviewed this manuscript. They aided me in maintaining the accuracy of the Treklore and they helped to sharpen my theoretical interpretation of characters and story lines. Mia Cameron, a member of the Northern California Cherokee Association, offered significant insights into the images of Native Americans on Trek.

Two other reviewers, Anntarie Sims and Dorothy Ige, reviewed the manuscript for academic content. And, Buddy Butler introduced me to the writings on black screen images that resulted in the development of the major analytical framework used to critique Star Trek. Their help was greatly appreciated.

Lastly, I must thank my son, Marquis, and my father, Robert. Marquis sacrificed a lot of hours with mommy so that this project could be finished. And, my father, well my father just walked through the room every now and then and said, "Daughter, I sure will be glad when you finish that book so you can rest".

MULTICULTURAL COMMUNICATION
AND
POPULAR CULTURE

RACIAL AND ETHNIC IMAGES IN
STAR TREK

Chapter 1
Introduction

Multicultural communication is the creation and sharing of meaning among individuals and groups within a geo-political system. A geo-political system refers to physical territory, land or geography occupied by an aggregate of peoples connected by one governing body. The aggregate of peoples can be described as a whole as a culture, nation, or society. The groups of people that comprise the whole can be described as tributary groups. These groups are distinguishable from the power dominant or mainstream on the basis of race, ethnicity, gender, age, class, ability, religion and sexual orientation.

As Americans, we are required to engage in multicultural communication every day. People of colour and people of various ethnic groups are rapidly increasing in numbers. In 1984, for the first time in American history, white males did not dominate the work force. In the 90's women and people of colour comprise 75% of the work force. By the year 2010 Latino Americans will represent 11% of the population and African Americans will reach 14%. Asian Americans will contribute 6% of the population by that date which means that by 2010 the American population will be 31% people of colour. (The British spelling ‘colour’ is used when referring to the pigment of a people. The American spelling, color, is used when referring to hue, shade or tint of animals or objects.)

It seems that multicultural relations are becoming more difficult even as the American population continues to diversify. A great many of these difficulties occur due to conflicts over the allocation of resources. However, a secondary source of multicultural conflict stems from the misconceptions, erroneous assumptions, and misinformation that the various groups have about each other. These misconceptions develop due to the lack of cultural knowledge about the various tributary groups and stereotypes that grow out of interpersonal and group communication. Misconceptions about the various ethnic and racial groups can also stem from the lack of authentic interpersonal and collective interactions among the groups, and stereotypical depictions of ethnic and racial groups that are both reinforced and created though popular culture. These stereotypes initially grow out of interpersonal, group and organization communication. They are then incorporated into written and visual forms of popular culture.

Popular Culture

Popular culture is a phenomenon that effects intrapersonal, interpersonal, group and national relationships. It is the manner in which the majority of peoples in a society acquire, borrow and pass on cultural objects within and between groups. It is only in recent history that popular culture has been shared through technological means such television, radio, and film. In earlier periods, people talking to people was the main medium of popular culture.

Popular culture is important because the way people see themselves and others reflected in the popular culture mediums such as TV, art, films, books, music and even mythology shape the way they see themselves and interact with each other. Likewise the absence of a particular image can influence the decisions of ethnic and racial tributary groups. Garret Want, who plays Ensign Harry Kim on *ST:Voyager* supports this point. "I used to play tennis in college and I wanted to turn professional, but there were no Asian-American role models to inspire me" (*ST: Voyager*, 1996, p.8).

Popular culture can influence self-identity and self-concept because it both mirrors and creates visions of who we are. For example, my son is an African American youth who has never lived in an African American community. He has only me, his single mother, and a few relatives to teach him what it means to be African American. Unfortunately much of what he knows about what it means to be African American is what he sees on television and what he hears in the popular music of today. Many of the images of African Americans on shows ranging from Cops to Martin to In Living Color are not positive.

Just as images in popular culture can influence self-identity they can also influence multiracial relationships. During the late 70's, when Alex Haley's Roots was originally televised, black-white relationships in this country were strained. I myself was never able to watch the series for fear that I would be unable to function in my doctoral program and work settings due to the anger generated by the program. Many African Americans who did watch reported that this was exactly what happened. They went to work and school angry at whites: and blacks were not the only ones affected. Whites reported feelings of denial, anger and guilt from watching the series. They became jumpy around blacks and some even became apologetic. Discussions around the nation were centered on black-white relations.

The Nature of Race and Ethnicity

In most cultures race is considered an important means of categorizing and dividing people. Race is a social construct devised by humans to talk about naturally occurring phenomena among people: variations in skin colour, hair texture, facial features, etc. Since race is an artificially constructed classification system it is arbitrary; that means it has no anchor in reality.

Furthermore the notion of race is imprecise. It is imprecise because the so called "racial markers" used to define each racial group appear in all groups of people. In all racial groups there are people with straight to curly hair, broad to thin noses, fair to dark skin, thick to thin lips, and flat to high cheekbones. Racial identification is not an infallible method of classification. Racial characteristics, because they are physiological, are biologically transmitted from generation to generation. The social interpretation of race constantly influences human relationships.

> This is of critical importance to the physically different or racial minorities, such as Negroes, Indians, and Chinese and Japanese-Americans. As long as their visibly physical difference is socially defined as relevant, they are precluded from learning their way out of minority status. (Mack & Duster, 1974, p.48)

Physical variances among groups of humans such as skin colour, type of hair, shape of the eyes, like symbols, have no meaning except that which the perceiver attributes to them. However, because humans deny economic, political and educational parity among groups based on physical variations, those differences become "relevant." Decisions about education, medical care, employability, neighborhood composition, who one should love and who one should hate are made on the basis of physical characteristics.

Just as race influences interpersonal and group interactions so does ethnicity. Ethnicity is a method of classifying humans on the basis of factors such as language, values, ways of thinking, world perspectives and traditions. Ethnic groups are people with certain behavioral, cognitive, communication and affective styles that set them apart from the larger society. Members of an ethnic group share a common set of cultural traits, have a sense of community and tend to judge others according to their group standards. Furthermore, membership is stable, enduring and ascribed at birth. Lastly, ethnic groups tend to occupy certain territory within the larger society with concentrated groupings in certain areas of cities, states, or regions of the country (Friedman, 1991, Chapter 1; Marger, 1985, p.9-10).

"Ethnic" is a political term, which has been used in the past to identify only those people not in power. The term originally meant heathen, people of neither Christian nor Jewish beliefs. The word ethnic has also been used to mean quaint or primitive. Power dominant groups consider themselves 'the society' and therefore without ethnicity. The fact of the matter is that all people have ethnicity regardless of the level of power associated with the group. African Americans, Asian Americans, Euro-Americans, Latino Americans, Middle Eastern Americans and Native Americans all have an ethnic heritage.

Fortunately notions about dominance and ethnicity are changing. This can be evidenced by the hearings that have been conducted all over the United States by the Office of Management and Budget in preparation for the census in 2000. The office is seeking suggestions on how to change the ethnic categories on the census to more accurately reflect the American population and its tributaries. Gerhard Holford, a participant in the hearings "proposed four new categories of European Americans... Scandinavian, Celtic, Germanic and Slavic" (Lewis, 1994, p. A1). Holford testified that "White Americans are a multi-ethnic group...They do not think, act and vote alike" (Lewis,1994,p. A1).

While in the past a general lumping together of Euro-Americans as "white" was preferable to specific ethnic identities this is no longer the case. Now even those who are considered members of the power dominant class understand the advantages of discovering and claiming their ethnic identities. An excellent example would be the 1995 election held in San Francisco for the mayoral seat. The incumbent, Frank Jordan, was referred to by the news media as an "Irish American candidate." Willie Brown was consistently referred to as "an African American candidate".

The term race can be defined as a group of people identifiable on the basis of physiological characteristics biologically transmitted from generation to generation. Their relations are determined by blood, which Sollors labels as descent (Friedman, 1991, pg. 19). The term ethnic indicates a group of people identifiable by traditions, values, ways of thinking, world perspective and language, which Sollors labels consent (Friedman, 1991, pg.19). Ethnic groups can be differentiated from one another on the basis of cognitive, behavioral, and affective styles.

Relationship Between Race and Ethnicity

While race and ethnicity have been used interchangeably they are not the same. The major difference between race and ethnicity is the ability to change one's status. Racial characteristics are difficult to change within one lifetime while ethnic characteristics can be changed within that period. Within a generation or two, a family could erase cultural and ethnic differences between themselves and the larger society. They could educate or earn their way out of minority status, but people who look different from the power dominant group in society will always face resistance because of how they look (Milner, 1983, p.226). Duster & Mack (1974) and Milner (1983) point out that no level of education (learning) can change a person's designation as a "minority" if the person looks different from the power dominant group in society.

Labels and Categories Arbitrary

The labels used to categorize groups of humans are arbitrary means of identifying people. The concepts are not so clearly differentiated in real life because one group of people can be identified in several ways. There are racial groups that include many ethnic variations, for example, Asian Americans. Asian Americans would include Chinese, Japanese, and Vietnamese

Americans, all of which are from the same racial group, but have different ethnic backgrounds: different languages, traditions, values and religions. Then there are groups sharing a common ethnic heritage, say for instance, Latinos, but who come from several racial groups including African, Native and Euro-American. The concepts of race and ethnicity overlap to a great extent because many racial groups also differ from one another ethnically.

Movement Among the Groups

While membership in a tributary group is fairly stable it can be altered. People do change their membership from one group to another, but not often. Religion, class, and ethnicity can be changed. Before 1980 East Indians were categorized as "white" according to the U.S. Census Bureau, now they are categorized as Asians. Before 1960 Spanish speaking people were forced to check black or white, on the Census. Now they can check Latino. Furthermore people routinely change their racial/ethnic designation on paper for the purpose of educational, occupational and social gain.

For a vast majority of the population humans remain in the same gender, ableness and sexual orientation categories throughout life. They have no choice about aging since it is a natural occurrence in the life cycle. But, people have more choice about religion, class or ethnicity. They can consciously choose to change them. An individual can have gender reassignment; there is a trend to start new careers at 60-65 forcing us to rethink the term elderly; and there is a political movement afoot to refer to hearing impaired people as the "Deaf Community", an ethnic rather than a disabled group. There is movement among the various tributary groups because the way people identify themselves changes across the life span and across life experiences.

Who Is Responsible for Racial and Ethnic Labels?

The labels for various groups originate from several sources including the larger society, the group itself, family units and individuals. The federal government of the U.S. designates people with Spanish surnames and who speak Spanish as a first language as Hispanics. This is an "official" definition. However, there are individuals and sets of people among Hispanics who do not refer to themselves as such, but rather Puerto Rican, Cuban, Mexican, Latino, Chicano and La Raza (Fisher, 1980).

The term "Latino" is a political term like ethnic. That means the word has many political and emotional implications. Latino refers to those people who were conquered in the New World by Spain and no longer retain tribal, clan or community affiliation. Spanish people refer to themselves as Europeans.

Myth has it that Columbus was lost when he reached the shores of America and thought he was on the Indian subcontinent, therefore he labeled the original inhabitants of this country "Indians." The dominant culture identified the indigenous people of America as Indians. The indigenous people identify themselves according to their tribal names and affiliations.

Russell Means is a member of the Lakota tribe. He has for many years been central to the American Indian Movement (AIM). Means offers an alternate theory for the naming of the indigenous people of the New World. He wrote:

> There is also some confusion about the word Indian, a mistaken belief that it refers somehow to the country, India. When Columbus washed up on the beach in the Caribbean, he was not looking for a country called India. Europeans were calling that country Hindustan in 1492. Look it up on the old maps. Columbus called the tribal people he met "Indio", from the Italian in dio, meaning "in God". (Means, 1991, p.72)

It is highly possible that this was the actual beginning of the myth of tribal Americans as edenic, children in paradise.

White Americans have identified people of African descent as coloreds and Negroes. The people have identified themselves as Blacks, Afro-Americans and African-Americans. Self-definition is very important to group identity.

Many people of colour report having discussions in the home, community and church about the meaning of their ethnicity. While oppressed peoples spend more time than power dominant people searching for the meaning of their ethno-racial identity, there are individuals who choose to identify with a group other than the one of origin. This may happen when they physically look like the power dominant group and wish to take advantage of that fact. Blacks, Mexicans and Native Americans who were very fair and wanted to accrue the same advantages as whites have "passed" as whites in this society.

Of course biracial people are able to choose the group they wish to identify with. For instance, the larger American society designates persons with any measure of black ancestry as black. This is so regardless of the race of the other parent. However frequently these mixed children choose to identify themselves with the race of the non-black parent. Their identity depends on what they are taught in the family and what they determine is most beneficial for them.

Biracial people struggle in order to come to grips with who they are and what that means in the larger society. Virtually all of my students who identify themselves as biracial express anger and resentment at society's tendency to invalidate or negate their existence by not recognizing the multiple sources of their ethno-racial identity. Furthermore, they voice resentment at the tendency of other individuals and society to tell them, the biracial person, who they are. The biracial person feels that his/her ethnic identity is a familial and personal choice, which cannot be decided by outsiders.

Other cases of individuals born in one group, but identifying with another, are children who belong to one racial group and are raised in a family outside the group. Friends of mine, a couple, who are white and Filipino/white have adopted a black child. They live in an all white neighborhood and are devout Mormons. Without considerable effort on the part of the parents while the child is growing up, or on the part of the child when she is of age, she will not identify with African Americans, but with white Americans. While she is without a doubt of African racial heritage her ethnic heritage and perspective will be European. Racial and ethnic identities are multidimensional terms, which include both physical and cultural characteristics and cannot be determined solely by outside appearances.

Racial and Ethnic Classifications

For political reasons, the allocation of state and federal funds, in order to implement affirmative action and to provide a tool for talking about group experiences humans in the U.S. are categorized by the arbitrary standards of race and ethnicity. A person can be recognized as belonging to a particular group by self-identification, group recognition and inclusion, family self-identification or government designation.

The major ethnic groups in the United States include African Americans, Asian Americans, European Americans, Latinos, Middle Eastern Americans and Native Americans. These groups can be defined as follows:

African American- origins in the original people of the African continent (Egypt, Ghana, South Africa, Nigeria), the Caribbean, West Indians, and Haitians. Origins in any black racial group, not of Latino heritage. Includes individuals ranging from dark to fair skin.

Asian/Pacific Islander- origins in any of the original people of

East Asia (China, Japan, Philippines and Korea), Southeast Asia (Vietnam, Cambodia, Thailand, Laos) South Asia (Bangladesh, Burma, India, Pakistan, etc.) and the Pacific Islands (Fiji, Samoa, Tonga, Hawaii, etc.).

European American- origins in any of the original people of western Eurasia (England, France, Germany, Italy, Portugal, Spain, Sweden, western Russian, etc.). People ranging from dark to fair skin.

Latino American - origins in any of the Spanish people who settled in the New World or of the New World people that were conquered by Spain (including Mexico, Puerto Rica, Cuba, and Costa Rico); who do not identify themselves by tribal or community affiliation (Native Americans). Also any person with Spanish as a first language or a Spanish surname except people from Spain. Includes racial groups ranging from dark to fair skin.

Middle Eastern American- origins in any of the people of Southwest Asia (where Asia, Africa, and Europe meet) including Turkey, Iran, Iraq, Afghanistan, Saudi Arabia, Israel, Kuwait, etc. People from dark to fair skin.

Native American- origins in people originally inhabiting the continental U.S. and Alaska who maintain cultural identification through tribal affiliation or community recognition.

Designating all of these groups as ethno-racial (ER) groups seems reasonable because in addition to the people having similar physiological traits there are always consistent and significant cultural traits that set them apart from other groups. For the remainder of the text ER refers to: any group distinguishable from the general population in terms of language, culture, traditions, values, religion and/or physical traits.

Stereotypes

There are stereotypes of every racial and ethnic group in the country. A stereotype is a classification of people on the basis of what appears to be characteristics that they have in common. Though some traits included in a particular stereotype may be true, the fact is that there are always exceptions to the rule. Furthermore, stereotypes tend to exaggerate characteristics and are often based on misinformation.

A stock dramatic ploy used in popular culture is the insertion of stereotypical characters in a story line. Stereotypical characters serve several functions. They can be used to:

> (1)keep the action of the story moving; (2) provide detailed character sketches without wasting time on unnecessary descriptions; (3) create simple heroes and villains motivated by the polarized notions of good & evil; and (4) create a specific emotional response in the audience by using an emotionally ladened figure (Hoppenstand, 1983, p.171).

An emotionally ladened figure is one that triggers very strong affective responses in the audience. The figure could trigger positive emotions like Timmy's mother on *Lassie* or negative emotions like Darth Vader of *Star Wars*.

There is nothing wrong, per se, with using stereotypes in popular culture since the presentation of a story is limited by time. The problems begin to occur when audiences are unable or unwilling to distinguish stereotypes of groups from the reality of human beings. When we fail to recognize that another human being is unique, even though s/he holds membership in several tributary groups, then effective communication is not likely to occur.

Popular culture makes extensive use of stereotypes. They can be seen in the characters that actors portray in film and television, in folk art, even in the lyrics of a song. Star Trek is no exception to the rule. The creative forces responsible for Trek frequently use stereotypes of groups. While those creative forces generate new ethnic and racial images several of the traditional ones are still used. As educated consumers of popular culture we should be able to recognize stereotypes and question the use of them.

Significance of Popular Culture

I spent my teen-age years watching *Lost In Space*. This series featured a family (the Robinsons), a technician, a stow-away and a robot, lost in space. Bill Mummy played Will Robinson and the robot was constantly shouting "Danger, danger, danger Will Robinson!" It was exciting to lose myself in that vision of the future and imagine what life would be like on another planet. Unfortunately based on that particular vision of the future people like me would not be there.

Science fiction became a passion for me again when I began watching TOS in reruns during the early 70's. A black character, Uhura, was a series regular. She was a senior officer on a starship and she was a communication specialist and I was in love with Star Trek. I had just completed my B.S. in Secondary Education with an emphasis in Public Speaking and here was a black female, starship officer working as a communication specialist. Though I had already chosen my career path it was wonderful to have my decision affirmed by the presence of a black female communication specialist, even if she was just a fictional character.

Dr. May Jemison, the first black female astronaut, and the only real astronaut to appear on ST, responded to Uhura in a similar manner. In an interview Jemison said of Uhura, "Her character was an affirmation. I would have gone into space no matter what, but sometimes you see people you can identify with, a person who allowed you to reaffirm that you could do it" (Logan, 1994, p.22).

Seeing Uhura on Trek was as momentous for me as the first time I saw a picture of an African American speech scholar. I attended college on a predominately white campus. There were other black students in the communication program, but I had never seen a black speech professional or even heard of one. During my junior year, while completing a speech assignment for a rhetoric class, I came across a book with a picture of the author, a black man named Arthur L. Smith now known as Molefi Asante. Though I was well on my way to completing a speech degree I sat in the library that day and gazed at the picture. I hugged the book close to me as I felt the thrill of validation. It was good to see a speech scholar who was black like me. I knew then that there were others out there and that day I felt less isolated in my chosen profession.

Herein lies the power of popular culture. When consumers of popular culture see themselves portrayed in a positive light they feel confirmed and connected. It is the product of all the life experiences shared by people in common and is therefore representative of the non-elite (Hoffman, 1995, p.xi, xii and Inge, 1989, p.xxiv). While it is true that it can distort and misinform, poplar culture can also serve to validate and motivate.

> Popular culture refers to those systems or artifacts that most people share and that most people know about ...television is an immensely rich world of popular culture, as nearly everyone watches television, and even if not everyone sees the same shows, they are likely to know in general about the shows that they do not see. In speaking of popular culture, then we are concerned with things, like television, that are part of the everyday experience of most people. (Brummett, 1994, p.21)

There are many types of culture including high, popular and living. High culture is observed among the monied and privileged: the power dominant in society. Descriptions of it are generated from the observations, investigations, theories and philosophies about the life of people in the upper strata of society. Living culture is how the masses of people "do life" from day-to-day. The waking, the eating, the sleeping, working, playing, ways of coping, and ways of improving life for the generations to come are the content of living culture.

Popular culture grows out of the common experiences of the people and is replicated, amplified, and transmitted by technological means. It can be an accurate representation of living culture, but most often it is overly simplified, at times distorted, and frequently inaccurate. Cultural artifacts including ideas, values and mythologies become popular because they present the old and familiar of living culture in new ways.

> The very essence of popular culture is its ability to provide its public with a sense of the familiar, while at the same time also infusing this with enough variety to ensure continued interest. All forms of popular culture walk the fine line between ...conventions and inventions. (Berger, 1992, p.vii)

The creative forces driving ST are masters at balancing familiar conventions with exciting inventions. They so often advanced the territory in terms of the screen presentation of minority characters that I became caught up in their use of new images and paid no attention to their use of traditional mythic characters. I was so busy applauding the successes and triumphs that I failed to recognize the weaknesses in terms of the presentation of minority characters on the show.

The portrayal of women and minorities in popular culture is important to American society (Seggar, Hafen, and Hannonen-Gladden, 1981).

> Within the state-of-the worlds of...television

> programs are embedded representations…which inscribe simplified, compartmentalized, and encased conceptions of race, culture, gender, power, personal agency and identity. The program's depictions have consequences on the ways children situate their identities of race and gender, as well as personal and social agency…
> (Voithofer, 1996, p. 2)

Interactions between the races and the sexes are affected by television's limited and often stereotypical portrayals of human beings. For example, I know of several heterosexual couples who reported that their relationships were permanently altered because they saw the film *Waiting To Exhale* (Terry McMillan) together. Likewise, I know several gay and lesbian couples who had some serious discussions about their relationships after viewing the film, *The Bird Cage,* together.

The social categories of specific groups represented in popular culture are highly simplified and generalized signs (Fiske, 1983, p.222). They implicitly and explicitly represent a set of values, judgments and assumptions concerning the behavior, characteristics and/or history of a group of people (Fiske, 1983, p.222). They then influence the way people perceive each other and their relationships.

> Thus, the study of... stereotypes remains an important area for the student of American popular culture. The more we understand about the impact of these images and their history, the more we will be able to understand about the state of our multi-racial culture... (Geist, 1983, p.170)

The influence of TV viewing on the larger society is obvious. The presentation of a professional black woman in a space adventure influenced real life events. After the 1969 season of TOS NASA began to recruit minorities into the space program. They hired Nichelle Nichols. It was almost twenty years later when we saw actual African Americans in the space program as astronauts. Colonel Bluford was the first African American male astronaut and Dr. May Jemison was the first black woman astronaut. Dr. Jemison also appeared in an episode of TNG as a transporter technician in Descent, Part 1" (1993).

That television viewing can influence the self-esteem of all viewers is evidenced in the following statements. "High TV entertainment viewing is accompanied by low self-esteem among black but not white audiences" (Tan & Tan, 1979, p.129). Many critics believe that images of a group which are projected in popular culture influences the self-esteem of Native American children: that these images may in part be responsible for the high suicide rate among Native American teens (Ganje, 1996). The Hibernian Council of the city of New York works to change the image of Irish people as has hard drinkers. They feel that the image induces young Irish American to drink as part of their ethnic identity.

It has been proven that television watching can lower-self-esteem, but it is also evident that when used properly television can improve the self-esteem of viewers. Based on these suppositions: that society is influenced by popular culture; popular culture is still fraught with stereotypes of minorities; and multicultural relationships are influenced by the stereotypes presented in popular culture; the conclusion must be that it is essential for scholars and viewers to continue to monitor popular culture.

My purpose here is to explore the minority presence on ST to determine if the writers and producers of the show were able to move beyond the mythic stereotypical presentations of people of colour. In view of the fact that:

> television's portrayal of women and minorities and the potential impact of these portrayals are issues of critical importance to the American society. [And]

> To the extent that the viewers' beliefs, attitudes, and behavior are affected by what they see on television, relations between the races and the sexes may be affected by television's limited and often stereotyped portrayals of men and women, both white and nonwhite. There should be ongoing research to serve as a barometer of change, or the lack of it. (U.S. Commission of Civil Rights, 1977, p.47)

The Nature of Star Trek

Star Trek: The Original Series (ST:TOS) first aired on September 8,1966 and ran until 1969. The ST premise was pretty simple: a group of people lead by a captain, doctor, and science officer go out into the galaxy to explore. The mission was explained in the prologue of every show.

> Space, the final frontier. These are the voyages of the Starship Enterprise. It's five year mission. To explore strange new worlds, to seek out new life and new civilizations. To boldly go where no man has gone before.

The seventy-nine original episodes gave birth to an American popular culture phenomenon that has spanned 30 years and shows no signs of stopping. While the original airing of the show drew a small audience (contributing to the cancellation of the series), it took on new life in syndicated reruns, which began in 1969 (Okuda, Okuda & Mirek, 1994). A much broader audience viewed the show in the early 70's so that by 1972 the first Trek convention, which was held in New York, drew an overwhelming 3,000 people (the organizers expected a couple of hundred) (Okuda, Okuda & Mirek, 1994).

The tenacity and loyalty of Trekkers and a popularization

of the show with general audiences aided by better time slots in reruns spurred a resurgence in the Trek universe. Eight Star Trek feature length films were produced between 1979-1996. In addition to the films three new episodic shows have appeared since 1987 including *The Next Generation* (TNG), *Deep Space Nine* (DS9), and *Voyager* (V).

The actors, producers and writers of the series are frequently asked, "why is the show so popular?" Arthur C. Clarke answered the question in this way:

> At a dark time in human history 'Star Trek' promoted the then unpopular ideals of tolerance for differing cultures, and respect for life in all forms--without preaching and always with a saving sense of humor. (Clarke, 1995, p.11)

Ursula LeGuin voiced the same sentiments.

> The continuing mission of the Starship Enterprise has been to take us out of the smog of fear and hate into an open space where difference is opportunity, and justice matters, and you can still see the stars. (LeGuin, 1994, p.32)

Both of these authors of science fiction point to the inclusive nature of Trek and its ability to help us think of what could be. But perhaps Avery Brooks alluded to one of the more significant issues.

Star Trek as Mythology

Avery Brooks was the first black student to graduate with a Masters of Fine Arts at Rutgers, he is a tenured faculty member of that institution and most importantly, he is the portrayer of Commander Sisko on DS9. Brooks refers to Star Trek as a mythology in the same vain that the series *Hawk* was (Reeves-Stevens, 1994). Hawk was an earlier series Brooks played in about a black man who was an independent contractor with a gun. In this myth Hawk was strong, educated, and did not need the approval of anyone. In the sense that Star Trek and Hawk are about fictional people, places and situations they are myths. "A myth is an unverifiable and typically fantastic story that is nonetheless felt to be true and that deals with a theme of some importance to the believer"(Bierhorst, 1976 p.3).

The word 'myth' is derived from the Greek word 'mythos' and originally meant word or story. All cultures have mythologies and they serve several functions. "Human beings have traditionally used stories to describe or explain things they could not explain otherwise" (Leeming, 1990, p.3). Myth allows people to study human nature through the discussion of the stories. Myth can exemplify how the universe should be, even if it has not yet been attained.

Myths can be thought of as conveyors of information and values about a culture. Therefore, they can have an instructive purpose. Mythology speaks of the familiar, which is comforting, and allows individuals to recognize their common ground. Mythological stories can aid in role playing, allowing a listener or viewer to step right into a larger than life story to become part of the action. Mythos provides an opportunity to escape from the daily routines of life and play for just a little while.

People, as an aggregate, are constantly searching for who they are and myths help them to define themselves. Furthermore myth exemplifies the struggle of good and evil, right and wrong, and most often shows the triumph of good over evil in the long run. Many strongly held beliefs in a society are reinforced through myth.

Not only does myth affirm strongly held beliefs in a society it also allows people to celebrate their strengths and gain new insights into their weaknesses. Myth helps a people celebrate the heroic figure, the heroic ideals, and the heroic deeds. It enables them to move towards redemption for wrongs and evils committed by past and present generations.

Star Trek is an American myth that does all of these things. The original episodes were individual morality plays. They made us think about right and wrong. Star Trek allows us to take a look at a future where people are working on being inclusive. It ignites our imagination so that we think about the "what ifs". The original series let us cheer for the good old American red blooded male, who took matters into his own hands, was not afraid to act and would fight to defend not just the many, but also the few. And though the galaxy was dominated by humanoids of Eurocentric descent Trek showed more women and people of colour in roles of authority than any other TV serial of its time.

The Trek mythology certainly has its problems. One is the white male dominance of the known universe. The tendency of the Federation to play big brother to the Alpha quadrant of the galaxy is a second problem. The third difficulty with the myth is the predisposition to interfere with other cultures on the basis of Terran standards in spite of the prime directive. Four, there are virtually no fat people in Starfleet and five, there are few significant relationships among the women. These are just a few of the problems with the series, not to mention the fact that most of the time Captain Kirk gets the girl.

The good thing is that the creative forces following in the footsteps of Roddenberry, Michael Piller, Jerri Taylor and Rick Berman, are continuing to expand the myth, to improve upon the idea. Who knows, the Star Trek myth may be as enduring Beowulf.

Star Trek as a Rhetorical Vision

Over and over again, viewers, writers, actors, and producers are asked, “Why is Star Trek so popular?” Of course Star Trek is good entertainment, but it is much more than that. It is a rhetorical vision that has much credibility in this nation.

> A rhetorical vision is essentially a view of how things have been, are, or will be. Rhetorical visions structure our sense of reality in areas that we cannot experience directly, but can only know by symbolic reproduction...such visions give us an image of things in the past, in the future, or in faraway places. (Littlejohn, 1996, p. 172)

Fantasy themes are smaller units of rhetorical visions. Fantasy theme analysis suggests that groups, be they small like families or large like nations, shape and explain reality by telling stories or narratives. These stories have re-occurring themes and eventually come to make-up larger rhetorical visions. Fantasy themes and rhetorical visions have characters, plot lines, scenes, and sanctioning agents.

> Characters are the heroes, villains and other players. The plot is the development of the story. The scene is the setting and the sanctioning agent is the person or ideals that lend credibility to the story (Littlejohn, 1996,p.172).

The narration of a fantasy theme or rhetorical vision will be judged successful on the basis of coherence and fidelity. Coherence is how well the story hangs together internally, externally, and character wise. Fidelity has to do with truthfulness: whether or not the story rings true. A story with fidelity presents a set of values that are taken as good reasons by the listener (Littlejohn, 1996 p. 174). The fidelity of a story is judged by the following: (1) the story must be a tale of values; (2) the values must be appropriate for the theme, thesis and characters; (3) the values should have positive consequences for the people; (4) the values should be consistent with the people's own experiences; and (5) the values must be part of the ideal for human conduct (Littlejohn, 1996, p 174). Add to these things the proper mix of convention and invention and you have begun to answer the question of why Trek is so popular.

First of all, Star Trek does present the viewers with a rhetorical vision. It shows us how things could be in the future. The show is an epic saga, which helps us to imagine what could happen if we but follow our ideals. The show provides us with a "fully imagined future world, where harmony and humanism have triumphed and the shackles of time and space can be cast aside..." (Zoglan, 1994, p. 74). On the bridge of the Enterprise "people of various races, cultures and planets work in utopian harmony" (Zoglan, 1994, p. 76). Here is a story that gives us hope that humankind is better that we might think and that it has much more potential to be explored.

Star Trek has all of the ingredients of a good rhetorical vision. It has heroes and heroines in the Federation crew. They include Kirk, McCoy, Spock and Uhura: Picard, Riker, Troi and Worf; Sisko, Odo, Kira, and O'Brien; Janeway, Chakotay, Kim, and Tuvok. The list of villains is endless; the Klingons & Romulans, the Jem'Hadar & the Borg, the Cardassians and the Kazons are just a few.

The story has been developed over a thirty year period from the first five year mission to being lost in space. Therefore the plot is broad in scope. The setting is said to be one of the last frontiers, space. The ideals that are believed to be true by most people in this country and authority figures that take the series seriously are the sanctioning agents.

Our nation's theoretical tolerance for human diversity, the frontier spirit, peaceful exploration, and the bringing together of people from many walks of life for the common good are ideals that guide this nation. They are also all sanctioning ideals included in Star Trek. The worth of the individual, the right to cultural development, inventiveness, and flexibility can also be added to the list.

Besides the incorporation of national ideals that bring credibility to Star Trek there are also many authority figures, opinion leaders, and institutions that deem the show worth while. In the mid 70's a seminar on physics as presented in ST was offered at the University of Missouri. During the time that I worked on my Ph.D. there I could never get into the course because it was full. An article titled "Using *Star Trek: The Next Generation to Teach Concepts in Persuasion, Family Communication, and Communication Ethics* was published in a 1993 issue of *Communication Education* (Winegarden, Fuss-Reineck and Charron). In 1994 the American Association for the Advancement of Science conducted a meeting to discuss the educational role of Star Trek among both children and scientists (Mestel 1994). Professors Sharf and Roberts of the New England School of Law have published an article detailing how they have used *Star Trek: The Next Generation* to demonstrate legal concepts. And lastly, in the Communication Studies department of San Jose State University I teach a course titled the Fundamentals of Intercultural Communication as presented in Star Trek. This is a very limited list of educators and professionals that have "sanctioned" ST.

After Star Trek was cancelled in 1969 NASA hired Nichelle Nichols to recruit minorities for the space program. Stephen Hawking and Colin Powell are among its viewers. Academicians around the world conduct scholarly investigations of the show. There are now books titled *The Physics of Star Trek, The Metaphysics of Star Trek* and *The Meaning of Star Trek.* In February of 1997 San Francisco State University held a scholarly conference about Star Trek. The conference was another example of how people in highly respectable institutions regard the series. Due to the ideals explored and the people and institutions who express interest in Star Trek the show is highly sanctioned (has high credibility).

While there is a bit of unevenness in coherence from episode to episode and series to movies, in general the writing is tight and the stories are well organized. They also build on each other, serial to serial and serial to movies. And for the most part the characters have become believable over time as we have seen them react in situation after situation.

The fidelity of the show is apparent in that it rings true for many, in terms of how things should be. The first 79 episodes were said to be a series of morality plays. That continues to be true for many of the subsequent stories. The values seem appropriate for the situations presented in the episodes and decisions being made by the characters. For the most part the values presented have positive outcomes and tap into what we consider ideal human conduct. Or at least the stories make us think about the issues. For those who watch the episodes the stories can become a sort of shorthand for explaining. "It was like that episode..." is frequently heard in my classroom discussions.

Lastly, Star Trek tells the old familiar stories in new ways: the story of the explorer, the settler, the strong individualist, and the adventurer. It tells the tales of the underdogs, the oppressed, and the disenfranchised. It also tells the tales of the rich and powerful. And even while the writers are telling the old stories they push the envelop. They push the audience to the edge in thinking about tolerance for gender, racial, and cultural diversity. They challenge us to examine attitudes towards the elderly, the young, the disabled, and gays & lesbians. On Trek we get to see a crew that is multispecies, a people that change genders with host bodies (the Trill), a blind man navigating a starship (Geordi), and a child genius saving the crew (Wesley Crusher). The saga has even enabled a man who is folliclely challenged (bald) to become a sex symbol (Picard).

The upcoming chapters in this text are based on a series of convention papers, articles and essays that I have written on black images in Star Trek. I had no intention of writing this work, but after I had produced about 100 pages on black images in Star Trek I thought, "Why stop there?" Because the chapters began as works designed to stand alone there may be a measure of overlap in terms of discussion of characters. Furthermore, as the chapters evolve the analysis of specific characters may include different insights depending on the variable I was critiquing at the time.

Conclusion

Chapter 1 contained a discussion of the basic concepts pertinent to the text including multicultural communication, popular culture and the nature of Star Trek. Chapter 2 provides a review of literature relevant to black images on screen. Chapter 3 is an analysis of blacks in TOS. An analysis of Worf, Sisko, and Yates from TNG is contained in Chapter 4 as well as an analysis of ST: V. Chapter 5 contains an analysis of black images in DS9 and Chapter 6 explores the notion of blacks as alien. Asian images are investigated in Chapter 7 and Chapter 8 lifts up for discussion the images of Native Americans in Star Trek. In Chapter 9 Latino images are discussed and the theory of racial and ethnic images on screen is explained in Chapter 10. We are about to take a journey to the stars to discover how people of colour are portrayed in the Trek universe.

References

Bierhorst, J. (Ed.)(1992). *Myths and tales of the American Indians*. New York: Indian Head Books.

Clarke, A. (Spring 1995)(Collector's Edition) Forward: Reflections on the Final Frontier. *TV Guide: Star Trek*. Radnor, PA: News America Publications, p.6-11.

Fisher, D. (Ed.)(1980). *The third woman*. Boston: Houghton Mifflin Company.

Freidman, L. (1991). Celluloid palimpsests. In Lester Friedman (Ed.) *Unspeakable Images: Ethnicity and the American Cinema*. Urbana, IL.: University of Illinois Press. pg. 11-38.

Ganje, L. (1996). Native American stereotypes. In Paul Lester (Ed.) *Images that Injure: Pictorial Stereotypes in the Media*. Westport, CN: Praeger Publishers.

Hoppenstand, G. (1983). Yellow devil doctors and opium dens: A survey of the yellow peril stereotypes in mass media entertainment. In C. Giest and J. Nachbar (Eds.)(3rd. ed.) *The Popular Culture Reader*, Bowling Green, OH: Bowling Green University Popular Press. p. 171-185.

LeGuin, U. (1994)(Collectors Edition). My appointment with the Enterprise. *TV Guide*. Radnor, PA: News America Publications, 31-32.

Leeming, D.(Ed.) (1990). *The world of myth: An anthology*. New York: Oxford University Press.

Lewis, M. (July 15 1994). U.S. ethnicity test is multiple choice. *San Jose Mercury News*, A1.

Littlejohn, S. (1996). (5th ed.) *Theories of human communication*. Belmont: Wadsworth.

Mack R.W. & Duster, T.S. (1973). *Patterns of minority relations*. New
York: Anti-Defamation League of B'nai B'rith.

Chapter 2
Black Images and Stereotypes

Racial and ethnic images in the media are very important because they shape racial attitudes and self-perceptions. The media is so powerful that Spike Lee maintains that it is the new frontier in managing the ideas and minds of the people. He wrote, "Presently in America a war is being fought. Forget about guns, planes and bombs, the weapons from now on will be the newspapers, magazines, TV shows, radio, and FILM" (Lee, 1992, Preface). The images of blacks on screen dates all the way to back to Edwin Porter," a mechanic turned movie director" (Bogle, 1995, p.3). In 1903 Porter filmed a character called Uncle Tom in a twelve minute piece of film. Here is when the first stereotypical image of blacks made its debut. Since that time the images of blacks have proliferated to include five traditional stereotypes and one new image.

The images of blacks seen on screen are most often designed to fulfill certain goals, be they political, social or economic. Not only that, but story lines involving blacks are frequently set in standard contexts where specific issues are addressed.

> Black [characters] exist primarily for white spectators whose comfort and understanding the films must seek....There are no simple stories about black people loving each other or hating each other, or enjoying their private possessions without

reference to the white world, because the spaces for these stories are occupied by newer forms of race relation stories.
(Diawara, 1995, pg. 406)

This chapter is focused on the exigencies (motives) for shaping black images in a particular way, the six predominant characterizations of blacks and the relationship between black and white characters on screen.

The terms African American and black are used in this text depending on the other concepts contained in the sentence and the poetics of the sentence. While African American is considered the politically correct term for people of African descent in the U.S., they refer to themselves as both African American and black.

Exigencies

Van DeBurg, in his work titled *Slavery and Race in Popular Culture* (1984) and Bogle in his *Toms, Coons, Mulattos, Mammies & Bucks...* (1995), suggested that the presentation of black characters is rarely creative, original or accurate. Images of blacks, whether in movies or television, have been shaped to fit the stereotypes of an era, the political and social demands of the period and the ego needs of the dominant society (Bogle, 1995; Guerrero, 1993).

The political and social demands of an era can range from a war effort to a social protest movement. At times, black characters have been shaped to fit a new consciousness of the dominant culture, hence the humanized Negro of the 50's and 60's. Social changes that influence the black archetypes include integration and the separatist movement. The federal government, at various times in American history, has requested that films depicting blacks in a specific light be produced to encourage a new direction in race relations in the country (Bogle, 1995; Guerrero, 1993; & Kern-Foxworth, 1994). Political goals, social demands, and the ego needs of the dominant society inform the molding of black images on screen.

Other motives for shaping black screen images include the need to justify colonial imperialism and the desire to justify missionary work. The need to fuel fantasies of the exotic and different are important shapers of black images. Black stereotypes are also used to justify the continued exploitation of blacks as servants and entertainers (Buskin, 1986). Black males are often portrayed as criminals in order to justify the wholesale incarceration of blacks. And lastly the images of blacks are used to aid in the self-identification of whites (Jewell, 1993).

The tendency of Eurocentric societies to perceive reality in opposites is another motivation behind the creation of black mythic types. The fabricated impropriety of black men and women underscores the fabricated appropriateness of white men and women. If there is no model of wrong then the concept of right is weakened. Stereotypes allow a method of self and group identification by projecting a manufactured image onto another group. Screen images help to do this.

Stereotypes of African Americans moved from toms, coons, mulattos, mammies and black bucks at the turn of the century to jesters and servants in the 30's. In the 40's the stereotypes were guised as the entertainers, the new humanized Negroes and the problem people. The 60's ushered in the stereotype of the professional black, caretaker administrators and militant people. The 80's produced the racially black, ethnically white characters (Bogle, 1995 & Guerrero, 1993).

Traditional Mythic Characters

The images of blacks on screen are designed to fit a particular mythic or stereotypical framework. A mythic character is a rigid role with stereotypical traits, distinguishable from other mythic characters and easily recognizable. These characters are considered mythic because they are distorted images of blacks and they are one dimensional. The black mythic characters are archetypal in that they are broad brush stoke representations, even caricatures of blacks.

Black mythic characters were not manufactured by writers and directors, but grew out of interpersonal and public discourse, group communications (both large and small), the print media (fiction and non-fiction) and were finally plastered on the screen (silver and boxed) in larger than life form. An examination of these images and stereotypes is essential because they at once create, reflect, reinforce and alter racial attitudes and relations throughout society.

Several authors have inventoried the reproduction of certain types of black characters. They include Edward Mapp, James Murray, Gary Null, Daniel Leab and Thomas Cripp (Smith, 1997, pg.3). However it was Donald Bogle who brought these works together to develop a comprehensive taxonomy of characters. While several authors have used somewhat different labels such as "Sambos" and "Superspades" (Leab), "Sapphires" and "Jezebels" (Jewell) it was Bogle who showed us how most of these can be folded in five basic mythic characters. Bogle's *Toms, Coons, Mulattos*...in 1973 and his second edition of that work in 1985 set the broad parameters for the discussion of black images on screen. Virtually every subsequent work on black screen images has referred to Bogle.

Many critics insist that Jewell's *From Mammy to Miss American and Beyond*; hooks' *Reel to Real*; Smith's *Representing Blackness*; and Lester's *Images that Injure* must be consulted in order to truly understand black screen images. However, the truth of the matter is that most of these people quote Bogle extensively; write only about one or two stereotypes; or are more concerned with the origins and consequences of black mythic characters than Bogle has been. His work is clear, concise and broad in scope. Therefore, Bogle's classification of black stereotypes figures heavily in the upcoming discussion.

Tom

The first mythic character is Tom, the good Negro. Tom is content with his lot. Even though he is chased, harassed, hounded, flogged, enslaved and insulted he keeps the faith. A tom never turns against the white 'massa'. He remains hearty, submissive, stoic, generous, selfless and kind. One of the reasons the tom character has been around so long is that he never shows anger. (Bogle, 1995; Kern-Foxworth, 1994; and Van DeBurg, 1984).

Coon

The coon is a second mythic type. He is a Negro included in the story as an amusement object and black buffoon. A coon can be no count, unreliable, crazy and lazy and is often characterized by his antics (Bogle, 1995). There are three subcategories of the coon including the pickaninny, Uncle Remus and Rastus (Bogle, 1995; Kern-Foxworth, 1994; and Van DeBurg).

Pickaninnies are black children and because of their childlike state they are considered harmless. Their popping eyes and hair standing on end identifies them. The pickaninny can be a pleasant diversion from the worries of the day.

Uncle Remus is a first cousin to Tom. He is harmless, congenial, quaint, naive, comical and philosophical (Bogle, 1995). He exudes contentment with his place in the system. The Rastus type character usually appears in slapstick comedy. His most famous pictorial representation is the chef on the Cream of Wheat box (Kern-Foxworth, 1994).

Mulattos

The tragic mulatto is the third broad mythic character. This character is likable and sympathetic, no doubt due to white blood. She is seen as a victim of racial inheritance because she had been tainted with black blood (Jewell, 1993). The tragic mulatto tends to have more sex appeal than the pure black mammy or tom (Bogle, 1995). Most often the tragic mulatto is female. The character could be mixed, of black and white parentage, or pure black, but very fair. White actors often portray mulattos.

Mammy and Other Female Characters

Mammy is a fourth mythic character and she is a female coon. She is highly independent, very dark, fat, cantankerous with no sex appeal. This character has also been called a "handkerchief head" due to the depiction of her with a bandanna or scarf around her head (Bogle, 1995; Kern-Foxworth, 1994; and Van DeBurg, 1984). A variation on mammy is Aunt Jemima. She is a female tom blessed with religion (Bogle, 1995). The aunt jemima is a mammy who has wedged herself into the dominant white culture. She is sweet, jolly, good tempered, more polite than mammy, and never headstrong (Bogle, 1995; Kern-Foxworth, 1994).

Gant (1972) suggested two other mythic types in addition to the mammy used to depict black females. They include the siren, and the innocent. In more recent times the siren has been referred to as the Jezebel (Jewell, 1993). This would be a black woman who is a seductress and woos men into dangerous or fatal situations like Sunshine in the movie Harlem Nights. The siren could also be a woman who men fall for because of her neediness, but the love causes the man to put himself in jeopardy.

A black woman, who is naive, lacking in experience and in need of protection would be considered an innocent. We don't see many of those on the screen unless they are embodied in the mulatto.

Jewell in *From Mammies...* identified the Jezebel and Sapphire stereotypes. The Jezebel is also known as the bad-black girl. This black female character is most interested in having sexual encounters. She was embodied in the Jackee Harris character on 227, Sandra Clark. Before Jackee was seen on 227 she played a prostitute, turned entertainer, on one of the soap operas.

On the street is where we will find most of the Jezebels, working in the sex industry or seeking after white men for status. Usually she is a mulatto or she is very dark.

I think that the Jezebel stereotype is an attempt to justify the forced sexual relationships between white slave owners and black slave women. If there are Jezebels among black women then no white man can ever be accused of raping black women. Instead the woman will be accused of inviting or causing the sexual exploitation.

Sapphire of course is named after the wife on *Amos and Andy*. Jewell wrote that Sapphire is really a combination of Mammy and Aunt Jemima. Her existence, unlike the other black female stereotypes is predicated upon the existence of a no-good, lazy black male mythic character (Jewell, 1993, pg.45). He provides a target for her nagging. Sapphire is described as a black woman with an attitude. She is argumentative and verbally critical, maybe even verbally abusive. The Sapphire might be shown with hands on her hips and/or fingers in the face of her target. Sapphire is an updated Mammy. In the black community in the late 80's it was not unusual for a black woman to say, " I had to put on my Sapphire scarf" when she felt the need to be assertive or verbally put someone in his/her place.

Black Bucks

The black buck, a fifth mythic character, was fine tuned in W.B. Griffith's *Birth of a Nation* (Bogle, 1995). This stereotype moves from the black buck to the black brute. The black buck is a big, bad nigger, oversexed, savage, violent and frenzied with great lust for white women (Bogle, 1995). The black brute is barbaric and out to raise havoc. They dominate with physical violence and are depicted as suffering from sexual repression; they occupy the status of subhuman or feral. I would say that the black buck and the black brute are at two ends of a continuum describing what whites consider to be an out of control, oversexed black man. From what I can tell the major differences between the black buck and the black brute are intensity & duration of emotions and extremism in behavior. The brute would be to the right of that continuum.

The New Mythic Type
Professional Black Women and Men

The term "professional" can be used in several ways. Professional can refer to a person who is an expert at his or her job regardless of occupational status. For example, one could be a professional telephone operator, which is a semi skilled job. But, the person who does the job exceptionally well might be referred to as a professional. The word professional could also refer to the job someone does for a living, for example a professional cook or driver. Most of us cook and drive, but not professionally.

Lastly, the term professional can refer to a level of education and placement in the work force. These work force levels go from unskilled labor, semi-skilled labor, and skilled labor to the administrative/management level. When I use the term professional I am referring to a person who is college educated and therefore is acquainted with both the practical and theoretical aspects of a job. The practical aspects include the how of the job. The theoretical aspects include the "what should be" and the "why" of the work. A professional would be able to do the mechanics of a job and develop guidelines and policies that direct the process. Professional black men and women have become a new staple of TV and movie land.

There is in fact a stereotype of the black woman whose archetype is perhaps found in *Julia* and has reached its zenith to date in Claire Huxtable. This alternate image shall be referred to as the 'Professional Black Woman' (McLaurin, 1989-1990, p.47). She differs from the earlier female mythic characters in that she is educated and is not serving anyone.

The professional black woman is considered a mythical character because "earlier findings... have found black females, for the most part, to be grossly over represented in professional roles on television when compared to actual labor market statistics" (McLaurin, 1989-1990,p.45). Furthermore, much of the character comes from myth because the professional black woman is seldom shown interacting with other people of colour (McLaurin, 1989-1990). Often the communication and relationship styles are one dimensional because of this. A prime example is the black female attorney, Jessica, on the soap opera *As the World Turns.*

The professional black woman archetype is described as follows: stylishly dressed, well groomed and slim. She has few ethnic markers and speaks General American English rather than black dialect (McLaurin, 1989-1990,p.47). She is found in an integrated setting, usually serving the token role. Most often the professional black women is childless and single, with work being the passion of her life (McLaurin, 1989-1990,p.48). She predominately appears in dramatic rather than comedic programs and rarely has a romantic life. The black professional woman seldom has close interpersonal relationships with any characters regardless of race and gender.

The professional black male stereotype follows along the same lines as the professional black woman. Characters such as Barney on *Mission Impossible*, the series, Virgil Tibbs in *In the Heat of the Night*, the movie and series, and Tenafly fit the professional black male stereotype. Detective Harris on *Barney Miller*, played by Ron Glass, and Tim Reid on *WKRP* in Cincinnati are all examples of professional black men.

Professional Black People

The professional black person grew out of the persistent appearance of professional black men and women. In the 60's there emerged, at first, what looked like black characters without categories. Bogle refers to them as the untyped black and the colourless black. The untyped black woman was neither mammy nor mulatto, but a multidimensional character frequently appearing in Art House films of the 60's (Bogle, 1995, p.204; Kern-Foxworth, 1993). The colourless black was an African American who was so enmeshed in white culture that except for physical features s/he could not be distinguished from whites (Bogle, 1995).

> White writers, producers and directors did all they could to make audiences forget the blackness of a black star. They had no cultural identity ethnic edges had been sanded down so that while they looked black everything about them seemed expressed in a white cultural context. (Bogle, 1995, p.268)

In fact Douglas, a black woman and a former TV executive, called television the "bleached world of blacks" (1980). Bogle refers to the phenomenon of racially black, ethnically white characters as the blackface fixation.

As the 60's moved into the 70's, the seventies into the 80's and so forth it became apparent that the "untyped" and "colourless" black characters were appearing frequently enough to form a new category, the "professional black person". Both men and women fit this category. They are intelligent, educated, career people, functioning in integrated work settings and existing in isolation from other people of colour. They speak General American English and work by the book. Frequently the black professional person is colourless in terms of culture. Unlike the faithful sidekick who plays second banana to a white character, the professional black person either holds an autonomous position within an organization or s/he is a member of a team.

What makes the professional black person mythic character new and different is his/her autonomy in the organization and the amount of power wielded in the work environment. The professional black person will have a measure of formal power inherent in the position s/he holds within the organization rather than power derived from association with a white person. The professional black person is also different from other mythic characters in that s/he works as a member of a cohesive team, rather than as a servant to the team.

One of the functions of the professional black person is to serve as a conservatising force in the organization (McLaurin, 1989-1990). They most often spout the party line, support the status quo and insist on playing by the book (Butler, 1996). Furthermore they tend to be keepers of the traditions and think in legalistic ways.

There are five traditional archetypal black characters. From the turn of the century until the late 50's the traditional mythic characters included toms, coons, mammies, mulattos, and black bucks. In the 60's through 90's the new professional black archetype has been prevalent. The major differences between the five traditional characters and the professional black character are as follows. Mythic characters are severely limited in their choices of work due to racism. They are limited to a much greater extent than other racial groups in society. Traditional mythic characters will be domestics, entertainers, sidekicks, etc. They have no legitimate power. The power that a traditional black character might have would be derived from their association with a white character in the story or based on some interpersonal characteristics. The professional and often personal lives of traditional black characters are completely dependent upon relationships with whites. Furthermore, the traditional mythic character appears to favor the dominant society over his/her own.

Professional black characters, on the other hand, are in specific jobs because they chose to be. While racism continues to influence the life of the professional black characters they have infinitely more choices for careers than traditional characters. Their professional and personal well being are no more impacted by supervisors than anyone else in the organization. The professional black has legitimate power based on their position in the organization, not their relationship with a white person. Lastly, the professional black character makes career and personal choices based on what is appropriate for him/herself, not what is 'white'. The basic difference between traditional and professional black characters is choice and recognition of self-worth.

The Guises

As the decades passed variations of the mythic characters appeared in several guises and created the illusion that the screen representation of blacks had moved beyond the stereotypes. Guises are variations on mythic characters designed to fit current images. There is a bit more flexibility in the role boundaries, with traits that coincide with dominant culture behaviors. Often guises are difficult to recognize and may appear to be new. They include villains, court jesters, servants, entertainers, troubled people, angry militants (Bogle, 1995) and care taker administrators.

The villain is often used to camouflage black bucks. Drug dealers and pimps are popular 90's versions of the black buck. Court jesters camouflage the coon. i.e. J.J. on *Good Times* who constantly exclaimed "dy-no-miiite"! Servants are thinly disguised house slaves and appeared in such early TV shows as *Beulah, The Jack Benny Show, and The Stu Erwin Show* (Wilson and Gutiérrez, 1985).

The caretaker administrator has been a popular guise in the 90's. It is a variation on the tom character and the faithful servant guise. The caretaker administrator is a black person in a position of responsibility without authority. The role could be that of captain of a police precinct, mayor, or manager in a company. Caretakers are considered such because, while they are in a visible role of responsibility, they have no real decision-making power: he or she is there simply to facilitate the matriculation of paper work. Caretaker administrators usually serve as foils for the white main characters that work outside of the system. One of the first was the police captain on *Starsky and Hutch*. A more recent one is Captain Banks (Bruce A. Young) on *The Sentinel* (UPN).

The Sentinel is a police officer whose five senses have developed beyond the normal human. He is like a walking crime lab. The Sentinel has a young sidekick, a doctoral candidate, who makes sure he is safe while he is focused on evidence. Captain Banks is the superior officer to the Sentinel. Basically Captain Banks yells and worries a lot. Every now and then he goes out into the field. He has very little power.

Toms evolved from house slaves, to servants, to intelligent, faithful sidekicks to caretaker administrators. At times they have been guised as the new sensitive Negro. Coons began as pickaninnies and evolved into jesters then entertainers. Black bucks moved from field slaves, to convicts, to militant angry men, to drug dealers, to black super heroes and villains.

The tragic mulatto has not changed much, but the mammies have. They have developed from the female house slave, to the maid and the servant (Bogle, 1995 and Van DeBurg, 1984). In the 80's and 90's the guise has broadened to include the secretary, nurse, teacher, school principal and barkeep. These are all societal roles that involve nurturing and looking after the needs of others to the exclusion of self.

With the original black archetypes, which were crystallized in Birth of A Nation, the black characters were very visible, but without power. The new mythic archetype, the professional black person, differs from previous mythic characters and guises because s/he is not paired with a more powerful white partner as in the movie *Lethal Weapon*. He is not serving a white employer as Mac did on *Night Court* and he is not simply holding down the fort as Captain Banks does on *The Sentinel*.

There are many variations or guises of the six black mythic characters that have emerged from the literature relevant to black images on screen. They include villains, entertainers, jesters, servants, and care taker administrators.

Standard Themes

Once the mythic types were introduced on the screen then themes emerged that dominated stories with black characters. These included slavery and the old south (Guerrero, 1994), blacks as a social problem, integration and separatism (Bogle, 1995) as well as the themes of the changing south, the new south, and colour blind society. The movie version of *In the Heat of the Night* with Rod Steiger and Sidney Poitier was a great example of the changing south theme with a professional black person. An example of the new south theme, complete with sidekick and professional blacks, is the television version of *In the Heat of the Night* with Carroll O'Connor and the late Howard Rollins.

Slavery as a Standard Theme

By its very nature popular culture is formulaic. Whether it is art, music, novels, film, or television there are certain formulas used in the products of popular culture. In film and television this formulaic approach allows the audience to identify with the story lines and main characters. When the producers of popular products stray too far from the formulas, become too inventive, the product usually does not gain popularity (Giest & Nachbar, 1983, Part Six). One of the most popular formulas or themes in stories surrounding blacks is that of slavery. Guerrero wrote that

> While the slavery motif and the plantation genre have ended in most of their outright inscriptions, fragments of the motif still resonate as sediment themes, metaphors, and icons in the content of many contemporary films (1994,p.40).
>
> Slavery and resistance to it, is such a central and formative historical experience deeply rooted in the social imagination of all Americans, cinematic

> expressions of slavery have become sedimented in a range of symbolic or latent content of many films depicting African Americans (Guerrero, 1994, p.43).

Basically the use of the slavery motif supports one of two views. The first is that slavery was a system necessary to provide structure and sustenance for the child like African. Here, the media is used to rationalize "the original white hegemonic impulse" (Guerrero, 1994, p.35). The second use of the slavery motif is to demonstrate the barbaric and inhumane nature of the system and reaffirm that it is always best to fight oppression.

> What would be desirable in future cinematic inscriptions of slavery would be the production of black and other independent features that artfully historicize and politicize the issue in a way that not only reveals slavery's past but at the same time, by allegory, allusion, or otherwise, communicates its relevance to all Americans today. (Guerrero, 1994, p.35)

The science fiction genre provides several advantages in the polemics of slavery. It displaces the story in time and place. At the same time it connects the oppression and injustice of the ante-bellum south with today's inner-city experience (Guerrero, 1994). Furthermore it allows discussions in both the public and private sectors about the issues of slavery while providing a measure of emotional safety for all parties involved.

The appropriate use of the slavery motif can allow black Americans to understand themselves in the context of American and African American culture. It can also enable white Americans to understand themselves in the context of American and Eurocentric culture. This understanding can bring about the ability to finally move past the issue of slavery or transcend it (Guerrero, 1994).

Standard Contexts

When black characters appear in stories they are placed in certain contexts. Those contexts include plantations, churches, the south, prisons, ghettos, inner cities, and crime ridden and drug infested areas. They are also frequently placed in service industries, athletic arenas, the sex industry and entertainment.

Binary Relationships

Imbedded in the standard themes incorporating whites and blacks in close associations are certain formulaic binary interpersonal relationships, two characters orbiting together, like two stars. They are the huckfinn fixation (Bogle, 1995) and the miss daisy syndrome (which Bogle refers to as the master servant syndrome). The huckfinn fixation reads as follows, "A good white person opposes the corruption and pretenses of dominant white culture. In rejecting society the white person takes up with an outcast" (Bogle, 1995, p.140). The outcast is usually "a trusty black who never competes with the white man and serves as a reliable ego padder" (Bogle, 1995, p.140).

This sort of binary relationship can be seen on *Walker: Texas Ranger*. On this show Cordel Walker (Chuck Norris) is a white Texas Ranger with a black sidekick by the name of Trivet (Clarence Gilyard). Often at the core of the huckfinn fixation is the notion of black-white male bonding (Bogle, 1995).

The lethal weapon pattern is a variation on the huckfinn fixation. Here a white person who is a misfit in white society or who is seen as a maverick is paired with a black person. The maverick and the black person are paired for two reasons: (1) according to American society "blacks don't fit either" and (2) a black person would not have the power to reel the other person in. The black character validates the white character, provides emotional support and serves as back up.

This binary relationship was fine-tuned in the *Lethal*

This binary relationship was fine-tuned in the *Lethal Weapon* movies. A television version of it can be seen on the 1996 mid-season Fox replacement show *Swift Justice*. In this series Max Swift, a former police officer and a computer wizard, protects those in distress. He works outside of the formal law enforcement structure and is given certain cases to work on by his former partner and sidekick Paterson, who is black.

The miss daisy syndrome is frequently the binary relationship in a major theme involving a white person with a black who serves him/her. The syndrome is named after the movie, *Driving Miss Daisy*. Two other television examples are *Designing Women* with Anthony & the four Georgia Peaches and *I'll Fly Away*.

Relationship of Black Characters to the White Community

All of the mythic types and guises can be categorized by their relationship to the white community. They are either non-assimilated or assimilated (Banks, 1977). A non-assimilated or traditional black character "contains all the stereotypical baggage associated with ethnic black culture and is frequently found [in] ethnicoms"(McLaurin, 1989-1990,p.47) like *Martin* and *The Wayans Brothers*. The assimilated or novel character "generally possesses all the positive attributes normally associated with white characters and is frequently found in integrated programming" (McLaurin, 1989-1990, p.47).

Harriet and Carl, in the television series *Perfect Strangers*, exemplify assimilated blacks. At a newspaper where two cousins work Harriet is the elevator operator and Carl, her husband, is a police officer. While on *Perfect Strangers* Harriet and Carl were shown as assimilated characters. In their spin-off show *Family Matters* they are non-assimilated.

Most black characters can be traced to one or a combination of the mythic types or guises with an assimilated or non-assimilated relationship to the white community. Furthermore the story lines can be traced to specific themes. For example, Guinan of TNG could fit the mammy, handkerchief head, mythic character and Worf the black buck. Tuvok, while he is a professional black Vulcan, is also an advisor to Captain Janeway on *Voyager*. In the first season of DS9 Benjamin Sisko was a muted administrator. Dr. Leah Brahms, a character who eventually married Geordi on TNG, was a flawed mulatto. Geordi, himself, was a professional black man with one major flaw-- he was sight impaired. All of the aforementioned characters are assimilated into an integrated society.

Black Characters on TV Today

Black characters seldom move beyond the five mythical stereotypes or the quise of them. These images are designed to answer specific social needs of the dominant society including providing plentiful, cheap labor, justifying the exploitation of a people and their resources and supporting war efforts. It is seldom that a black character is explored beyond the stereotype.

The images of blacks on screen have been limited since they first appeared. Primarily they have been limited to the five basic black mythic stereotypes including toms, coons, mulattos, mammies, and black-bucks. These stereotypes were guised as the decades wore on by black characters such as the villains, entertainers, servants, and caretaker administrators. The 60's ushered in a new stereotype, the professional black person. This character is considered a mythic stereotype because it is portrayed much more often on screen than it appears in real life.

There are several story themes, which traditional employ black characters including slavery, ill-fated interracial love, the old south, and the new south, racial harmony, and prison stories.

Relationships between blacks and white are also shown in stereotypical ways. They include the huckfinn fixation, the miss daisy syndrome, and the lethal weapon pattern. Black characters can appear as novel, assimilated blacks totally submersed in white culture or unassimilated in white culture while totally submersed in their own community. The unassimilated character has little interaction with people from other races or ethnicitys.

While the professional black character is usually working as an assimilated novel entity in an all white setting they still broaden the categories for which black people are acceptable characters. Furthermore, the professional black character wields formal power within an organization commensurate with his/her position in the organization. He/she is not there to serve or nurture the white characters.

Based on my own survey of the 1996-1997 season of television programs images of black men have improved considerably over the past decade. Figure 1 contains a list of most of the current shows that have black men as heads of household, lead role, or team member. While the images of black women have continued to improve they have not had the same success in leading roles as black men. With the exception of *The Burning Zone, ST: Next Generation*, and *Voyager* all of the shows listed in Figure 1 revolve around black male leads.

Figure 1

TV Show and Occupation of Head of Household or Lead Male Character

Babylon 5	Doctor
Baywatch and Baywatch Nights	Police Officer and investigator
Cosby	Retired from airlines
Family Matters	Police Officer, students
Fresh Prince of Bel Air	Judge, students, butler
Goode Behavior	College professor Philosophy
Hanging with Mr. Cooper	Teacher
Homeboys in Space	Pilots of freighter ship
In the House	Athlete and doctor
Jamie Foxx Show	Hotel clerk
Living Single	Accountant

Living Single	Accountant
Malcolm and Eddie	Café owner, mechanic
Martin	Game show producer
Moesha	Owns car dealership
New York Undercover	Police Officers
Sister, Sister	Owner limousine service
Sparks	Lawyers
St: Deep Space Nine	Station Commander
St: Next Generation	Navigator and security officer
Steve Harvey Show	Music teacher, coach
The Burning Zone	Investigator and Security Chief
The Cape	Astronaut
The Parent'Hood	College professor Communications
The Sentinel	Police Captain
Voyager	Tactical Officer
Walker: Texas Ranger	Texas Ranger
Wayans Brothers	Work in father's café

Only three of the shows listed in Figure 2 have black female leads, *Living Single, Touched by an Angel, and Moesha.* Shows in Figure 2 like those in Figure 1 were also taken from my own survey of prime time television in the Fall-Spring season of 1996-1997. This survey is not an exhaustive one, but it is fairly representative of what is on television today.

Figure 2

TV Show and Occupation of Lead Black Female Or Black Female Supporting Role

Cosby	Wife
Family Matters	Security guard
Fresh Prince of Bel Air	English Professor, weather reporter

Hanging with Mr. Cooper	Principle, teacher
In the House	Student, gym personnel
Jamie Foxx Show	Hotel owner, Hotel clerk
Living Single	Magazine editor, lawyer, actress, Costumer
Moesha	Student, teacher, café owner
Sister, Sister	Students, seamstress
Sparks	Lawyer, receptionist
ST: Deep Space Nine	Freedom fighter
ST:Next Generation	Barkeep
Steve Harvey Show	Principal
The Cape	Astronaut
The Parent'Hood	Law school graduate
Touched by an Angel	Instructor of angels
Wayans Brothers	Security guard

Conclusion

While the images of blacks on television have become broader in scope and more in-depth there are still areas that have not been addressed. There is a need for more shows with black women lead characters and there is a need for more shows that feature working class blacks. Presently, blacks in the professional ranks are over represented on television and it gives the impression that they are better off economically than they actually are.

One other goal for writers and producers of TV and film images is to create more stories that present integrated communities. While many parts of the country and many large cities continue to have segregated neighborhoods there are communities where people live in integrated settings. We are seeing some of this in educational settings such as *Nick Freno: Licensed Teacher* and *The Steve Harvey Show* on the WB network. Viewers need to see stories set in the home where the neighbors are diverse.

References

Banks, C. (1977). A content analysis of the treatment of black Americans on television. *Social Education, 41*, 336-339.

Bogle, D. (1995). *Toms, coons, mulattos, mammies, & bucks: An interpretive history of blacks in American film*. New York: Continuum.

Berger, A. (1992). *Popular culture genres: Theories and texts*. Newbury Park: Sage Publications.

Brummett, B. (1994). Rhetoric in popular culture. New York: St. Martin's Press.

Butler, B. (1996). Interview. Professor of Theatre, San Jose State University.

Byrd, M. (Nov. 1995). Images of Blacks in Star Trek: The Original Series. Paper presented at the Speech Communication Association Convention, San Antonio, TX.

Diawara, M. (1995). Black American cinema: The new realism. In Martin Michael (Ed.) *Cinemas of the Black Diaspora: Diversity, Dependence and Oppositionality*. Detroit: Wayne State University Press.

Giest, C. (1983). From the plantation to the police station: A brief history of black stereotypes. In Christopher Giest and Jack Nachbar (Eds.). *The Popular Culture Reader*. Bowling Green: Bowling Green University Popular Press.

Guerrero, E. (1993). *Framing blackness: The African*

American image in film. Philadelphia: Temple University Press.

Hoffman, F.W. (1995). *American popular culture: A guide to the reference literature.* Englewood, CA: Libraries Unlimited.

hooks, B. (1996). *Reel to real: Race, sex and class at the movies.* New York: Routledge.

Inge, M.T. (1983) (2nd ed.). *Handbook of American popular culture.* New York: Greenwood Press.

Jewell, K.S. (1993). *From mammy to Miss America: Cultural images & the shaping of US social policy.* New York: Routledge.

Kern-Foxworth, M. (1994). *Aunt Jemima, Uncle Ben, and Rastus: Blacks in advertising, yesterday today and tomorrow.* West Port, Conn.: Praeger.

Lee, S. with Wiley, R. (1992). *By any means necessary: The trials and tribulations of making Malcolm X.* New York: Hyperion.

Logan, M. (May 14-20). The magnificent seven. *TV Guide:* Radnor PA: News America Publications.

Marger, M. (1985). *Race and ethnic relations.* Belmont, CA: Wadsworth, Inc.

Means, R.(1991). Fighting words on the future of the Earth. In *Questioning Technology: Tool, Toy or Tyrant*? John Zerzan and Alice Carnes (Eds.). Santa Cruz, CA: New Society Publishers. pp. 71-82.

Mestel, R. (February 1994). Education...the final frontier. *New Scientist, 141*(1914) , p.11.

Milner, D. (1983). *Children and race*. Beverly Hills: Sage Publications.

Myers, K. (1994). Boldly going where no law school class has gone before. *The National Law Journal, 17*(14). p.A17,col.1.

Reeves-Stevens, J. & G.(1994). *The making of Star Trek: Deep Space Nine*. New York: Pocket Books.

McLaurin, P. (1989-1990). From Beulah to Claire Huxtable, you've come a long way girl, or have you: A black woman and television. *Missouri Speech and Theatre Journal, 20,* 39-50.

Nemeses, L. (1992). *Star Trek: The next generation companion*. New York: Pocket Books.

Root, R. (1987).*The rhetoric of popular culture.* New York: Greenwood Press.

United States Commission on Civil Rights (95th Congress, 1st Session, 1977). Window Dressing on the set: Women and Minorities on Television.

Van DeBurg, W. (1984). *Slavery and race in American popular culture.* Madison: University of Wisconsin Press.

Wilson II, Clint, and Gutiérrez, F. (1985). *Minorities and media: Diversity and the end of mass communication.* Beverly Hills: Sage Publications.

Seggar, J., Hafen, J. & Hannon-Gladden, H. (Summer 1981). Television's portrayals of minorities and women in drama and comedy drama 1971-80. *Journal of Broadcasting, 25*(3),pp. 277-288.

Tan, A. and Tan, G.(Winter 1979). Television use and self-esteem of Blacks. *Journal of Communication.* pp. 129-135.

Voithofer, R.J. (1996). *Making identities: Challenging representations of language, gender, and race in high tech television programs.* In Proceedings of Selected Research and Development Presentations at the National Convention of the Association for Educational Communications and Technology (18th, Indianapolis, IN.).

Zoglin, R.(November 28, 1994). Trekking onward. *Time Magazine.* New York: Time, Inc.

Movie Review: *Star Trek: First Contact*

It is the day before legendary Zephram Cochrane achieves the first warp flight. It is also the day before First contact, but something is very wrong. The attacking ship is Borg." (Fisher, 1996, 46). The problem is that the Borg are not supposed to be in the 21st century. They are trying to erase the past so that the Federation will not exist in the future. Captain Picard and his crew must go back to the past to keep the Borg from destroying Earth. This is the opening sequence of the 1996 Star Trek movie, *First Contact.*

Alfre Woodard played the lovely, strong, and fierce Lily Slone. She was one of the four leading characters of the story. Slone was not a mammy, a servant, nor a prostitute. She was a colleague of Zephram Cochrane the physicist who was pivotal in the development of faster than light space travel. She was a freedom fighter and was able to capture and hold at bay non other than Picard himself. Even more exciting was the fact that this black woman was allowed to retain her natural beauty: she wore no wigs, weaves, or falls. She sported a short afro, which was something we have not in the movies seen since the 60's and 70's. Even when garbed in a satin gown her head was crowned in its original glory of short, tight curls.

Lily took Jean Luc to task when he was seeking revenge. And the big surprise--she did not offer to sacrifice her life to help Picard save Data. When Lily realized that Picard was going to stay aboard the Enterprise to save Data I fully expected her to say, "I'll stay with you." What a delightful surprise to hear her say, 'You go save your friend" and then turn and leave the ship. Here was a black female character that was not expendable.

Johnathan Frakes, who plays Riker, also directed the eighth Star Trek movie. He said that Patrick Stewart (Picard) and Alfre Woodard (Lily) were great together. "Their characters were sort of Tracey/Hepburn" combination "connecting as actors, as people and across the same work ethic. They look great together." (Fisher, 1996, pg 46). The depiction of a black female as a heroine, freedom fighter, scientist and unexpendable is the kind of characterization that helps break stereotypes. Bravo Star Trek. My score ****

***Fisher, D. (1996). Star Trek: First Contact. *Star Trek Communicator*, #109, pg. 44.-50**

Chapter 3
Blacks on the Original Series

Star Trek: The Original Series first aired on September 8,1966 and ran until 1969. The seventy-nine original episodes gave birth to an American popular culture phenomenon that has spanned 30 years

and shows no signs of stopping. TOS has been described as a series of morality plays set in space. The television series "Star Trek: The Next Generation" has supplied philosophy instructors with some superb examples of moral dilemmas dressed up as good entertainment. (Rosenstand, 1994,p.165)

Not only has Star Trek been described as a series of morality plays, it has also been referred to as a good ol' western set aboard a space ship (Roth, 1985).

According to Roddenberry's vision of the future, people of African descent had made it to the stars. Black viewers hung on to the sight of the few black characters presented in the series because it was better than what had been shown in previous episodic television. Many African Americans were given their first reason to watch science fiction because TOS showed blacks as commissioned and non-commissioned crew members in a space adventure. These characters stood out in contrast to the background of white characters, but exactly what images did they portray? This is an important question because the images of blacks on screen influence the way the entire society views African Americans.

Six major black characters represented the only people of

African descent in the Alpha quadrant, a heavy burden to carry. In view of the fact that the sample of people of African descent was small it is important to understand who they were and how they were portrayed.

Character Sketches

James Kirk: White male, captain of the Starship Enterprise. Originally from Iowa. In his time period the youngest to command a starship.

Mr. Spock: Vulcan/human male, science officer. Culture valued management of the emotions and the triumph of reason over feelings. They were long-lived, empathic and stronger than the average human.

Dr. McCoy (Bones): White male, medical doctor, Southerner. Frequently argued the merits of emotions and intuition over logic and reason with Spock.

Montgomery Scott (Scotty): White male, engineer. Always able to deliver what the captain ordered from the engines even when it seemed impossible.

Sulu: Asian male, helmsman. Born in San Francisco. At times served as tactical officer and acting captain. Hobbies included fencing and gun collecting.

Chekov: White male, Russian, navigator.

Black Characters
Uhura

Lt. Uhura, played by Nichelle Nichols, was a black female and a permanent member of the bridge crew (Trimble, 1976). Based on my survey of the 79 episodes and the cast members that appeared in each I calculated that Uhura appeared in 82% of the episodes. In Nichols' autobiography titled Beyond Uhura (1994) a detailed description of who Uhura the character was supposed to be is included.

> She would be a citizen of the United States of Africa. And her name would be Uhura...derived from Uhuru, which is Swahili for freedom...Uhura was far more than an intergalactic telephone operator. As head of Communications, she commanded a corps of largely unseen communications technicians, linguists, and other specialist who worked in the bowels of the Enterprise, in the comm-center. A linguistics scholar and a top graduate of Starfleet Academy, she was a protégé of Mr. Spock.(p.144-145)

This was the character outline sketched out by Roddenberry and Nichols.

Of all of the black characters Uhura has been written about most often. "Nichelle was one of the first Black actors to be cast as a regular featured character on a network television series in the 60's (Park, 1988, p.9).
The other was Bill Cosby in *I Spy*.

Women played a larger role in Star Trek than any other series at the time. Modern women may see Uhura as nothing more than a glorified telephone operator. But, in 1966 just to have a woman in contact with Starfleet at all was a breakthrough (Editor, 1988).It was a ground breaking stroke to make her part of the command crew.

Uhura's first appearance was in the episode *The Corbomite Maneuver*. Her presence on the bridge fulfilled two minority categories, women and African American. Her job basically included running the communications center from the bridge. According to Deegan she "filled the traditional female role of translating linguistic meaning"(1986, p.209). Uhura also served as the opponent of several female aliens threatening the crew or ship.

Of all the black characters Uhura was the only one that was overtly identified as African. In the episode, *Is There No truth in Beauty?*, written by Jean Lisette, the Medusan ambassador to the federation inhabits Spock's body in order to navigate the ship back home from an uncharted region of space. As Kollos, the ambassador, coexisted with Spock he sees Uhura and says, “She walks in beauty, like the night"(Byron, 1815).

In the episode *The Savage Curtain* a re-creation of Abraham Lincoln referred to Uhura as a "Negress." This was an appropriate word for Lincoln's time period. Uhura did not appear to be uncomfortable with the label.

Uhura's memory was wiped clean by a space probe gone astray (Nomad) in The Changeling. She had to relearn the Swahili language from the use of language tapes. The choice of first language, the name Uhura, and overt comments about her racio-ethnic markers indicated Uhura's origins. She was the only black character identified as such.

In the *Star Trek Encyclopedia* (1994) Uhura is reduced to a "highly skilled technician" (p.357) even though she was an officer. Apparently even in a fictitious universe it is difficult for a black person to hold on to her rank! In this reference guide Uhura is extolled for being a talented musician. She sang in two episodes, *Charlie X* and *The Conscience of the King*.

Nichelle Nichols made television history when she was part of the first interracial kiss to be aired on serial television. *Plato's Stepchildren* is the episode in which this famous kiss appeared. The story line concerned a race of people with psychokinetic powers. The set was similar to a Greek or Roman court where the ruling class was said to have engaged in many perverted pleasures.

The kiss between Kirk and Uhura was shown as a perverted desire of the Platonians. They enjoyed forcing the characters to do things they wouldn't normally do. This black woman and white man had to be forced to kiss. Nichols wrote that two versions of the encounter were taped, one with a non-kiss and one with a kiss. In order to keep the network from choosing the non-kiss version that tape was destroyed (Nichols, 1994, p.161).

Uhura had one particularly violent experience during the series. Apparently she was raped in the episode titled *The Gamesters of Triskelion.* Kirk, Uhura, and Chekov were trapped on Triskelion, a planet used to train newly captured aliens for life as slaves and gladiators. Each Enterprise crew member was assigned a personal trainer. Uhura's trainer was a hulking white male. In attempting to subdue Uhura the trainer raped her in her retention cell. The cameras cut away from the scene. Kirk called out, "Uhura, are you alright?" as she screamed. Unfortunately even Captain Kirk could not save her from this brutal attack!

Based on the taxonomy of black characters discussed in Chapter 2, Uhura was a professional black woman-entertainer. She was not a server, that was Yeoman Rand's job. She was not the nurturer, those duties belonged to Dr. McCoy (Bones) and Nurse Chapel. As far as her character was developed in the 79 episodes, Uhura was single, childless and had one passion, her job. She was characterized as an "entertainer" because she sang in two episodes. She was slim and spoke General American English. Her relationship to the larger space community was assimilated. While she was not colourless in that ethnic markers identifying her as black were presented across the episodes, she never communicated or interacted in any recognizable way as a black woman.

Uhura had the power associated with a member of the bridge crew and had no close relationships with either men or women. She fit the professional black person mythic character.

Daystrom

Daystrom won the prestigious Nobel and ZEE-Magnees prizes in 2243 at the age of 24 for his breakthrough in duotronics, which became the basis for computer systems aboard Federation starships for over 80 years.(Okuda, Okuda and Mirek, 1994, p.69)

Dr. Richard Daystrom was played by William Marshall and appeared in the episode *The Ultimate Computer*. Daystrom was a 23rd century computer scientist, inventor of comptronic and duotronic systems (Okuda, Okuda and Mirek, 1994). He came aboard the Enterprise to test his new computer M-5. It was designed to run the ship without human crews and Daystrom was testing it in war game simulations. The computer circuits in M-5 had been imprinted not only with the neural engrams of Daystrom's brain, but also with his insecurities. M-5 almost killed 500 members of Starfleet on other ships before it was convinced to self-destruct. "The failure of his creation pushed Daystrom over the edge of insanity and he was committed to a rehabilitation center for treatment" (Okuda, Okuda and Mirek, 1994, p.69).

The writers presented Daystrom as a "mad scientist". He was portrayed as insane because he dared to think that humans could be replaced with machines. His experience aboard the Enterprise served to underscore one of the major premises promulgated throughout the show, pure reasoning and logic can never replace intuition and emotions: technology is never a substitute for humans.

While the writers implied that Daystrom was mad because he tried to put machines before humans, I would suggest that he was driven insane by racism. As Daystrom began to experience a nervous breakdown he talked about the fact that people sneered at his accomplishments and called him a boy wonder. But he went on to say that while they laughed "they stole my work and used my ideas" (STO: *The Ultimate Computer*, 1968).

Daystrom's story was a familiar one for African American scholars. The appropriation of intellectual and scholarly property from African American scholars by white scholars has been a topic for formal discussion in many present day professional and academic associations. Apparently it was still an issue in 2260. While the author of the story, Laurence N. Wolf, and the teleplay writer, D.C. Fontana, presented the viewers with a black scientist devoid of ethnic markers the correlation between his race and the stealing of his work was obvious to many black professionals.

The character of Daystrom fit the professional black male mythic type. He was colourless in terms of ethnic identifiers and he spoke a high register of General American English. Daystrom had one passion, his work. He was shown out of context in that he had no links with other people of colour. Daystrom wore the guise of "villain" because he sought to put technology---machines, before man. He was the perfect antagonist as the brilliant, but crazy, "Negro".

Masters

Lt. Charlene Masters, played by Janet MacLachlen, appeared in the episode Alternative Factor (1967). Don Ingalls wrote the episode. The basic plot revolved around "A mysterious rip in space opened between our universe and an antimatter universe, threatening the existence of both" (Okuda, Okuda and Mirek, 1994, p.7). The rip was evidenced by the appearance of a man called Lazarus as matter and anti-matter.

One bonus feature of this episode was "the casting of black actress Janet MacLachlen as Lt. Charlene Masters, another high ranking responsible female" (Greenberger, 1991, p.24). More important to this discussion than the fact that Masters was a responsible female was the fact that she was a black female and an engineer! Masters was identifiable as a person of African lineage because of her skin colour and she was wearing a short natural. It could be assumed that she was a highly competent engineer because she was in charge of the engine room in the absence of Scotty.

Though a competent officer, Masters was unable to defend herself and was overcome in the engine room by Lazarus. She was forced to show a "feminine frailty" that is required of women to "mask their actual competency... within a world dominated by patriarchal assumptions and masculine authorities" (Jenkins, 1991, p.184). Jenkins suggested that most women in science fiction are forced to do so. Masters was no exception.

As with the previous characters, Masters was a professional black person. She spoke General America. English and was slim. Like Uhura, Masters was working as a novel, assimilated black. Masters was another of the racially black characters with no ethnic identifiers. In this limited role we were to learn nothing of her background.

Boma

Don Marshall played Lt. Boma (Okuda, Okuda and Mirek, 1994). The story line in *Galileo Seven* placed several crew members in a shuttle craft on a planet where they were under attack by big, fury, stone age creatures. The central issue in this episode, written by Oliver Crawford, was Mr. Spock's apparent lack of emotions, therefore humanity. Spock chose to leave a dead crew member unburied, refused to say a few words over the body when the others insisted on burial, and predicted that one crew member would have to be left behind if the shuttle craft was to reach orbit. All of these decisions were based on the fact that the shuttle craft and crew were under heavy attack from the indigenous beings and Spock was trying to save the crew.

Mr. Boma's role was to be the voice of the status quo. He stood out among the crew members in admonishing Spock for his lack of respect for Earth customs. He, Boma, insisted on burying the body of his fallen comrade even though he risked death to do so.

In this episode someone, perhaps casting agent, producer, director or author, decided to use a black character to employ pathos in the long running series debate over logic and emotion. Contrary to the Euro-Western tradition of casting logic as highly preferable to emotions, in this episode emotion was extolled as a virtue. A black character espoused the lines supporting the role of emotions in decision-making. This was ironic in view of the fact blacks are frequently criticized by whites for being "too emotional" and "overreacting". This is exactly what Boma was doing, but it was shown as preferable to logic in this instance. Boma's reactions were not typical of people of African descent who, in the face of life threatening situations, know when to work on escape and "let the dead bury the dead." Otherwise, we would have perished as a race long ago.

Boma fit the professional black mythic type. He was a member of a hand-picked crew chosen to be on the shuttle. He spoke General English and wore an executive type afro. He could be identified as black only on the basis of his racial markers: skin colour and hair texture. His lines could have been spoken by any one of the people on the shuttle. Boma was an assimilated character interacting with no other people of colour. He spoke as a conservatising force or check on Spock's behavior.

Stone

Commodore Stone was the senior administrator at Starbase 11 in the episode titled *Court Martial*. Percy Rodriguez played the Commodore who had commanded a starship earlier in his career (Okuda, Okuda and Mirek ,1994, p.323). Here again the character was not overtly identified as being of African ancestry, but obviously was. Stone played the care taker administrator who advised Kirk to resign his commission rather than fight a court-martial action. The boy wonder, the youngest ever to command a starship, Kirk of course chose to stand and fight for his rights.

Stone was the senior officer at the court-martial proceedings and was the one to dismiss the proceedings after Ben Finney, the crew member that Kirk was supposed to have killed was found alive. Stone was an early version of the care taker black administrator, chosen to serve as the foil for the young, white, maverick central character.

Stone was a professional black person with high occupational status: he administrated a starbase. He spoke General American English. While Stone was racially black he was ethnically white. There could be no distinctions made between Stone and other Starfleet brass. He espoused the party line, encouraging Kirk to resign rather than to bring disgrace to himself and Starfleet.

M' Benga

Dr. M'Benga was played by Brooker Bradshaw (Trimble, 1976). In *The Star Trek Concordance* M'Benga is described as a tall, slender elegant African (1976). M'Benga was never identified as being of African heritage, but his name and appearance suggested it. He appeared in two episodes, *That Which Survives* and *The Private Little War*. M'Benga was a medical officer who had interned on Vulcan. Consequently he was the only doctor in the Federation who knew more about Vulcan physiology than Dr. McCoy. With the exception of Uhura, M'Benga was the only black character to appear in more than one episode.

M'Benga was also a professional black character. He was a medical doctor, fully assimilated and he interacted with few people outside of those in the infirmary.

Against the backdrop of the Eurocentric dominance of the Star Trek universe stood six black characters, the first of whom was included in the cast to "add a little colour to the bridge" (Nichols, 1994, p.145). These characters held the positions of Commodore, doctor, and lieutenant. Most were never given the responsibility commensurate with their rank. We never saw Uhura in charge of the communication corp, we never saw M'Benga practice except under the auspices of McCoy, we never saw Daystrom emerge from the asylum, and we never saw Commodore Stone away from Starbase 11. Even so three of the characters have enjoyed extended life in other forms of Trek popular culture.

Trek books, Cartoons and Films

The Star Trek universe is vast including television series, movies, cartoons, comic books, novels, and literature produced by the fans themselves (Trimble, 1976). Most of the writing stays within the foundation principles developed by Gene Roddenberry in the original series, but the stall of writers who produce novels and fans who write for newsletters and fanzines extend the story lines and characters to fill-in the blank spaces. In seventy-nine episodes the audience could be shown very little about the personal lives of the characters and all of the stories of space adventure could not be told. Therefore many character lines were more carefully developed in novels and movies based on TOS including the lives of three characters Uhura, Daystrom and M'Benga.

Uhura

One fan asked, “How does Uhura feel about her lack of promotion...what does she try to do about it...How would she handle an emergency or a case of sexual harassment? (E. Osbourne, 1987, p.171). These questions were partially answered in the Classic Trek novel series, fanzines and the movies. Henry Jenkins in his essay titled, "Star Trek Rerun, Reread, Rewritten: Fan Writing as Textual Poaching", (1988) suggested that many women were fans of the series because it fanned "the desires of traditional women..." with the "suggestion of non-traditional feminine pleasures of greater and more active involvement for women within the adventure of professional space travel" (p.182).

Furthermore Jenkins hypothesized that "some have been devastated over the repeated failure of the series and feature films to give Lt. Uhura command duties commensurate with her rank"(p.182). Because "these promises were unfulfilled" fans and professional writers extended the Uhura character and added greater texture. They engaged in answering the "what ifs."

In novels based on TOS Uhura obtained a Ph.D. in linguistics. She was known throughout the Federation for her work in improving the "universal translator" which was first introduced in the episode written by Gene Coon titled *Metamorphosis*. Uhura took language samples from each new culture the ship encountered which enabled linguists to develop grammars for those languages.

In the novel *ST: Uhura's Song* (Kagan, 1985) the lieutenant was also credited with collecting music samples from across the galaxy which facilitated in the understanding of various cultures and propagated the study of xenomusicology. She was again connected with music in the book The Tears of the Singers (Snodgrass, 1984). And, Uhura was instrumental in saving the galaxy from extinction in the book *The Three Minute Universe* (Paul, 1988).

Daystrom

Daystrom left the Ultimate Computer episode insane. However, later he either regained his sanity and founded the Daystrom Institute of Technology or the Institute was founded in his name by others. Dr. Leah Brahms, a character appearing in TNG: *Booby Trap,* was said to have attended the Institute. In the last episode of TNG Geordi told Picard that his wife Leah was working at the Daystrom Institute. That time period was 25 years after TNG seven year voyage. While no one actually said what happened to Dr. Daystrom himself his work was recognized and he received the credit he deserved. The Daystrom Institute continued to train the best engineers in the Federation and provide leadership in engineering technology (Okuda, Okuda and Mirek, 1994).

Dr. M'Benga

While the good doctor did not appear in any more episodes of TOS, nor the movies, he did appear in several of the Trek novels. He never had a major role in the stories, but continued to be an intermittent presence on the ship.

Conclusion

If the media is to aid in the development of positive self-esteem in young African Americans and improved multicultural relationships in society more realistic images of blacks must appear on the screen. TOS both aided and hindered this process. It aided the process by breaking from the traditional mythic black characters and presenting blacks in roles that portrayed them as competent members of the organization. The creator of Star Trek, Gene Roddenberry, and his stall of writers took one step forward with the professional black character. So, the series did actually take the viewing audience "where no man has gone before" in its presentation of individual black characters. However, in upcoming chapters we will see how Roddenberry and his posse hindered the development of positive self-esteem in young African Americans by stepping back into theatre and film history in the use of the black buck.

References

Bogle, D. (1995). Toms coons, mulattos, mammies and bucks: *An interpretive history of blacks in American film.* New York: Continuum.

D'Ignazio, F. (Mar 1991). The starship Enterprise: New opportunities for learning in the 1990's. *Language Arts, 68*(3), 248-252.

Editor, (December 12 1988). *The New New Yorker, 64*(43), 37-38.

Greenberger, R.(1991). *The alternative factor, Star Trek 25th anniversary special.* New York: Starlog Communications International.

Guerrero, E. (1993). *Framing blackness: The African American image in film.* Philadelphia: Temple University Press.

Jenkins III, H. (June 1988). Star Trek, rerun, reread, rewritten: Fan writing as textual poaching. *Critical Studies in Mass Communication, 5*(2), 85-107

Kern-Foxworth, M. (1994) *Aunt Jemima, Uncle Ben, and Rastus: Blacks in advertising, yesterday, today and tomorrow.* West Port, Conn.: Praeger.

McLaurin, P. (1989-1990). From Beulah to Claire Huxtable, you've come a long way girl, or have you: A black woman and television. *Missouri Speech and Theatre Journal, 20,* 39-50.

Nemecek, L.(1992). *Star Trek: The next generation companion.* New York: Pocket Books.

Nichols, N.(1994). *Beyond Uhura: Star Trek and other memories.* New York: G.P. Putnam's.

Okuda, M., Okuda, D. and Mirek, D. (1994).*Star Trek encyclopedia: A reference guide to the future.* New York: Pocket Books.

Osbourne, E. (1991)., Star Trek, rerun, reread, rewritten: Fan writing as textual poaching. In H. Jenkins III, *Close Encounters: Film, feminism, and science fiction,* Constance Henley (Ed.). Minneapolis: University of Minnesota Press, 171-198

Rosenstand, N. (1995).The moral of the story : An introduction to questions of ethics and human nature. Mountain View, CA: Mayfield Publishing Co.

Trimble, B. (1976). *Star Trek concordance.* New York: Ballantine Books.

Chapter 4
Blacks on *The Next Generation*

The second installment of ST occurred eighteen years after the original show was canceled. *Star Trek: The Next Generation* began in 1984 and ran seven years until 1991. The plot for TNG was an extension of the one for TOS. It was framed in the prologue of the show.

> Space, the final frontier. These are the voyages of the Starship Enterprise. Its continuing mission: to explore strange new worlds; to seek out new life and new civilizations; to boldly go where no one has gone before.

Character Sketches

Jean Luc Picard: White male, French, captain of the Enterprise-D. Cerebral leadership style.

William Riker (Number One): White male, Canadian. First officer. Hobby, playing jazz.

Beverly Crusher: White female, medical doctor.

Worf: Black male, Klingon, Chief of Security.

Geordi La Forge: Black male, chief engineer. Blind, wore visor.

Deanna Troi: White female, Betazoid, counselor. Empathic abilities.

Data: White male, android (being made of artificial and biogenetic materials). Different from robot in that robot has only mechanical components. His quest was to become more human.

These characters were dubbed "The Magnificent Seven" (Logan, 1994) and that primary ensemble included two black characters, Geordi and Worf. By the second season Whoppie Goldberg had convinced Roddenberry to add her to the series. The number of permanent black crew members increased from one in TOS to three in TNG.

In addition to the three recurring black characters on the show in the episode titled *The Masterpiece Society* a black man served as the interpreter of his society's laws. In the episodes *The Booby Trap*, *Galaxy's Child* and *Aquiel* mulatto/black women appeared in romantic relationships with Geordi. Nicholai, Worf's foster brother, was married to a black woman in *Homeward*. These are just a few of the black characters that appeared in the series. This analysis is not intended to be an encyclopedic review of all of the black characters in TNG, but rather an analysis of the series regulars and story lines where blacks played prominent roles.

Geordi: The Tinker

Geordi La Forge (LeVar Burton) appeared on the first show and figured prominently in the second year of the show. He was blind from birth and wore a Visor, which enabled him to see beyond human sight. Ironically enough in the first season Geordi served as navigator. During the second season he was promoted to Chief Engineer, a job performed on the Enterprise-A (TOS) by Scotty.

As an engineer Geordi was always building or repairing equipment on the ship. He was a gifted engineer in that he made improvements to the ship before they were even thought of by Starfleet's theoretical engineers. Geordi worked on his best friend, Data, more often than the doctor did. Therefore I have anointed Geordi "the tinker".

Geordi fit the black professional mythic type. He was highly educated and in a position rarely filled by blacks on screen, he was an engineer. He followed in the footsteps of Barney on *Mission Impossible*, Bill Cosby on *I Spy* and Ivan Dixon on *Hogan's Heroes* in breaking one stereotype of black males as having no technical know-how. Geordi spoke General English and was not ethnically identifiable as black.

What was new in the presentation of Geordi as a black image was the insight the audience was given into his personal life. He had a father, played by Ben Vereen, and a mother, played by the late Madge Sinclair. Both were Starfleet officers. Geordi's best friend was the android, Data.

While one would hardly think so, Geordi was a "nerd". He was cool, but he was a nerd. No, not like Steve Erkel of *Family Matters*. Erkel is a coon nerd. Geordi was a professional nerd. Instead of the black horn rimmed glasses he wore a visor.

Geordi was highly competent with mechanical things, mathematical relationships, etc., that's why he was a good engineer. He was also very articulate. But here's what the Star Trek

Encyclopedia entry says about him. "Although brilliantly proficient as a starship engineer, La Forge had difficulty building relationships with women" (Okuda, Okuda & Mirek, 1994, p.168). In this same source Geordi was said to be suffering from low self-confidence (1994, p.124). This facet of Geordi's character was based on a stereotype of engineers in general. The stereotype of the engineer is that he/she relates very well to mechanical things, but not to people.

Geordi always seemed to be chasing after the wrong woman. We saw him in the holodeck with the character Christi Henshaw, where he tried to create a romantic evening. She eventually told him she didn't have romantic feelings for him (*Transfigurations*, 1990). Then there was Dr. Leah Brahms a brilliant engineer who studied at the Daystrom Institute. Geordi fell in love with her holographic image first (*Booby Trap*, 1989). When he met her in real life it was a no go. She was married and very stiff (*Galaxy's Child*, 1991). A third romantic relationship was with Lieutenant Aquiel Uhnari played by Renee Jones (*Aquiel*, 1993). This one turned out to be successful. Aquiel was initially assigned to an outpost where the one other officer serving with her was killed. She went on to another assignment at the end of the episode.

There were two questions circulating among black female Trekkers, "Why was Geordi chasing after women who were light, bright, almost white" and "why did the main black character have to have something wrong with him?" The first two women that Geordi was interested in fit the mulatto image. They were women who could have been very fair black women or olive skinned white women. While the third woman, Aquiel, was identifiable as black, the relationship with her came late in the series, 1993.

Based on my conversations with other black Trekkers it was evident that black viewers were watching closely in the beginning to see what parameters were established for the Geordi character. In 89', 90', and 91' he was involved with the mulatto women. It seemed as though a black woman with black features was not good enough for Geordi. The habitual pairing of Geordi with very fair women was troublesome for many black female viewers who wanted to know, "why he couldn't he be in love with a woman who looked black?" Even though Geordi did actually have a relationship with Aquiel, in the last episode, *All Good Things...* he revealed that he had married Leah Brahms. It was a disappointment for black female viewers to see an eligible black man dating "as close to white as possible".

Perhaps Geordi was disabled because he was named after "the late, handicapped Star Trek fan George La Forge" (Okuda, Okuda and Mirek, 1994, p.168). But, it seemed as if a strong, intelligent black man, could not appear in a popular culture medium without some detractors. He had to be disempowered in some manner. It was done with the blindness and his ineptitude with women. Geordi was rendered harmless, no threat to white people in general.

Worf: The Warrior

Worf, played by Michael Dorn, was the only Klingon officer in Starfleet. His presence on the ship signaled a drastic change in the relationship between the Federation and the Empire. In TOS the Federation and the Klingon Empire were bitter enemies: in TNG they were allies. Roddenberry "wanted a Klingon on the bridge as a reminder to the audience that today's enemies can become tomorrow's friends" (Okuda, Okuda and Mirek, 1994, p.377).

Worf had a very interesting background. His parents were killed in an attack by the Romulans at Khitomer. Sergy and Helena Rozehnko, humans adopted him. Sergy was a member of Starfleet and rescued Worf from Khitomer. The Rozehnko's could have been Russian. Worf was raised with Nikolai, the birth son of the Rozehnko's. In 2366 Worf found out that he had a younger biological brother who survived the massacre at Khitomer. His name was Kurn. Worf also learned that he had a son, Alexander. At the beginning of the series Worf was a security officer serving under Lt. Yar. After she was killed he was promoted to security chief.

The family relations of Worf were a patchwork quilt because the character was not meant to be a regular. He "was originally intended to be little more than a costumed extra with elaborate makeup" (Okuda, Okuda, and Mirek, 1994, p.377), but the character grew and became much more complex.

The addition of Alexander as Worf's son added significant texture to the Worf role. He became not only a Klingon warrior, a Federation officer, the foster child of humans, but also a single father. His fatherhood was suddenly thrust upon him because soon after he found out he had a son, the mother was murdered. As a single parent Worf presented a very familiar character to the American viewing audience. Single parent viewers were able to identify with the struggle of learning to care for a child alone, the career issues relevant to that task and the interpersonal sacrifices necessary to achieve that goal.

In some ways Worf fit the black buck mythic type: he was violent. The writers used one incident to show just how violent Worf was. When the mother of his child, Ambassador K'Ehlyr, was murdered, Worf killed her assassin with a bat'telh (a hand held curved blade). Until the very instant that Worf killed the man I thought his Starfleet training would take over and he would stop himself. The killing of his lover's assassin indicated just how violent he was according to human standards. Though Worf was violent by human standards, he was considered weak by other Klingons.

Furthermore, Worf was sexually repressed. He purposely refrained from sex because "human women were too fragile" for sex with a Klingon. At several instances the Klingons were shown to have a mating ritual that combined sex and violence. As the show evolved Worf began to lust after a white woman, Counselor Troi. After repeatedly stating that humans were too delicate for Klingon sex he fell in love with the tiniest, most fragile appearing woman on the ship. Of course the sexuality of the black buck had to be rendered inert, so he and Counselor Troi were sexual only in her dreams or in one instance when she was experiencing alternative realities. While Counselor Troi was sexual with Riker and several other characters she was not allowed to be so with Worf.

Guinan: The Sage

> You are the most beautiful woman in the galaxy. You don't know how long I've waited to tell you that. I dream of a galaxy where your eyes are the stars and the universe worships the sky. You are the heart in my day and the soul in my night. (Riker to Guinan, *The Dauphin*, TNG)

Guinan appeared on the show in the second season (*The Child*, TNG). The role was specifically designed for Whoppie Goldberg. The character was named after a famed bartender, Texas Guinan, who ran a saloon during the period of Prohibition (Okuda, Okuda and Mirek, 1994, p.119).

> The news of Denise Crosby's departure prompted Goldberg to let the producers know---through her friend LeVar Burton--that she'd like to join the cast. Disbelieving, they ignored her until she finally called the TNG office and said, "Hey, I know I'm no blonde, but...! (Nemecek, 1992, p.64)

Goldberg did not appear in most of the episodes because the producers had to work around her schedule. According to Marina Sirtis, the actress who plays Counselor Troi, the writers basically worked Guinan in when Goldberg could be there. Therefore, Guinan was a recurring rather than permanent role.

Guinan's people, the El Aurians, were annihilated by the

Borg and she was one of the last surviving members. Her age was calculated to be over 500 yrs. She had been married several times and had several children. Guinan had the gift of being able to sense anomalies across time and space continuums. She was able to discern when events were out of kilter.

In a lecture at a 1990 Trek convention held in Kansas City, Mo., Marina Sirtis, the actress who played Counselor Troi, talked about the Guinan character. She said that since Guinan had to be written around Goldberg's schedule the character was often given the lines that would have been given to Troi. Guinan did serve in the traditional role of a bartender, the listener\counselor. Her people were listeners and at one point Guinan found herself engaged in therapeutic listening with Troi (*The Loss*: TNG). Troi lost her empathic abilities for a period of time and suffered an identity crisis. She wondered if she could still be a counselor without her empathic abilities. Guinan helped her understand that she still had the ability to counselor others if she used her other capabilities.

In an initial analysis of the Guinan character I placed her in the traditional mythic category of mammy. She was in the role of nurturer, she served others. Guinan was not part of Starfleet so she had no formal authority on the ship. Any power that she had was a function of her personal relationship with Picard, the fact that he trusted her completely and her ability to listen and counsel well.

In my mind, the mammy category was the place for Guinan because she fit so many aspects of that character up to and including the "handkerchief" on her head. She spoke her mind, dispensed advice, listened, fed people and in general mothered the crew.

Even with the aforementioned facts in view, the case can be made for categorizing Guinan as a sage woman. The sage woman is one who teaches, guides or mentors others with knowledge born of study and experience. She is wise, comfortable with herself and has moved past the ambitious cravings which drive most of us.

Regardless of her physical circumstances the sage woman

is free. She is free because her spirit cannot be bought or sold. While she does not seek to control others she is always in control of her response to them and her environment. The sage woman combines ancient knowledge with the new. Sage women often live on the fringes of society. They frequently work with the forces of nature and spirit to bring harmony to life. Every society has women in this class. Guinan was such a woman.

Guinan dispensed advice in a very different manner than Counselor Troi. Troi's work was based on professional techniques coupled with her Betazoid empathic abilities. Guinan's counsel was based on the wisdom gained through 500 years of living. She had at her command, not just the facts, not just the formal training, but acumen that could only come from critical thinking and emotional assessment across a broad variety of experiences spanning a great deal of time and territory. Her knowledge could be compared to that of Yoda, in *Star Wars,* who was a master Jedi.

The most important factor that would differentiate Guinan the sage from Guinan the mammy is choice. Guinan was living in an age when her choices were no more limited than anyone else's. We can assume that having lived 500 years she had in fact done most of what she wanted to do. There was the distinct impression that she was a bartender on the Enterprise because she wanted to be. She had nothing to prove, she was at peace with herself and it appeared that she knew that she was in the right place at the right time. This element of choice distinguishes Guinan from the mammy in that mammy had no choice. In slavery she had no choice and even when living free many black females were forced into the mammy role in the labor market because their job choices were limited. It was either that or field work.

Though "much remains unknown about Guinan, largely because Star Trek's producers made a conscious decision to keep her background a mystery..." (Okuda, Okuda & Mirek, 1994, p.119) she gave the impression that she had many powers. This was hinted at in the episode *Q Who*? when it was revealed that Guinan knew Q. Q was a being from a race that survived in a group consciousness. They had powers that most humanoids would associate with gods. They could travel through space and time without the aid of machinery. They did not die unless they chose to. They could change matter, energy, space and time to their liking. The Q were extremely powerful beings. An individual Q appeared in the first episode of TNG as he came to judge humanity. After the first two episodes Q popped in whenever he wanted to. He was a great nuisance to the crew and could not be defeated by force.

When Guinan and Q met in the *Q Who?* episode they both threw up their hands in a sort of dueling stance one might take when battling with magic, Q backed off. He did not approach Guinan in the carefree manner that he used with Picard and the rest of the crew. This implied that Guinan had powers even Q respected. Therefore, I say again that Guinan was a bartender on the Enterprise because she chose to do so, not because her options were limited, beyond anyone else's. This then, along with her other characteristics, endowed her with the essence of a sage rather than a mammy.

Martin Benbeck: Interpreter of the Law

The character of Martin Benbeck (Ron Canada) appeared in only one episode of TNG. That episode was *The Masterpiece Society* and featured a culture where all of the people were genetically engineered to perform specific functions. They had what was considered a perfectly balanced society and it was called the Genome colony (Okuda, Okuda & Mirek, 1994). The crew of the Enterprise came in contact with the Genome society because a stellar fragment was headed for their planet. The Genomes lived in a biosphere which provided a perfectly balanced environment. The planet outside was uninhabitable. The Enterprise was attempting to evacuate the colonist to safety. The colonist refused because it would destroy the balance of their society, thus in effect destroying the society.

Martin Benbeck was seen early in this episode as "the interpreter of the society's laws" (Okuda, Okuda & Mirek, 1994). As Riker, Data and Counselor Troi worked to convince the people to evacuate Martin advised that the colonist should have no contact with the outsiders for fear of altering their society. Benbeck acted as the "moral voice" of the colony, a role played by African Americans in U.S. society.

Rev. Joseph Lowry, while president of the Southern Christian Leadership Conference, made such a statement in a speech at Central Missouri State University (CMSU) (1989). In his speech to commemorate the 20th anniversary of the Association of Black Collegiates on the CMSU campus Lowry referred to African Americans as the "moral conscience" of America. He posited the notion that blacks have a unique voice in America in that they can lift up for discussion the rights and wrongs, the justices and injustices of this society and no one can tell them to "go home" because they did not come here of their own free will. Therefore, Lowry said, black Americans could raise a louder voice of concern about the discrepancy between what should be and what actually is in America, than other groups who immigrated here. He said that it is the "creative tension generated by this paradox", blacks acting as the moral conscience of the country even though they are at the bottom of the hierarchy, that produces the energy necessary to move America towards improvement.

Martin Benbeck was a black man genetically engineered to act as the moral voice of his society. He was a conservatising force as he spouted the party line and supported the status quo. Martin did this even though the status quo had the potential of leaving his society vulnerable to total destruction by a stellar fragment.

It is interesting to note that a black man was chosen to play the role of the moral conscience of a society, a role played by African Americans in real life. Benbeck fit perfectly, the modern mythic stereotype of the black professional. He spoke General American English, held an autonomous position in the organization and acted as a conservatising force. Benbeck was a character that we are all familiar with.

Captain Scott: Legend in Her Own Time

The accounting of black characters on TNG would not be complete without the mention of Captain Tryla Scott (played by Ursaline Bryant). She appeared in only one episode, *Conspiracy.* She is note worthy because she was the youngest person ever to earn command of a starship (Okuda, Okuda & Mirek, 1994). When Jean-Luc met her he said " Are you that good?" and Capt. Scott answered, "Yes I am!" Scott's record means that she beat ol' Jimbo's record! Scott was among a trio of captains who met secretly with Picard to tell him of a plot to take over Starfleet. She appeared again at Command headquarters on Earth where Picard met with three top admirals of Starfleet. Unfortunately in 2364, after her graduation from Starfleet, Captain Scott was taken over by an extragalactic intelligence that attempted to gain control of Starfleet. She lost her life in the line of duty. The girl was bad!

This characterization of a black female was definitely not of the traditional mode. Scott was a professional black woman, but more than that she had to be outstanding in both her academics and leadership abilities to achieve what she did. Here again Trek writers broke away from the basic stereotypes of blacks.

Conclusion

Geordi was a black professional, a cool nerd, and a typical engineer. In many ways he was a new black character. On the other hand Worf fit the traditional black buck mythic type. He showed the classic characteristics. And then there was Guinan: she displayed all of the trade marks of the mammy mythic type. Even so those trade marks were coupled with the element of choice, elevating her to the status of sage. Martin Benbeck filled a traditional, role for blacks, the moral conscience, while Captain Scott broke all of the molds.

So we see that in this second outing of ST the creative forces driving the popular series mixed convention with invention. In some ways the images of blacks were new, in many ways old.

Geordi was a black professional, and a cool nerd. He had a life outside of the Enterprise, a mother and a father and a healthy interest in romance. Worf was a black buck, but he became much more than that. He was a warrior, a single parent and a man trapped between two societies. Guinan was a bar keep, in what appeared to be a mammy role. But closer inspection revealed her to be the sage woman who choose to be what and where she was. She did not listen and serve because there were no other options, she did so by choice. We only saw a thumb nail sketch of Benbeck because he appeared in only one episode. He was a one dimensional professional black man stating the status quo. Captain Scott, well Captain Scott was in a class of her own.

I believe that the creative stall producing TNG showed new images of black characters for several reasons. One, the show aired in the mid 80's when some of the improvements called for in the 60's had been implemented. We saw blacks in a wider spectrum of occupations in the larger society. Furthermore, the characters were broader and had greater depth than those of TOS because TNG ran for seven years. In the course of 79 episodes, the number of TOS, there was little time to flesh out the characters. With a seven year run and 177 episodes of TNG, the writers had the opportunity to add depth and breadth to these characters. The characters spilled out of the confines of the traditional mythical stereotypes to provide multidimensional black images.

References

Logan, M. (May 14-20, 1994). The magnificent seven. *TV Guide*. Radnor, PA: News America Publications.

Nemecek, L. (1992). *The Star Trek: The Next Generation companion.* New York: Pocket Books.

Okuda, M. Okuda, D. and Mirek, D. (1994) *The Star Trek encyclopedia: A reference guide to the future.* New York: Pocket Books.

Movie Review: *The Fifth Element*

The Fifth Element was touted as the *Star Wars* for the 90's. While the movie was released in 1997 it was clearly a throw back to another era. Luc Besson, author of the book and screenplay also directed the movie. He said that he started the piece 22 years ago when he was 16 (circa 1975). That is surely evidenced by the formulaic story and the stereotypical characters in the movie. Because I am a science fiction fan I looked forward to seeing *The Fifth Element* despite the fact that it did not look good even in the promos. I was disappointed.

In a nutshell the plot is as follows. After 300 years the ultimate evil again threatens to engulf our planet. The only way to stop it is to find the fifth element so that it can be combined with the other four. Then the evil will be stopped. The first four elements are based on the notions of the ancient alchemists and include fire, water, earth and air. The fifth element derived from the other four is life. In this movie the fifth element is the Supreme Being. There are three main characters of interest to me here. Korben Dallas (Bruce Willis) is the New York cab driver who must find the fifth element. Leeloo (Milla Jovovich) is the Supreme Being or fifth element. And last, but not least is Rudy Rhod (Chris Tucker). He is a radio talk show host who lives his life on the radio.

Korben is the typical all American hero. He is white, male, the leader. He is in search of the perfect woman. What he finds is the so-called perfect being. So the universe as we know it is about to come to an end and his greatest concern is finding the perfect woman. Along comes Leeloo, a white girl, with breasts and hips that are so negligible that a few strips of cloth cover them adequately. She has read-orange hair, a waif-looking face and she speaks something that sounds like baby talk. Since she is the Supreme Being she is able to overcome this problem half-way through the movie. But I wanted to scream when we finally saw her and she represented the perfect being/woman. There was no room for the rest of us girls. Though she was very strong she looked helpless and talked baby talk, I guess just what a sixteen year old male would be looking for in a woman.

Then, the piece-de-resistance, Rudy Rhod, a black shock jock and a true s/he man arrived on the scene. Gleiberman described Rudy as a "super-freak entertainment queen…like Rodman, Little Richard, RuPaul and Urkel…" rolled into one (*Entertainment Weekly@aol.com*, 1997). Rudy was obviously a man (he didn't shave his mustache), but he wore male and female clothing including dresses and blond wigs. He screwed everything that was moving regardless of gender. And when poor Rudy was scared he bucked his eyes like Stepin Fetchit. Rudy was a buffoon, driven by sex, and displaying high sexual ambiguity. For me it was difficult to watch.

Then there was the familiar Coolie. Hovering outside of Korben's living cubicle high in the sky was an old Chinese man. He was in a houseboat such as can be seen today in waterways at the edge of many overcrowded Asian cities. He was selling Chinese food from his boat and sporting the "Happy to serve you Mr. Charlie" smile. I almost hurled!

Last, but not least, there was the President of the Federated Territories, a man of African descent. He played the role of black care-taker administrator. Unlike the president in *Airforce One* who saved the day with his military training or the president in *Independence Day* who lead the world's fighting forces to victory, the president in *The Fifth Element* simply sat by the TV and radio listening for news.

Chapter 5
Blacks on *Deep Space Nine* and *Voyager*

DS9 has captured the imagination of the American viewing public because it is the first addition to the Star Trek universe where a black character has the lead role. Avery Brooks began to play the role of Commander Benjamin Lafayette Sisko in 1993. Having a black man in the commander's role in a space adventure can have a significant impact on the self-esteem of black viewers, particularly children. Brooks, a professor of theatre for 20 years at Rutgers University supports this point. When asked what were the tangibles for playing the role Brooks said, "Because I am brown and American and male, it is important...for our brown children to have the chance to see something they might never otherwise imagine" (Logan, 1994, p.10).

Character Sketches

The original ensemble on DS9 included Commander Sisko, his son Jake, a Trill called Jadzia Dax, a shapeshifter named Odo, Major Kira of Bajor, Dr. Bashir: Chief medical officer, the chief engineer: 'O'Brien, and Quark, the bar owner.

Benjamin Lafayette Sisko: Black male, Commander of Deep Space Nine. Starfleet Officer. He has great religious significance to the Bajorans because he met their Prophets. Sisko is referred to by the

Bajorans as the Emissary. His favorite pastime is watching baseball in the holodeck.

Jake Sisko: Black male, son of Benjamin. Wants to be a writer. Friend to Nog, a Ferengi teen-ager on the station.

Jadzia Dax: White female, Trill. Jadzia embodies two entities, a humanoid host and a small symbiant. The symbiant lives in her abdominal cavity. Jadzia is the humanoid host; Dax is the "being inside of her. The symbiont "being lives an extremely long time and therefore may inhabit several host bodies. Jadzia is the seventh or eighth host for Dax. Dax has been a friend of Sisko's through two hosts, Curzon and Jadzia. Sisko knew Curzon Dax when he was an old man. Even though Dax is now hosted by Jadzia, a young woman, Sisko still refers to Dax as "old man".

Odo: White male, shapeshifter member of the Founder race. Odo is the constable of DS9. He can change himself into any shape or texture. He can hold a form for about 17 hours before he returns to is gelatinous state for rest. Odo is conservative and standoffish.

Major Kira: White female, Bajoran. Kira is the second in command on DS9. She is from Bajor, the planet that owns DS9. She was a freedom fighter against the Cardassians. She reveres Sisko because is a religious figure to her people.

Dr. Julian Bashir: Asian Indian male, chief medical officer. Graduated second in his medical class because he made a small error on his exams. Plays darts and holodeck games with O'Brien. Bashir was genetically enhanced as a child because he was mentally challenged.

Miles O'Brien: White male, chief engineer. Assigned from he Enterprise. Married to Keiko with one daughter, Molly and a son, Yoshi.

Of the original permanent characters, Sisko and his son were the only black ones. In the fourth season Worf came on board. Another addition was a black actress in the recurring role of Sisko's love interest, Kassidy Yates. At the end of the second season the Jem'Hadar made their entrance. While the Jem'Hadar characters are covered by layers of latex it was apparent to me that they were played by black actors.

The third installment of ST aired 24 years after the original show was canceled. *Star Trek: Deep Space Nine* began in 1993 and is yet in the developing stage. It is too early to tell where it will stand in ST history, but an initial analysis shows that the creative team responsible for the show has continued the Roddenberry tradition of mixing the old with the new. Even so, one critic wrote, "...this series is far stronger [than Next Generation], for it is more than just a spin-off -- it's a wholly new show with its own vision and its own messages for our new world" (Jarvis, 1995, p. 120).

The Wormhole

One of the plot devices used to change the premise of DS9 from the other Trek shows was the use of a stationary structure and a transit point (wormhole), rather than a ship. The wormhole allows instantaneous transit between the Alpha and Gamma quadrants of the Milky Way Galaxy. The Alpha quadrant is where all the familiar races on Trek reside. The Gamma quadrant is where the new sentient beings populating the show originate. The wormhole serves the same function as the Panama Canal. It allows quick passage between very great distances. The distances could be reached with normal travel, but the time, money and hazard of normal-time travel make it unattractive. The DS9 bible described the wormhole as follow:

> The wormhole is located in the Denorios Belt, which is located within Bajoran space. It contains a

> 'charged plasma field'. The region is almost invisible to the naked eyes, except for the presence of light blue streaks of space dust. (Reeves-Stevens, 1994, p. 104).

The wormhole provided the dramatic device to enrich the Trek universe with new worlds, peoples and conflicts.

Captain/Commander Benjamin Sisko

The role played by Avery Brooks in DS9 is that of Captain Benjamin Sisko. Sisko was sent to administrate a space station deserted by the Cardassians. At that point he held the rank of Commander. In the first episode Sisko's wife, Jennifer and her death were reviewed in flashbacks. His son, Jake (Cirroc Lofton), was also introduced. In the third year of the series, Sisko's father, Joseph Sisko, was introduced *(Homefront*, DS9, 1995-96). Sisko is from New Orleans and his father, played by Brock Peters, runs a restaurant there.

Sisko carries the weight of a religious icon. He is called the Emissary by the Bajorans because he met with the beings that inhabit the wormhole. The Bajorans refer to these beings as the Prophets.

In the first season Sisko looked every bit the company man; short executive Afro and clean shaven. While he showed some independence in asserting his authority on the station with Major Kira and Odo he did not appear to have much power. He appeared to be stiff and subdued. Sisko handled most situations in clear Starfleet fashion and appeared to support the status quo.

Audience members did not respond well to the character, I believe, due to their expectations of a Starfleet Commander and their earlier exposure to Brooks as Hawk in *Spencer for Hire*. In that TV series, Brooks played a modern day hired gun: he was an independent enforcer. He was extremely powerful and he answered to no one. Later, the Hawk character was moved to a spinoff titled *A Man Called Hawk.*

It has been virtually impossible not to compare the execution of the Hawk and Sisko characters. The characters were different in many ways, the most important being their relationship to the larger society. Hawk was independent, no family ties and self-employed. Sisko is a single father and a company man.

Sisko fits the professional black mythic type. He holds an autonomous position within Starfleet. His authority is not dependent on a personal relationship with any one person, but is commensurate with his rank. He is very articulate and speaks crisp General American English.

I would say that, in addition to being a professional black person, Sisko in the first year was little more than a caretaker administrator. There was a general sense among audience members that Brooks was being muzzled, he was not allowed the full range of what he could do with the character. This could have been due to the complexity of the character and the need to develop the rest of the ensemble.

By the second season, Sisko had added a beard. This took the edge off of the clean-cut look and made him appear a little less conventional. Perhaps the clean-cut look did not fit well with the unconventional nature of the assignment. The station does not have the spit and polish look of a Federation vessel, certainly not the Enterprise.

Furthermore, Deep Space Nine is a highly volatile setting, far away from the Federation. Many unusual situations occur due to the diversity of the traffic through the wormhole and the curious power relationships supporting the station. It was built by Cardassians, now owned by the Bajorans, but manned and protected by the Federation. Having a clean cut, by the book Commander simply didn't work well.

By the end of the second season Sisko had a starship, the Defiant, under his command. It was a prototype ship filled with more firepower and engine power than the outer structure could handle effectively. Most importantly, it has a cloaking device, a technological advances not available on other Starships. The cloaking device makes the ship invisible, but uses a great deal of energy.

At the beginning of the third season, Sisko was promoted to Captain. He kept the beard and sported the bald look. He now looked more like the Hawk character. Sisko has been allowed to appear more powerful and more independent.

Perhaps the gradual unfolding of the Sisko character was planned, but it appeared as though the creative forces behind Trek had a black male character in a new role that they were uncertain about how to handle. He was a black man in charge on a permanent basis. He was not a coon, not a tom, nor a black buck. Neither was he so intellectual that he was without sexual energy. This could be an intimidating image for the white viewing audience. Perhaps this is the reason *A Man Called Hawk* did not last. Whatever the reason, in the first one and a half seasons of the show, Sisko was developed in such a manner that he presented no threat to the white male viewing public.

Despite some difficulty with the interpretation of the Sisko character, this presentation of the professional black person has broken many stereotypes. For one, Sisko has been allowed to have a normal love life. It is normal in the sense that he actually has one, he is not sleeping with prostitutes nor is he paired with a white female.

After a reasonable period of grieving the loss of his wife, Sisko fell in love with the alter ego of the wife of a visiting scientist (*Second Sight*, 1994). Nidell was her name and she was racially identifiable as black. By the end of the second season he met Kassidy Yates, the black woman I have dubbed "freedom fighter." A black male character with a normal love interest is rare in television drama.

The second bit of inventiveness for the Sisko character is that he is a single parent. Since the death of his wife Sisko has raised Jake alone. The relationship between Jake and his father is not like any other father-son relationship on television. It is not just different from any black father-son relationship, but different from any father-son relationship shown on television. It is unique in two ways; the amount of talking that goes on between the two and the amount of physical affection displayed even though Jake is almost eighteen.

Sisko has never raised his voice to Jake. He has high trust in him, he encourages him and supports him. But beyond this, when Sisko looks at his son he seems to be looking at the most precious thing in the universe. Sisko's look is filled with love and tenderness that he is not ashamed to display.

Furthermore, Sisko touches Jake in a manner not common among TV fathers. He hugs him, he touches him in the chest, stomach and back regions frequently and he kisses him. Sisko kisses his son on the forehead and on the cheek. Even now that Jake is taller than his father there are scenes where Sisko kisses him. The relationship between Sisko and Jake displays a level of love and interpersonal intimacy more often reserved for father and daughter. This level of intimacy between father and son is unusual and a sheer joy to watch on the screen. The loving black father is an image sorely missing from popular culture.

Seeing Benjamin, his father Joseph and his son Jake brought another image to the TV screen that was new. Showing three generations of black men who loved and cared about each other and spoke to each other with respect added a new dimension to the black family image. Benjamin touches his father with the same tenderness that he touches his son. Joseph looks at Benjamin the way Benjamin looks at Jake. Benjamin shows respect for his father, his father shows pride in him.

The appearance of Brock Peters in *Homefront" Parts 1 & 2* provided the audience with an opportunity to see Benjamin and his father resolve an issue of personal rights. Benjamin was brought to Earth to act as head of security to reduce the threat of the Founder's infiltrating Earth. As head of security, Benjamin ordered every member of Starfleet and his or her family members to be tested to make sure he/she was not a Founder (shapeshifter). Benjamin's father refused such a test on the grounds that it interfered with his personal rights. Naturally, Benjamin was very upset since he ordered the test and if his own father wouldn't take it then he would have trouble forcing the test on others.

In the second part of *Homefront* the elder Sisko consented to have the test, but Benjamin declined to force him. They both sought to please each other. This inclusion of the elder Sisko provides the audience with a rare opportunity to see black men across generations behave as a functional family. This image is missing from the dramatic series format.

The only other black male image on episodic television rivaling the Sisko character was Hawk. In fact "Brooks sees his role as Sisko as part of a continuum linked with his other major television role, Hawk" (Reeves-Stevenson, 1994, p. 178). In an interview Brooks said,

> let's go back even further to "A Man Called Hawk. "That was the first time, as far as I understand it, that we had a brown, contemporary, mythological hero in the history of television... Tell me another one who did not answer to anybody, who didn't have a badge, who did not need to be sanctioned by white males. (Brooks, 1994, p. 178)

While Brooks sees Sisko as a continuation of Hawk, there are some real differences between the two. Sisko is a family man, a company man and must be sanctioned by someone higher in the organization. Hawk was none of these things. Even with the differences between them, Sisko and Hawk are in a unique category in terms of black male images on screen. The viewing audience has been fortunate to have Brooks play both of them.

Kassidy Yates: Freedom Fighter

Late in the second season, the character of Kassidy Yates (Penny Johnson) began to visit the DS9. She is a black female and captain of her own transport ship. Jake met her and soon afterwards began to lobby for his dad to meet her. Eventually Yates and Sisko began to see each other on a regular basis.

Yates is identifiably black and her image is that of a professional black female. She speaks General American English and presents no black ethnic markers. Her hair and make-up are always perfect.

She and Benjamin experienced some slight difficulty in moving toward the commitment stage of their relationship. When she told him she was taking up residence on the station he simply said, "That's a big step." She was expecting a more definitive response. They were able to overcome that hurdle and establish a normal relationship, at least as normal as a relationship between two career people could be.

As for Kassidy Yates, during the last episode of the third season, we saw her and Benjamin in bed. It was a scene that depicted the deep caring between the two. Unfortunately, later that day Sisko was informed that Kassidy was suspected of working for the Maquis.

The Maquis is a group of freedom fighters comprised of Bajoran rebels and former members of the Federation. The group was named for and patterned after a French underground group that resisted the Nazis in World War II. The literal meaning of the word 'maquis' is a scrubby underbrush or vegetation cover in the Mediterranean. It is described as dense and nearly impenetrable.

The Maquis are rebelling against a peace treaty signed by the Federation and the Cardassians. In the peace treaty certain worlds that were in the Federation now lie in Cardassian territory and vice versa. The former Federation worlds in Cardassian territory claim that the Cardassians have harassed them, confiscated their communities and turned them into subjects of Cardassia. They have lost all of their rights of independence, yet they had no say in the negotiations. Therefore, they have formed a resistance group that occasionally mounts raids against the Cardassians, disrupts cargo shipments and fights to defend the displaced planets.

Odo soon proved that Kassidy had been planted on the station to get close to Sisko. The captain was devastated when he learned that the accusations were true. What Kassidy did not know was that she had been used as a decoy to divert Sisko's attention while the Maquis hijacked a shipment of equipment from the station. Sisko allowed Kassidy to escape once the plot had been discovered, but she returned to DS9. She made sure her crew was safe from prosecution and then she turned herself in.

Kassidy let Sisko know that she had actually fallen in love with him and returned in order to salvage what she could of the relationship. Sisko turned her over to the proper authorities, but not before kissing her and assuring her that he would wait.

When it became apparent that Kassidy was a member of the Maquis, Sisko was naturally disappointed. He felt duped because his trust had been violated. There were moments when there was deep disappointment for me as a viewer because I wanted Kassidy to be one of the good guys. But the fact is that there is no more appropriate characterization of the black woman than that of freedom fighter.

The Maquis have a just cause; they are fighting to resist oppression by the Cardassians and to protest their sell-out by the Federation. Kassidy chose to fight with them. Here, then, is the inventiveness of the ST writers. There are very few black women characters as freedom fighters, though we know from African American history there were many. For example, Josephine Baker, a black entertainer and freedom fighter, was honored by France for her work in the French resistance during World War II (*Academic American Encyclopedia*, 1992). Baker worked with the resistance movement to thwart the German occupation of France. Other black female freedom fighters include Fannie Lou Hamer, Harriet Tubman and Angela Davis.

Kassidy then follows an excellent tradition. She is not a mammy, a coon, an innocent, or a female buck. She is a freedom fighter, a new image for black women in popular culture, though a traditional role for them in real life.

Worf: More than a Warrior

Though Worf came to DS9 from TNG, he continues to be the only Klingon officer in Starfleet. Again, his presence on both the Enterprise and Deep Space Nine brings attention to the relationship between the Federation and the Klingon Empire. In TOS the Federation and the Empire were bitter enemies: in TNG they were allies. Now on DS9 the Federation and the Empire are enemies again.

Worf has suffered many losses due to his allegiance to the Federation. He is a man caught between two worlds, not quite at home in either. Worf said,

> I have lived with humans so long, I no longer think like a Klingon. For a long time, I have tried to walk the line between the Empire and the Federation. I told myself I could live in either world, that it was my choice. But the truth is I cannot go back to the Empire. (Moore & Sayers, 1996, p. 53)

The Empire has spurned Worf, yet he does not feel comfortable in human culture. He has been stripped of his family heritage. Worf's last surviving biological family member of his generation, Kurn, has been dishonored because Worf chose to serve Starfleet during the current hostilities between Starfleet and the Empire.

During his first season at DS9 Worf lost his brother Kurn

(*Sons of Mogh*, DS9, 1996). The House of Mogh, Worf's family, had been dishonored on the home world, Qo'nos (kronos). Kurn had requested that Worf take his life in the Klingon suicide ritual of Makto'Vor. Worf obliged him, but Dax and Dr. Bashir saved Kurn's life. Because Kurn was deeply depressed after finding he was still alive he became a danger to himself and others. Worf decided to have Kurn's memory erased. Along with that his DNA and appearance were altered to conceal his identity forever. Worf then had a friend of their father, Noggra, take Kurn as his son. When Kurn awakened he was told that he had an accident and a complete loss of memory. As Noggra's son Kurn's name is Rodek. When Kurn looked at Worf he asked him, "Who are you? Are you part of my family?" Worf answered, "I have no family" (Moore & Sayers, 1996, p.53). Worf's brother was lost to him because Worf could not serve the Empire.

While an initial analysis of the Worf character would place him in the black buck mythic type, the character is much more complex than that. He worked to learn and maintain his Klingon heritage and, by Terran standards, he was violent. However, by Klingon standards he was weak. When Worf tried to express his regret for the disgrace he brought on the family his brother Kurn replied, "You regret? What's next Worf? Do you want to apologize to me? Express your sympathy? How many human weaknesses will you display?" (Moore & Sayers, 1996, p.50). Worf is too human to be Klingon and too much of a Klingon to be human.

Another way of looking at the Worf character would be to see him as an ethnically mixed child. He is racially Klingon and ethnically a Klingon-Terran. Due to the dual nature of his identity, Worf is isolated and alienated. His character exemplifies the plight of the mixed race child in America, or the child who is adopted and raised by parents who are racially different from the child. Though an officer on DS9, Worf eventually exiled himself to live alone on the starship Defiant.

Of the several mythic black characters Worf is a combination of professional black person, buck, and mixed ethnicity (mulatto). In addition to that he is a single parent. While the single parent issue has not surfaced during his stint on DS9, it has followed, in my mind, as part of his identity. The writers of Trek took what could have been a very one dimensional character, the black buck, and added depth and texture to produce a new black image that is both realistic and honorable. Worf is a military man straddling two worlds, struggling to follow his own code of ethics that are neither Klingon nor Terran. In the midst of this struggle, he became a single parent. Worf represents a creative marriage of standard popular culture conventions with new inventions.

Tuvok

Commander Tuvok is a member of the crew on ST:V. He is the tactical officer and he is considered a friend by Captain Janeway. When the series first began Tuvok was an infiltrator of the Maquis. He worked for Starfleet, but was sent to find out what the Maquis were planning. He had been working with Chakotay and Tom Paris. He was not revealed as an infiltrator until the Maquis crew was beamed aboard Voyager.

What is new about Tuvok is that he is the first black Vulcan we have seen. Until this point Vulcans were white. Tuvok is the first indication that the Vulcan population might be multiracial. The script writers have not indicated that Tuvok is mixed with a race other than Vulcan. Tuvok is about 100 years old. He is a bit younger than Mr. Spock. He is married and has children. Tuvok has taken on as a student the character Kes. He is working with her to improve her mental capabilities. At one point Tuvok also worked with a character on board who was a murder. His name was Suder and he was a member of Starfleet. Tuvok performed a mind-meld with Suder and at one point lost control of his own emotions. Suder murdered someone on Voyager and he was confined to his quarters until the ship reached Federation territory. Tuvok worked with this character to help him control his violence.

Tuvok taught him several Vulcan control techniques (*Star Trek Voyager*, #9, 1996).

Tuvok undertook the task of training the Maquis crew while they were on board Voyager in order to bring them in line with Starfleet standards. He showed his compassion by saving a trainee from harm and won the respect of the Maquis crew.

Tuvok was in charge of the ship when Janeway and Chakotay were left on a planet because they were infected. He taught archery at Starfleet academy.

One of the most interesting episodes featuring Tuvok had him combined with Neelix. Due to a transporter mishap Tuvok and Neelix were combined into a single being who named himself Tuvix. The Tuvix character had the memories and capabilities of both Tuvok and Neelix. It took the Doctor a while to determine how to separate the two bodies and personalities. Unfortunately, in order to do so, Tuvix had to die. Janeway administered the chemical, which allowed the two to be separated.

Tuvix was a wholly unsatisfying episode in that the crew explored no ways to keep Tuvix alive. Janeway just killed him to get Tuvok and Neelix back. With the technology available the essence of Tuvix could have been kept in the computer. He could have been programmed into a hologram and then Tuvok and Neelix separated. It was highly unusual to see a Starfleet crew fail to explore options. And it was a shocking ending to have Janeway, in effect, kill someone.

Tuvok is heavily involved in Voyager. He is a professional black. Tuvok is a Starfleet officer with authority appropriate for his rank. And by choice he is a friend and confidante of the Captain.

Conclusion

Based on a cursory examination, the major black characters of DS9 seemed to fit the traditional mythic stereotypes of caretaker administrator, traitor and black buck. Upon a closer examination of the development of the characters across the series it became obvious that the black images were much broader than the stereotypes.

Sisko, the initial caretaker administrator, has become a much broader character. He is a religious icon, a single father, a grieving husband, a ship's captain, and a man with normal companionship and sexual needs. This is a new black male image.

While Worf, on the surface, fits the black buck mythic type he is much more than that. On DS9 he is a loving brother and a man who fits no where. He is disconnected from his Klingon heritage and he is too much of the Klingon to be human. For the time being he lives in isolation on the starship Defiant.

Kassidy Yates, what a breakout character! She is neither a mammy, aunt jemima, nor female buck. Neither has she served as a conservatising force in the story line. She represents the best tradition of black females, one rarely if ever seen on the screen, a freedom fighter.

It is apparent that the images of blacks on ST have continued to evolve with the predominant social political and economic circumstances. During a period when the first black woman flew in outer space (May Jemison), a black man actually had a chance of becoming president (that is, if he could have successfully dodged the assassins' bullets (Colin Powell), a black female served as Secretary of Health (Jocelyn Elders), and a black man served as Secretary of Commerce (Ron Brown), we saw new complex characters emerge on Trek. These characters have broken stereotypes and covered new ground in the quest to present more accurate images of blacks on screen.

References

Academic American Encyclopedia (Electronic Version). Canbury, CT: Groiler, Inc.

Brooks, A. (1994). In Judith and Garfield Reeves-Steven *The making of Star Trek: Deep Space Nine.* New York: Pocket Books.

Jarvis, J. (Spring 1995)(Collector's Edition). Avery Brooks: The private commander. *TV Guide: Star Trek*, pp. 122-124.

Moore, R. and Sayers, J (June 1996). Sons of Mogh. *Star Trek: Deep Space Nine,* #16, pp.50-54.

Reeves-Steven, R. & G. (1994). *The making of Star Trek: Deep Space* Nine. New York: Pocket Books.

Chapter 6
Blacks as Alien

One of the standard themes in science fiction is the exploration of dissimilarity. It is through science fiction that we can imagine and explore physical environments different from our own. It is through science fiction that we can experiment with morals and values unlike those in our own society. It is through science fiction that we can try on various interpersonal and familial structures. It is through science fiction that we allow ourselves to come to know the 'other' in society; the one who is close enough to self to be thought of as 'like me', yet different enough to represent alieness. Usually good science fiction incorporates some portion of all of these factors.

Along with the exploration of dissimilarity comes the uncovering of a number of society's greatest phobias. These could include the fear of the familiar stranger (the citizen who looks different from self), the fear of being overrun by immigrants, the fear of racial genocide, the fear of overpopulation, and the fear of ecological depletion. Along with these fears a host of others exist such as society's fear of death, of the dark, of heights (acrophobia), of insects, of reptiles, of the loss of freedoms, and of people who are different (xenophobia).

One of the strategic problems in translating science fiction stories to film and TV screens is the physical manifestation of difference. With the full range of make-up and prostheses (items which can be used to alter appearance such as beards, hairpieces, and latex facial features) make-up artists are able to create the fantastic. Add to that the use of computer generated and animated figures and the viewing audience can view truly out-of-this world beings. These are the technologically advanced methods of creating dissimilarity.

A simpler method of displaying differences among humanoids or sentient beings is the use of variations in skin colours. Witness the use of color to exemplify otherness on ST. There were the dark green Orion dancing slave girls and the mint green of Mr. Spock. Both the Andorians and the Bolians were blue. Data was created with clown white skin and yellow eyes, while the Borg wear the white of the undead. Then there is the bone gray of the Cardassians and the half black-half white of Lokai and Bele (*Let That Be Your Last Battlefield:* TOS). Whatever the colors have been, the one most important to this discussion is the racial and/or cultural blackness of the Klingons, the Ligonians, the Tamarians and the Jem'Hadar. Star Trek, like all other science fiction, uses skin color as one of the shortcuts to demonstrate otherness.

In TOS the Klingons and Romulans were the black people even though played by white actors in black face. Blackface is a theatrical term referring to white actors in darkened make-up. In the third episode of TNG the crew visited an all black planet, Ligon II. Captain Picard was stranded on a planet with a Tamarian who was played by a black actor (*Darmok*: TNG). And the Jem'Hadar are the black reptilian 'other' on DS9. Let's take a look at how racial blackness and otherness are coupled in Star Trek.

The Klingons

The early Klingons were black mythic characters played by whites. The Klingons first appeared in *Errand of Mercy* (1967) written by Gene Coon. The plot revolved around the Enterprise attempting to save what the Federation thought was a defenseless people from Klingons. The Organians did not need help since they existed, for the most part, in a pure energy state and had powers far beyond the Federation or the Empire. Klingons appeared in a total of five episodes: *Friday's Child, The Trouble with Tribbles, Day of the Dove*, and *Elaan of Troyius (Star Trek 25th...* 1991).

Klingons were a warrior society and arch enemies of the Federation. The entire Klingon culture was built around battle; without it they had no purpose. Klingons were presented as ruthless conquerors, pillaging the galaxy, and ready to die. They were described in one interview as "The mongrel hordes of space" (*Star Trek 25th...* 1991, p.28). The producers and directors of TOS reached right back through theatre history to vaudeville for the presentation of Klingons, white actors in black face. While the make-up used was not nearly as dark as that used in films in the early 1900's, the skin of the Klingons in TOS was obviously darkened.

The Klingons again made their presence known on TNG. In the second installment of the Trek serials the Klingon culture was explored much more fully than in TOS. The viewing audience came to know them as more than the enemy, but humanoids or sentient beings with their own rich culture. They were still primarily the black buck characters, but as with Worf, the Klingon people have been given depth and texture.

In TNG we meet Klingon women, Klingon children and Klingon elders. We come to understand their government, which is run by the High Council with officers and representatives from various "houses." We learn about their religion, which was founded by Kahless the Unforgettable. And we came to understand their peacemakers in *Star Trek IV: The Undiscovered Country.*

What I have noticed in the evolution of the Klingon characters is the colour-coding of their society. On TOS they were all the same color, white actors with dark make-up. On TNG a black actor was chosen to play the Klingon Worf. And Worf's biological brother is a very dark black man. However, white actors play members of the High Council, important leaders, even Kahless the founder of their religion.

Furthermore, by the time we see the Klingons in *STVI: The Undiscovered Country*, the entire group was played by white actors. The only black Klingon we see is Worf's father (played by Michael Dorn). Not only was this high echelon of Klingons played by white actors, they were also quoting Shakespeare, the whitest of white literature! The Klingons were spouting Shakespearean lines to demonstrate just how civilized their culture was even though they were envisioned as a war-like, violent people. (Pendergast, 1995). Lastly, one of the highest authorities in the land, the judge at the trial of Kirk and McCoy in *The Undiscovered Country*, was an elderly white man, who looked like Father Time or the Emperor in *Star Wars*.

It appears that writers, producers and directors of Trek are colour coding Klingon society, as many real societies are colour coded, awarding high social and occupational status to people with fair complexions. This is a very subtle phenomenon. With all of the latex and pancake make-up the actors are wearing some may say that it is impossible to tell what character is played by a black actor and what character is played by a white actor. However, if a viewer pays attention, he or she can perceive the difference. I think it registers at a sub-conscious level and that it reinforces the notion that people with light complexions are superior. There is nothing wrong with making the Klingon people multiracial, but the audience should be aware of this colour layering.

The reservation of certain roles for white actors is very similar to the racial stacking of players on an athletic team. Because of racial stacking, for a long time in football history, black players were not allowed to be quarterbacks. The rationale was that blacks could not think well enough to play the position.

Based on the racial images in Star Trek one would get the impression that only light Klingons are capable of leading. Only they are capable of nobility. While the warriors are mixed racially, the ships are commanded by white actors in dark make-up. And we have seen, perhaps, one black female actress play a Klingon woman.

This image of Klingon culture mirrors the impression people watching television might get about America or Israel. Uninformed people tend to think of Americans as white and they think of Israelis as white, because that's who the audiences see on television administrating those governments. At times internationals are surprised to find there are so many people of color in the U.S. and they are surprised to see dark Israelis.

Let's hope that the creative forces energizing the Trek universe don't stay in this rut too long. What rut? The rut of choosing white actors to play high status Klingons and black actors being limited to other positions. This is not in keeping with the notion of the "color blind" world imagined by Roddenberry.

The Romulans

Balance of Terror (TOS) was the first episode to feature the Romulans. It aired in 1966 and was written by Richard Matheson. In this episode Kirk matched wits with a Romulan commander in a cloaked Bird of Prey. The Romulan vessel was sent to test Federation defenses. Romulans were a warrior race from the planets Romulus and Remus. Spock identified them as an off shoot of the Vulcans. These people originally left the Vulcan home world because they did not believe in the Vulcan philosophy of peace as espoused by Surak.

While Vulcans, in the personage of Spock, were originally presented as green people, on the black and white screen they looked white and were eventually shown as such. They were the logical, reasonable race while Romulans, their darker cousins, were warlike and driven by emotions. While Romulans were not as dark as Klingons there were darker than Vulcans. The Romulans were seen in two episodes. In addition to *Balance of Terror*, they were also featured in the *Enterprise Incident*.

Romulans have appeared in TNG more than in TOS. In

TNG they are virtually all white. In the seven years of TNG there were two black Romulans, one female and one male. Though the Romulans are primarily white in TNG their costuming has become Asian in appearance. The hair is highly stylized with black color and block cuts. The uniforms are quilted and padded with rather pointed shoulders. They, the Romulans and their uniforms, look very militaristic. The creative talents behind Trek have not made an attempt to be consistent with the looks of the different species. They change from series to series and series to movies. Some of the visual changes are due to changing conceptualizations of cultures and people as they change from Trek team to Trek team. But most would agree that the majority of the changes are due to advancements in make-up techniques. The Romulans changed from TOS to TNG in racial characteristics, hair, and clothing. There have been no philosophical reasons stated for the racial changes of the Romulans.

The introduction of the Klingons and Romulans to the Star Trek universe was a clever use of the villain guise of the black buck. The writers and producers used the dark-light motif to exemplify good and evil. Some of the "baddest mo'fos" in the universe were dark while the good guys were white. Klingons and Romulans are identified as black bucks because they were depicted as violent, living for war and destruction. They were shown to have little regard for sentient life. Rank advancements were achieved through murder and subterfuge while warriors spent their evening singing of battles.

One Klingon woman appeared in TOS, Mara, a science officer aboard a Klingon ship in *The Day of the Dove*. And there was but one Romulan female. She was a ship commander and referred to only as "Romulan Commander". This female Romulan commander fell for the charms of Mr. Spock and asked him to leave Starfleet in order to command with her in the Romulan Empire. While she was being romanced by Mr. Spock Kirk was stealing secret equipment from her ship. She paid with the loss of her freedom.

In TOS the Klingons and Romulans fit the traditional black buck stereotype crystallized in *Birth of a Nation.* They were very effectively guised as the villains and were played by white actors in blackface. There was a consistent use of the dark-light motif by presenting the bad guys as dark skinned and the good guys as white.

During the seven year run of TNG the Klingons and Romulans have become much more than the one dimensional black buck stereotypes. The images of both races have been broadened and deepened. They have been broadened by the use of several different character types: not just the warrior, but the politician, not just the ship commander, but the average working citizen. The roles of the Klingons and Romulans have been deepened because the viewing audience has come to know them more intimately. So, there is greater knowledge about and a greater intimacy with these two cultures. They have become more than just the 'enemy'.

TNG: Ligonians

On the third episode of the first season of TNG the crew of the Enterprise encountered the Ligonians. The Enterprise visited Ligon II to negotiate for a vaccine to be used to stop a plague on Styris IV (*Code of Honor*). The negotiations fell through when the chief, Lutan, kidnapped Lt. Yar. While initially it was thought that he kidnapped her because he desired her sexually, it was later revealed that Lutan kidnapped Yar in order that she might fight his wife and kill her. Lutan's plan was to take his wife's land and rule without her. Yareena was Lutan's wife and was played by Karole Selmon.

Lt. Yar and Yareena fought to the death. Yareena was struck with a poisoned weapon. At that moment she was beamed up to the Enterprise and given an antidote to the poison. Her death satisfied tradition and she was able to demote Lutan to second

husband and make her lieutenant the first husband.

Ligonian culture was based on an Euro-Western image of a 40's tribal black culture. Tracy Torme, a Trek writing staffer, later said she was embarrassed by the image (Reeves-Stevens, 1994). The Ligonians were played by black actors and initially were to be based on the "honor is all" Japanese Samurai culture. The original idea was to make the Ligonians reptilian (Reeves-Stevens, 1994). Somewhere in the production discussions the concept of otherness was changed from reptilian to black.

The presentation of the Ligonians utilized several stereotypes of black culture. While Lutan was the chief, he held that position only as a privilege of his marriage to Yareena: the society was matriarchal. The matriarchal black family is an idea touted in the Moynihan Report as the downfall of the black family. In matriarchal societies property and rights are passed from woman to woman in the family. Secondly, Yareena had to physically fight to keep Lutan. This propagates the stereotype of black women fighting over men. To add insult to injury, Yareena had to fight a blonde, white women, Lt. Yar.

A third facet of the black stereotype is the black man lusting after a white woman. In every campaign to limit the rights of blacks, white males raise the argument that black men want freedom so that they can rape white women. When Counselor Troi was asked what she sensed in Lutan, she said she sensed his mild sexual interest in Yar. And the next thing we know Lutan has kidnapped Yar.

The black-white, male-female relationships in this episode were very formulaic. A black man sees a white woman, then plots to use her to get rid of his black wife. The black wife fights the white woman for her black husband in order to save her pride.

When I first viewed this episode of TNG I was excited to see a planet of black people. But now that I have analyzed what I saw, it has become apparent to me that the Trek writers presented recycled images of blacks. Lutan was the black buck and Yareena was the black woman being abandoned for a white woman. Yareena did not have a clue that the man she was fighting for was not worth having, since he wanted to have her killed. This story made use of traditional themes and stereotypes involving black people.

TNG: The Tamarians

The Tamarians were a race of humanoids that were faintly reptilian in appearance and were played by black actors (*Darmok*: TNG). The viewing audience only saw four Tamarians. Paul Winfield, a black actor, played the Tamarian captain: the name of the character was Dathon. The Federation had encountered these humanoids over a seven year period without incident. However, the Tamarians and Federation people were never able to verbally interact because the language of the Tamarians was unintelligible to the Federation listeners. The words they used were the same as Federation Standard, but they triggered no response in the Federation listeners because they and the Tamarians did not have a common meaning for them.

This is similar to the relationship between Japanese and Chinese writing. The Japanese use the same alphabet as the Chinese, but the Japanese characters do not mean the same thing as the Chinese characters do. Therefore, a Japanese reader might recognize the written characters of the Chinese language, but not understand the words (Wang , 1994). As it turned out, the Tamarians spoke in metaphor based on the mythology of their culture. This brings to mind two cultural groups in the US that use mythology extensively, the H'Mong and the Amerindians of the U.S.

The H'Mong are a tribal people belonging to a region rather than a nation. They originally resided in the Tibetan mountain range crossing Vietnam, Laos, Thailand, and Cambodia. Many have immigrated to the U.S. since the end of the Vietnamese war. They are considered preliterate (without a written tradition). The H'Mong take their family names from the mythology of their culture.

Not only does mythology figure prominently in H'Mong culture, but also among Native Americans. Among many Native American tribes the knowledge reservoir is imbedded in the tribal mythology. Therefore, among the H'Mong and Amerindians, mythology is used as a primary mode of intergenerational knowledge transfer and it is used to instruct the people on present day issues.

Though the Tamarians did not fit any specific black mythic stereotype their relationship with the Federation was symbolic of black-white relations in the U.S. The Tamarians and the Federation had met on seven occasions previous to the one recorded in Darmok. The Federation simply listed the Tamarians as unintelligible and went on their merry way. They did not send a team of linguistic experts to help decode the Tamarian language, nor did they send ambassadors (apparently the Tamarians did not have anything that the Federation wanted).

When Dathon, captain of the Tamarian ship, and Picard were stranded on a planet together Riker assumed that the Tamarians were responsible for the difficulty. Riker attempted to communicate with the Tamarian ship, but could not understand them. Rather than collecting as many language samples as possible in order to aid in translation Riker turned off the monitor.

The onus to make a meaningful interstellar contact lay on one Tamarian captain who was willing to endanger his life to bridge the gap between the Federation and his people. In a society where there is a communication problem it is usually the oppressed that spend a great deal of time trying to teach the oppressor how to understand the other culture.

While the Tamarians were not oppressed, they seemed to have technology and offensive power comparable to the Federation, it was more important to them than to the Federation to span the abyss created by the lack of contact. And for this Captain

Dathon lost his life.

When I reviewed this Next Generation episode in anticipation of writing this section it occurred to me that Captains Picard and Dathon were like two Americans from different ethnic and racial backgrounds trying to establish a friendship. Many Americans, be they white, black, Latino, Asian or Native, report that it is difficult to be intimate friends with people of a different culture. In order to be intimate friends there must be a high degree of common ground and a feeling of closeness intellectually, emotionally, and possibly physically. This closeness is troublesome to achieve when people share a geo-political system and a common language, yet have vastly different life experiences there.

When I attempt to maintain an intimate friendship with a white female I have to do a lot of explaining, over and over, to get her to understand the variables impacting on my children who are black males. My children face a higher than average probability of dying by gunshot wound before 18, joining a gang, using drugs, and dropping out of school. They must also be on constant guard for police brutality and unwarranted search and seizure. The lessons that I must teach my sons are not the lessons she must teach hers. By the time I get through explaining these things and the emotional cost of living in this oppressive country I have no energy left to be good "girlfriends."

Due to the fact that I have been assimilated into Euro-Western society I know much more about my white female friend's culture than she knows about mine. Therefore, I end up doing more work to establish understanding than she does. The episode *Darmok* (TNG) is an excellent example of what frequently occurs when members of the various tributary groups of the U.S. talk. It could be men to women, children to adults, Muslin to Christian to Jew, abled to differently abled; we frequently understand the words, but not the meaning.

While the Tamarians did not fit a black mythic type, their relationship with the Federation was symbolic of the relationship among the power dominant and the oppressed in terms of who takes the brunt of the responsibility for making multicultural relationships work.

DS9: The Jem'Hadar

The Jem'Hadar appeared in the last episode of the second season of DS9. In this installment titled, *The Jem'Hadar*, Sisko and Quark were captured by them while on a peace mission. They were depicted as the most formidable enemy ever met by the Federation. The first time they appeared in the series it was apparent that the Jem'Hadar were played by black actors. What bits of skin that showed beyond the greenish reptilian latex was black. By the second show that notion was confirmed.

The name of the group, Jem'Hadar, has an interesting etymology (linguistic history). Jem is a word originally found in the Persian and Arabic languages meaning aggregate of men (*Webster's Unabridged...*). Hadar is the name of a star in the Centaurus constellation (*Webster's Unabridged...*). So, Jem'Hadar could mean "men from Centaurus". However, what is more likely is that Jem'Hadar is a derivation of the word jemadar. Jemadar is an Asian Indian word for a lieutenant in the sepoy army. During the British occupation of India they enforced their rule through the use of a military comprised of Indian males called sepoys. The sepoys suffered the ultimate oppression and degradation in that they were used to suppress their own people.

In May of 1857 this changed. The sepoy army revolted against the British (Franda and Franda, 1992). The mutiny was triggered by a rumor that the British were introducing new rifle cartridges that were greased with animal fat. The sepoy soldiers were both Hindu and Moslem: to the Hindus the cow was sacred and to the Moslems the pig was unclean. The sepoy soldiers revolted and killed every European found in the city of Meerut. Of course the issue of rifle cartridges greased with animal fat was only one issue fueling the revolt. Other important factors were the

British rule of India in general and their attempts to change Indian society. The British made unlawful several Indian traditions such as child brides and the self-burning of Indian widows. The British also required some of the sepoy soldiers to serve outside of their country. This caused them to lose their caste. Many Indians considered the revolt at Meerut to be the first volley in the fight for Indian independence from Britain (*Academic American*, 1992). The Jem'Hadar of DS9 were probably based on the sepoy soldiers of India.

Over the course of the third year of DS9 the mysteries of the Jem'Hadar were unfolded. In the episode where Odo meets the race that spawned him, the Founders, we learn that the Jem'Hadar are a genetically engineered race. They were designed to be warriors and protectors of the Founders. The Founders, who have the ability to shapeshift into any desired form, always look Eurocentric in their human manifestation.

A second layer of protection for the Founders exist among the Vorta. The Vorta serve as the "overseers" of the field slaves, the Jem'Hadar. Like the Founders all of the Vorta have Eurocentric features with the addition of highly stylized hair and pointed ears. The Founders, along with the Vorta, and the Jem'Hadar are known as The Dominion.

In a second appearance of the Jem'Hadar (*The Abandoned*, DS9, 1995) a baby was found aboard a salvage ship in an incubator. The infant was stored with a shipment of vials that the child needed to survive. Without the enzyme the Jem'Hadar feel, irritable, ill, and violent.

When Sisko first saw the baby boy he held it in his arms tenderly and was a bit reluctant to let him go. The baby reminded him of his son Jake. Needless to say, the baby was black. In a few hours of leaving the incubator the baby attained the development of a ten-year-old and had full cognitive and language capabilities. Within three days the baby was a teen-ager, fully equipped with the warrior mentality and ready for battle. By the time the Jem'Hadar infant had reached the stage of adolescence (three days) he was covered with latex. Even so, the image of a young black baby boy was itched in the minds of the viewers.

Odo attempted to teach the young Jem'Hadar that he could choose to live his own life, not one dictated by the Founders. Major Kira told Odo it was a lost cause, the boy could only be what he was engineered to be. At the end of the episode the young Jem'Hadar could not free himself from his biochemical and mental slavery and Odo was forced to let him go. Odo had to admit to Kira that she was right. There never was a chance of freeing the boy.

The next outing of the Jem'Hadar found Dr. Bashir and Chief O'Brien trapped on a planet with them. One Jem'Hadar commander had been able to wean himself from the "white" and survive. He had brought his unit of men to the planet to see if he could get the whole group detoxed, thus breaking their addiction and slavery. He wanted Dr. Bashir to help him and the doctor agreed to do so. As Bashir tried to find an antidote or effect a cure, O'Brien destroyed the research. He said it was because he did not want to aid and abet the enemy. The Jem'Hadar were left on the planet. Their leader, though free of the chemical himself, felt that there was no hope for his men. He set out to hunt down the remaining Jem'Hadar and kill them. This was a bleak picture indeed. Here, then, are two episodes that leave the viewer with the message that empowering one's self and resisting slavery is futile, as futile as resisting assimilation by the Borg.

The most recent addition to the development of the Jem'Hadar culture occurred in the DS9 episode *To The Death* (1996). Here we got a full cataloguing of the Jem'Hadar experience. A group of Jem'Hadar were rescued from a damaged ship by Sisko. They were lead by a Vorta on a mission to kill a renegade group of Jem'Hadar who were attempting to effect an escape from their slavery. The Vorta overseer controlled the Jem'Hadar because he controlled the chemical they needed. He carried the vials in a locked container that could be opened only with his handprint.

The Jem'Hadar must have a dose every four hours. They refer to it as "the white" and it is fed into the body by a tube that is connected from the chest area to the neck. The viewer can see the white flowing into the bodies of the Jem'Hadar. They must recite this passage in order to receive their ration of the white: "We pledge our loyalty to the Founders from now until death." The Vorta answered, "Then accept this reward from the Founders."

The most chilling view of the Jem'Hadar was provided by Ometakline, the Jem'Hadar leader who helped the Vorta keep the soldiers in line. Ometakline, played by Clarence Williams III, a black actor, says of the renegade group, "They have broken their vow of allegiance to the Founders. It is our duty to punish those who break their vow of loyalty." These Jem'Hadar were willing to kill their own who fight to be free. This was the ultimate in internalized slavery; identification with the oppressor and self-hatred to the extent that group members kill one another for attempting to break the chains of bondage. At another point Ometakline said to Sisko, "We are more loyal to the Founders than the Vorta. Loyalty to the Founders is our reason for existence. It is the core of our beings."

More about the Jem'Hadar culture was revealed in a scene which occurred between a young Jem'Hadar and Jadzia (*To The Death*). Jadzia encouraged him to relax until it was time to fight. Here's what was revealed in this exchange. The young Jem'Hadar said:

> We do not need to sleep. We do not eat. The white is the only thing we need. Relaxation makes us weak. We cannot take pleasure in sex, for there are no female Jem'Hadar. We are bred in birthing chambers and are able to fight within three days of our emergence. None live to be thirty years old. Few live to be 15. Twenty is considered an honored elder. I am three years old. (*To The Death*: DS9 1996,)

The Jem'Hadar leader, Ometakline, killed his best friend for a minor infraction of the military rules. In contrast, Sisko confined Worf to his quarters when not on duty for the same offense. As the teams of Federation and Jem'Hadar prepared to go into battle, Ometakline and his men recited these lines to the Vorta: "I live to serve you." He then led the men in saying, "From this moment I am dead. Dead we go into battle to reclaim our lives. Victory is life."

At the end of this episode Ometakline (the Jem'Hadar) killed the Vorta overseer for questioning the loyalty of the men. They take the white and remain on the planet in order to hunt down and eliminate the remaining renegade Jem'Hadar. Ometakline left Sisko with the promise that the next time they meet they will be enemies; that he will kill Sisko for being too weak to punish Worf with death.

The Dominion as Allegory

The story line involving the Founders, the Vorta and the Jem'Hadar uses the standard theme of slavery, replete with the masters, the house slaves, and the field slaves. Within this storyline the writers explored ethnocentrism, repression, and resistance to slavery.

DS9 provided the displaced time and place to explore the slavery issue. The time is 2370; the place is outer space. The masters are the Founders, the Vortas are the house slaves, the Jem'Hadar are the field slaves engineered to be soldiers.

These elements of the story line are reminiscent of two works of fiction normally thought of as science fiction, but that actually belong to the class of Utopian literature. The two works are *Brave New World* by Aldous Huxley (1932) and *Nineteen Eighty-Four* by George Orwell (1949). In Huxley's work a world made stable by drugs is presented and there is the artificial production of sentient beings. The genetic engineering is used to produce people to function in particular occupations or class of jobs. In DS9 it is the Jem'Hadar. In Orwell's work there is the use of the master class on three continents ruling things from behind the scenes, manipulating the masses for their own benefit. In DS9 it is the Founders.

The Founders are an allegorical reference to the oppressors, slave masters and the power dominant in America. The Founders, like many of the founders of the U.S., were victims of discrimination and oppression. Escape from these conditions was the impetus for many groups to settle in colonial America. But, instead of transforming their society in order that neither they nor anyone else would be oppressed, the white American forefathers sought to enslave others, thus perpetuating the oppression.

This line of reason is also prevalent among extremist groups such as the Klan and the Aryan Nation. Very often these people have suffered from economic stress, discrimination on the basis of poverty, and the brutality of life in violent families. They have been hurt and made to fear, therefore they devise a system to perpetuate these experiences on other groups. In the DS9 saga, the Founders also failed to transform the galaxy to insure freedom for all. Instead they chose to move to the top of the power grid by enslaving others.

The Jem'Hadar fit the black mythic character, the brute: the guise, villains. Here are the characteristics of the black brute displayed in them. They are violent and live for war. They can achieve life only through victory in battle. They are sexually repressed: though the males are apparently heterosexual, there are no Jem'Hadar females. Their repressed sexual energies are channeled into war and violence.

The use of the 'white' is an allegory for the modern slavery happening in the poor and minority communities of America, drug use. As long as the Jem'Hadar live for their next dose of the white, they are controllable and cannot turn their energies toward freedom and self-empowerment.

Internalized slavery is evident throughout the Jem'Hadar

culture. They identify themselves only in the context of serving the Founders. There is intragroup crime, with one Jem'Hadar killing another in order to preserve the slave order. Even more chilling is the killing of rival groups among the Jem'Hadar, a symbolic representation of black on black crime. The masters need not be present in order for the system to work. This is a consequence of internalized slavery. *To the Death* was one of the strongest presentations of internalized slavery I have seen on television.

The short life span and the expectation among the Jem'Hadar that one will be dead before 30 years of age is an allegory for gang or thug life in American inner cities. Life with significantly reduced options and existence in a violent world where one has buried friends at the age of six can lead to fatalistic thinking. Without the vision and without individual and group efforts to help, the Jem'Hadar (inner city youth) see no way out. Parallels also exist between gang life and the Jem'Hadar lifestyle with the lack of fear, the worship of death, and substance dependence.

Lastly, the notion of biologically determined behavior has been central to the presentation of Jem'Hadar culture. This has been a stock argument among imperialists throughout time. Racists contend that certain groups are predisposed to violence and poverty. When Odo and Major Kira agreed that there was never any chance of the young Jem'Hadar breaking out of his slavery, there was no chance of him living a life without violence, there was no chance for self-definition and empowerment, they bought into the notion of biological determinism. In other words, the Jem'Hadar breaking away from the Founders was about as futile as resisting assimilation by the Borg.

Conclusion

It is too soon to determine how the use of the slavery motif on DS9 will impact on African American viewers or multicultural relations. It is too soon because the saga has not been finished. The story line has not been brought to resolution.

I would suggest that the lack of critical response to this story line could be detrimental to the viewing public. So far the message has been that it is acceptable to enslave others to protect one's race and that it is futile to resist oppression, especially chemical enslavement. If there is no dialogue among African American viewers about the theme of slavery as it has been presented on ST: DS9, the story line may serve to reinforce the violent conditions already present in our society. It may reinforce the notion that there is no way out for inner city youth. It is essential that this story line be monitored and that it be subjected to critical review because the framing of images and the treatment of standard themes in popular culture can influence real life situations.

If the creative forces driving DS9 follow the Trek formula and the history of the Indian jemadar, sooner or later the Jem'Hadar will fight to free themselves. The creators of Trek have demonstrated that resistance to assimilation by the Borg is not futile and that people must fight to be free as the Maquis are doing. I hope that the story line of the enslaved Jem'Hadar will soon demonstrate the same moral.

The Klingons, Romulans, Tamarian, Ligonians, and Jem'Hadar are all groups of 'aliens' that are played predominately by black actors or have had their skin darkened. Though all of these characters except the Ligonians wear heavy facial appliances, they present several indices of blackness. The Klingons and the original Romulans made use of the black buck stereotype. They were violent, war-like driven by emotions, with little regard for sentient life. The Jem'Hadar fit the categories of slaves, black bucks, and villains. The Tamarians represented the superior-subordinate relationship among whites and other racial groups in the U.S. The story of the Ligonians utilized several black stereotypes including the matriarchal black female, the black buck male, and the fighting black female. Trek writers and producers have used blackness to exemplify otherness or alieness. The viewer must be careful about equating the two in real life.

References

Bogle, D. (1995)(3rd). *Toms, coons, mulattos, mammies & bucks: An interpretive history of blacks in films.* New York: Continuum.

Franda, M. and Franda, V. (1992). Indian mutiny. In the *Academic American Encyclopedia* (Electronic Version). Canbury, CT: Groiler, Inc.

Guerrero, E. (1993). *Framing blackness: The African American image in film.* Philadelphia: Temple University Press.

Kern-Foxworth, M. (1994). *Aunt Jemima, Uncle Ben, and Rastus: Blacks in advertising, yesterday, today and tomorrow.* West Port, CT: Praeger.

Okuda, M., Okuda, D. and Mirek, D. (1994). *The Star Trek encyclopedia: A reference guide to the future.* New York: Pocket Books.

Pendergast, J. (1995) (Special Issue). A nation of hamlets: Shakespeare and cultural politics. *Extrapolation,* 36(1), pg. 10.

Reeves-Stevens, J. & G. (1994). *The making of Deep Space Nine.* New York: Pocket Books.

Van DeBurg, W. (1984). *Slavery and race in American popular culture.* Madison: University of Wisconsin Press.

Webster's encyclopedic unabridged dictionary of the English language (1989). New York: Portland House.

Chapter 7
Asian Images in Star Trek

On July 4, 1996, George Takei (pronounced T'Kay) commemorated the day by visiting the internment camp where he and his family were held during World War II. You see George Takei is Japanese and he and his family were incarcerated in an "internment camp" in the 1940's. Internment camp is a euphemism for what was actually a political prison, where Japanese Americans were held as a result of racism after the Pearl Harbor bombing. This incarceration of the Japanese American could be traced to racism since no German or Italian Americans were rounded up and thrown into camps even though the U.S. at war with Germany and Italy in World War II also.

In a television interview about his visit to the camp Takei said that he harbored no ill feelings about the experience, but that he had many childhood memories of it. Takei said, "I think a visit to the camp will reconnect me with those childhood memories" (July 4,1996)

What is so important about George Takei? After all, he was only one of many Japanese American children herded off to internment camps during World War II. What makes George Takei important is that he played Mr. Sulu in TOS. Sulu was a ground-breaking role in that he was an Asian and a permanent character of this space adventure. His presence added to the Trek mystique of being avant guard, ahead of its time, in dealing with multicultural issues. In the upcoming sections we will find out what was so ground breaking about Sulu's character by taking a look at images of Asians on screen.

Exigencies : Silk Screened Images

Remember, in the introduction of this book, Asians/Pacific Islanders were defined as people whose origins could be traced to any of the original people of:

1. East Asia (China, Japan, Philippines and Korea),

2. Southeast Asia (Vietnam, Cambodia, Thailand, Laos)

3. South Asia (Bangladesh, Burma, India, Pakistan, etc.)

4. And the Pacific Islands including (Fiji, Samoa, Tonga, Hawaii)

The political, economic, religious, and war aspirations of Euro-Western societies have driven the development of the mythical stereotypical images of Asians and Pacific Islanders in popular culture.

"For the most part, Hollywood's depiction of Asia has been...rooted in medieval fears of Genghis Khan and Mongolian invasions" (Marchettii, 1993, p.2). "In nearly all pre-medieval European mythologies there existed the belief that to the west lay a paradise or Eden where people lived in bliss and where society...was a virtual Utopia" (Hoppenstand, 1983, p. 175). The problem was how to reconcile the myth with the reality of the East. The answer was to deem the people of those lands to be heathens, the enemy, animal like, uncivilized and unclean. Based on these myths and lies it was then the duty of the European Christian to convert the heathens. And, it was necessary for the British Crown to subjugate the people in order that their resources might be used for the betterment of the world and not wasted on infidels who did no know the real worth of it. Here then, are the origins of the "yellow peril" stereotype.

Economic and social factors in the U.S. that have fueled the use of Asian mythic stereotypes were the need for cheap labor in the form of railroad workers, construction workers, house keepers and cooks. These images were determined by the needs of the labor force. When good, cheap labor was needed the Asians were shown in humble servile roles. When the labor market was flooded, Asians were the embodiment of the enemy.

Pacific Islanders are also subjected to these forces. Their images in Western cinema and television have been shaped by the impulse of Westerners to use their land for vacations, resources and military advantages. The image in popular culture of the Pacific Islanders has been "inviting, exotic, and more than a little erotic" (Brislin, 1996, pg. 35)

Another factor informing the image of Asians in the U.S. was the need to present the Chinese and Japanese as allies or enemies as the politics of war changed. Putting an Asian face on the enemy helped whip up support for World War II. Depicting them as 'good' allowed the U.S. to pursue the Chinese, Koreans and Japanese as allies when the conditions of war demanded it.

The most pervasive stereotype of Asians is the yellow peril (Hoppenstand,1983; Marchetti, 1993; and Wilson & Gutiérrez, 1985 & 1995). "The yellow peril was the fear held by Western society--in particular British and American societies--that Orientals would one day unite and conquer the world" (Hoppenstand, 1983, p.174). Asians were depicted as predators of Western society and were often portrayed as animals e.g. Splinter the ninja master in the Ninja Turtles mythology.

Myths about Asians

There are five basic myths or misconceptions about Asians that inform the stereotypical images of them held by Westerners. “The belief that Orientals are part of a great, undifferentiated horde that robs non-Orientals of economic resources" is the first (Hoppenstand, 1985, p.176). The second is that "Orientals are schemers and that their plots involve something dreadful for white society" (Hoppenstand, 1983, p.176). Myth three is "the notion that Orientals are blood-thirsty killers who possess a low regard for human life" (Hoppenstand, 1983,p.176). "The belief that Orientals [will] conquer the white man's world if left unchecked" is the fourth myth (Hoppenstand, 1983, p.177). A fifth myth is the desire of Asian men to ravage white women. The myth suggests that the greatest desire of Asian men would be to contaminate the white race by violating white women (Marchetti, 1993). These five misconceptions feed into the Asian mythic stereotypes that are seen on the screen.

Taxonomy of Characters

The Mastermind Villain

Max Rohmer in the dime novels of the Fu-Manchu series fine tuned the evil Oriental mastermind stereotype, during the late 1800's. The mastermind is an astute, strong character who plots the destruction of Western civilization (Hoppenstand, 1983). The person understands and utilizes Western science and Eastern magic. An army of assassins is always at his service. This stereotype was utilized over and over again in the form of Dr. No (the first James Bond movie), Wo Fat of the *Hawaii Five-O* series and Dr. Fu in *The Adventures of Fu Manchu* (Wilson and Gutiérrez, 1985 & 1995). We see these same evil masterminds in

Shredder of the Ninja Turtles and the principal Asian businessman in *Rising Sun*. Shu Khan was the bad guy out to destroy the world in *Mortal Combat* movie.

The Chinatown gangster is a variation on the mastermind stereotype of the Asian male. He frequently appears in martial arts and drug stories.

The Inscrutable Detective

Charlie Chan exemplified the inscrutable detective, an Oriental version of Sherlock Holmes. He has exceptional powers of deduction and often spouts what passes for Chinese philosophy along the way of the investigation. The detective is always self-effacing and at the service o& whites. A second example of the Chinese detective is Dr. Yat Fu of *Mysteries of Chinatown.*

The Martial Arts Expert

The work of Bruce Lee in *The Green Hornet* (1966-67) and his martial arts films did a great deal to develop the stereotype of Asians as martial arts experts. The martial arts expert is a combination fighter-philosopher. He is able to take on huge groups of enemies and never be defeated. As he fights the enemy the expert delivers words of wisdom. Cain in the original Kung-Fu series (70's) and Lou Kang, one of the good guys in *Mortal Combat*, would fit this category.

Even more astounding than the great feats of courage, which can be accomplished by the young martial arts experts are the wondrous feats they are able to achieve even as they become elderly. Examples of the aging martial arts experts include Cain and the ancient in *Kung Fu: The Legend Continues* (90's). In the movie *The Three Ninjas* the grandfather who taught his grandchildren the martial arts would also fit this category. The last example is the Pat Morita role in *Karate Kid*. All of these characters, which were between 65 and 90, were still able to take on the bad guys because of their martial arts expertise.

The samurai character, a variation of the martial arts expert, appeared in *Sho-Gun, Ninja Turtles III* and as a character on *Saturday Night Live* played by John Belushi. The samurai is a sword wielding Asian fighter that is afforded a great deal of honor in Japanese society.

Coolie

The humble servant image is highly prevalent among Asian images in popular culture. I'll call it the coolie syndrome. In its traditional configuration this character is comparable to the black house slave or servant character. The coolie was used for his cheap labor to help build the railroad. He would frequently be seen in movies of the early west wearing the cone shaped bamboo hat. (After a survey of graduate students from Korea, Taiwan, and Vietnam I found that none of these societies have a word or phrase for these hats. They are simply referred to as bamboo hats, like straw hats are in the U.S.) Sometimes the coolie would be the cook on a wagon train. He could also be seen joyfully pulling the rickshaw (jinrikisha) in Chinatown or in large Asian cities where whites were visiting.

A modern version of the coolie appeared in war films where Americans were stationed in Asian countries and had Asian gofers. The gofer frequently referred to the white GI as Mr. Charlie. A variation on this stereotype is the Chinese laundry man. The Chinese laundry man cheerfully served the white community and could be relied on for information when necessary.

Coolie is efficient, quiet and ready to sacrifice for the master/employer. He/she usually has no family. This image was promoted in the TV series *Bachelor Father, Bonanza* and *The Courtship of Eddie's Father* (Wilson and Gutiérrez, 1985, 1995).

The high tech coolie or the techno coolie is a recent

variation on the coolie stereotype. Coming out of high technology areas such as Silicon Valley, the term techno coolie is used to identify many Asians in high technology careers. The techno coolie is an Asian who is highly educated, but stuck in a low level, low paying job. These highly qualified people are often hired in entry level positions and never make it to management levels, due to racism. The employer gets a highly qualified worker at a fraction of the cost. In this type of system Asians quickly hit the "bamboo ceiling". (Hien, 1997)

Immigrants

The immigrant stereotype is often associated with Asians. However, Asians are seen not just as immigrants, but as model immigrants or model minorities (Lee, 1996). Asians are seen as such because of their high success rates in higher education and business in the US. One problem with the model immigrant image is that the existence of Asians who actually need assistance is obscured. A second problem is that the stereotype denies the existence of systemic racism in the US. People can point to successful Asians and say, "See, they made it." "The racism must not be so bad after all." When Asians internalize this stereotype they are unable to sympathize with other Asians who may be victims of circumstances or racism. The have-nots in the Asian community are effectively silenced.

Americans still do not view Asians as "Americans". Many Asians did travel to the U.S. as immigrants invited to work in specific types of industry, however there are millions of Asians who are native to America. Unfortunately, the Asian as immigrant is a recurring image.

Asian Female Stereotypes
Dragon Lady

The Dragon Lady was one of the earliest Asian female

stereotypes. This character first walked onto the popular culture scene in Milton Caniff's comic strip *Terry and the Pirates* (Hoppenstand, 1983). Caniff developed the dragon lady character as a variation of the mastermind. He described her as a character who combined the best of the Asian male villains with a seductive female (Hoppenstand, 1983). Rita Repulsa is a current dragon lady on the *Power Rangers*. Rita was the initial nemesis of the Rangers. She spent her time plotting to rule the Earth: unfortunately she needed to destroy the Power Rangers to do so.

In the second season of Power Rangers Lord Zed, a devil-like creature, upstaged Rita. In subsequent seasons Rita was married off to Lord Zed. This is similar to what happened to Hera in early Greek and Roman mythology. At first Hera was the central figure and Zeus was her son. In subsequent tellings of the Hera-Zeus relationship Hera became the wife of Zeus. Finally Zeus replaced her.

Scorpina, an aide to Rita, was also a dragon lady. She was one of the assassins in Rita's army. In the new version of the Power Rangers, Power Rangers: Zeo, Rita and Scorpina are gone.

The dragon lady is deadly, ruthless and frequently is involved with drug smuggling, spying and plots to destroy the West. She is a combination villain and seductress.

The Geisha/Lotus Blossom

The Geisha image became prevalent after World War II during the American occupation of Japan. There were, of course, earlier images of the Geisha in the 17-1800's, but the image became even more real after the American occupation (Marchetti, 1993). The Geisha was considered a highly polished prostitute, which was and is a misunderstanding of her function. The Geisha is an entertainer and companion and has been restricted by law from dealing in prostitution (Marchetti, 1993). She is trained in many of the arts including music, painting

and theatre. The art of conversation is one of her most sought after talents.

The Lotus Blossom is often portrayed as the ideal woman, the one every man would want. She is intelligent, yet does not upstage the male. She is docile, eager to please, malleable, childlike and vulnerable (Yang, Gan & Hong,1997) The Lotus Blossom is the Asian female who may be in the role of mother, servant or wife. While the wife, mother or servant may not be a Geisha she is expected to function as one. This Geisha-like woman speaks only when spoken to, can be seen, but not heard and is most interested in pleasing and serving her man. Self-interests are never a serious consideration for the Geisha-like woman. She never seeks sexual pleasure for herself. She defers to the wishes of her man and the good of the family.

The Geisha/Lotus Blossom image of the Asian woman is rampant throughout America. It can be evidenced in the number of American men who seek mail order brides from Asian countries. When asked why they prefer the Asian woman to the American woman men say, the Asian woman doesn't talk too much and is willing to follow him. He doesn't have to fight her for control. The mail-order bride is a variation of the Geisha fantasy.

Suzie Wong/Asian Harlot

Asian woman as prostitute is a widespread image of Asian females. The image was crystallized in the movie The World of Suzie Wong (Yang, Gan, & Hong, 1997;Marchetti, 1993), but appeared in earlier dime detective novels of the late 1800's to the early 1900's (Hoppenstand, 1983). The Suzie Wong mythic type uses her body to seduce men; to divert them from the narrow path. She fulfills his sexual fantasies and does not bother him again until he wants her. Often she is a character that must be saved from the excesses of her society by a white male or missionary. (For a more complete discussion of the Asian woman image on screen read Romance and the Yellow Peril, Marchetti, 1993).

Yang, Gan, & Hong in their book, *Eastern Standard Time* (1997), provide a list of dates and movies that crystallized specific Asian stereotypes.

Figure 3
Asian Stereotypes and Their Screen Origins

Date	Title	Stereotype
1926	*House Without a Key*	Oriental Sage
1931	*Charlie Chan Carries Own*	Second Banana
1931	*Daughter of the Dragon*	Dragon Lady
1936	*Flash Gordon*	Diabolical tyrant
1956	*Teahouse of the August Moon*	Lotus Blossom
1957	*Sayanora*	Sexless eunuch Asian male
1957	*Bachelor Father*	Houseboy
1960	*The World of Suzie Wong*	Asian Harlot
1961	*Breakfast at Tiffany's*	Goofy guy from Japan
1966	*The Green Hornet*	Asian sidekick
1972	*Kung Fu*	Inscrutable Ancient
1973	*Enter the Dragon*	Martial arts killing machine
1984	*Sixteen Candles*	Super Nerd
1985	*Year of the Dragon*	Brutal Chinese gangster
1986	*Gung Ho*	Japanese corporate drone
1993	*Rising Sun*	Japanese corporate predator
1994	*Falling Down and*	Rude Korean

	Menace to Society	storekeeper

Yang, Gan, and Hong (1997, pgs. 111-112)

Americans are only now able to see Asians depicted with any accuracy because of the surge of literature and films produced by them. But, it is still an uphill battle because Asians do not yet control enough production resources to take control of their images in the English speaking TV market. Though an Asian company owns one media conglomerate in the US, Columbia, the organization is driven by profit so it produces what the management thinks the viewing audience wants to see.

One example was the short lived *All American Girl*, sitcom that was centered on what was supposed to be a Korean family. The mother was an unbending matriarch, the father, a powerless shadow. The son was the model Asian and grandmother was a caricature of an assimilated Asian older woman. According to my colleague, Dr. Jeongwa Choi, who is Korean, there was nothing Korean about this family. The actors were racially Asian, but conformed to the white American image of what an American Korean family would look like.

Stereotypes of Pacific Islanders

Pacific Islanders are people who inhabit islands in the Pacific Ocean. Australia, the Americas and Asia border the Pacific Ocean. Many of the people of the Islands are of mixed ethnic and racial heritages. They are primarily Asian, mixed with African, and the descendents of the successive waves of European peoples who conquered them. Because of the beautiful setting of the Islands, white beaches, blue skies, and tropical trees & plants Western film makers have primarily used the Islands and the people as set pieces, just as other Asians are often used.

According to Brislin there are primarily four stereotypes of Pacific Islanders in popular media (1996). There are the pleasant, but ignorant natives who cling to their primitive traditions. Savage cannibals who are overcome

with superior Western firepower make up the second group. And the male stereotypes are rounded out by the self-inflated men who style and profile, but are easily fooled by the superior Westerners. Of course this stereotypes easily lends itself to comedy. Lastly there are the "shapely, sexy, uninhibited women ever willing to take a roll in the taro with a Westerner" (Brislin, 1996, pg 38). If you notice these stereotypes fit those of the Native Americans and Mexican Americans.

Brislin (1996, pgs.37-38) provided a list of movies and TV programs that helped to establish the stereotypes of Pacific Islanders.

Figure 4
TV Stereotypes of Pacific Islanders

Year	Television Show
1915	Aloha Oe
1932	Byrd of Paradise
1932	Wings over Honolulu
1937	Waikiki Wedding
1939	Hawaiian Nights
1960-61	Adventures in Paradise
1967-77	Hawaii Five-O
1980-88	Magnum P.I.
1995	One West Waikiki

Professional Asian Women

Though fairly rare in films and TV professional Asian women characters do appear. They would follow along the same lines as professional black women. They work as assimilated characters, speak General American English, have little or no dealings with other people of colour and they are devoid of ethnic identifiers.

Natsuko Ohama played the role of Amanda Cohen on the

TV series *Forever Knight*, 1994-95 (UltimateTV, 1997). Amanda Cohen was a professional Asian woman. She was a police captain on the night shift where one of the officers was a vampire. On the pilot of *Babylon 5* Tamlyn Tomita played the number two in command. The name of her character was Laurel Takashimoa. Unfortunately Takashimoa did not make it to the series.

Tomita, who is Japanese, also played a doctor during the first season of *The Burning Zone*. She was described as a consultant to an emergency medical team designed to respond to and contain exotic viral outbreaks around the world. Tomita, playing Dr. Kimberly Siroma, was a molecular geneticist. Her character survived only through the pilot episodes. The sitcom, *All American Girl* (1994), was based on the work of stand-up comedian Margaret Cho. Margaret is Korean and her "character personified a quick-tongued modern Asian woman with a distinctly 'American' attitude " (Wilson and Gutierrez, pg. 105). Another Asian female character was on *Power Rangers* and her name was Trina. This young lady attended high school and fought the evil of Lord Zed and Scorpina. Lastly, during the 80's a show called *Night Court* brought the actress Denice Kumagai to the small screen. Quon Le was the name of her character and the character was married to Mac, a black Vietnam vet.

Professional Asian Men

Of course for a discussion of professional Asian men Sulu and Kim lead the group as Star Trek Officers on TOS and ST:V respectively. In addition to these two there were professional Asian men on other TV programs. Sam Fujiyama who was a lab technician on Quincy was one of them. One of the most popular professional Asian characters was Charlie Chan. According to Brislin (1996), Charlie Chan was based on a legendary Honolulu police detective, Chang Apana (Hynson, 1997; Watanabe, 1996, Honolulu Police Museum, 1997). Apana was a real person of Chinese-Hawaiian descent. Though the Chan character was based on Apana, whites always played the role. The list of professional male Asian characters is not nearly as long as the list of professional female Asian characters. This is so because most often Asian males appear in a specific mythic role such as the monk, the martial arts expert, or the evil mastermind.

Standard Themes Involving Asian Characters

As with black characters there are standard ethnic themes that center on Asian characters. Wong and Jones identify themes involving Asians as miscegenation (interracial love affairs), tragic love affairs and cases of mistaken identity (Marchetti, 1993, p.2).

Interracial love affairs usually occur between white men and Asian women. These love affairs are used to support the need for racial tolerance or to warn of the dangers of race mixing. The dangers of race mixing are most often explored among Asian male-white female liaisons. The thinking is that a white female who is romantically involved with an Asian male has strayed from normalcy or has been forced into the sexual encounter because Asian men "tend to be depicted as either rapists or asexual eunuch[s]" (Marchetti, 1993, p.2). Therefore, no self-respecting white woman would chose to be with an Asian male. The imagined threat of rape of the white woman by Asians and African Americans could stem from the fear of whites that they will be biologically eliminated through massive interracial relationships.

I have listed here four exceptions to the rule of shying away from Asian male/white female relationships on TV and in the movies. They are the *Kung Fu* series (1970's & 1990's), *The Adventures of Lois and Clark* and; the movies *The Three Ninjas* and *Rising Son.*

In *Kung Fu* (1970's) Cain, the lead character, has been since the beginning of the show a racially mixed character. He is Chinese and European. The mix is always Chinese men with white women. Each of the Cain men has been married to a white female from great grandfather down to the modern Cain. In *Kung Fu: The*

Legend Continues, (1990's) Cain was married to a white woman and his son, Peter, appears to be completely white. Though the Cain men have been married to white women the series has seldom shown the women. In *Kung Fu: The Legend Continues* one episode revolved around the Cain that lived in the old west. He was married to a white woman and she was shown in one episode. However, the interracial nature of their relationship was not explored. In the opening of the show it was revealed that Cain had been gone from his wife for years. Soon after the episode he left again. Apparently he was never at home. So while the Cain men have been married to white women, the writers have not delved into the marriage or family relations.

Perhaps the mixed race of the Cain character made him more appealing to American audiences and allowed the series to gain popularity in its original run and the second incarnation. Bruce Lee, who helped to create the series, thought that the Cain role would be his, but the producers thought he would be too Asian. So they chose David Carradine to play Cain, a white actor that looks slightly Asian.

The Adventures of Lois and Clark series has been a true adventure because a Eurasian male actor has been paired with a white woman character. On this up-to-date TV series a Eurasian actor, Dean Cain, plays Clark Kent/Superman. His girlfriend, Lois Lane, is white. During the last season Lois and Clark were married. Since Superman came from another planet, Krypton, the writers have not been forced to deal with his racial characteristics. In fact many viewers are not aware that Dean Cain is Eurasian. This is a loss for the Asian community.

A third example of mixed race relationships was shown in the movie *The Three Ninjas*. The three lead characters in this movie had a Japanese grandfather and an American grandmother. She was a tall blonde, but was only shown once in a picture with her husband. Apparently she had died before the story took place. The mother of the three Ninjas did mention her Japanese heritage at several points during the movie.

Unfortunately, in *Rising Sun*, starring Sean Connery and Wesley Snipes, Asian men and white women were shown in a stereotypical manner. The Asian businessmen were shown to have a stall of white prostitutes, which they housed and cared for to be used for their carnal pleasure. They were white women who had "strayed from normalcy". The character played by Sean Connery had an Asian mistress, a woman at least 30 years his junior. She was physically disabled and disdained in her own culture. Apparently the Connery character saved her from the streets. The white male/Asian female relationship was shown as charitable and noble: the Asian male/white female relationships were shown as immoral debauchery.

The first standard theme featuring Asians, interracial relationhips, is very complex. White males with Asian females are acceptable. Asian males with white females are not acceptable unless the character or the actor is Eurasian. Then and only then is he worthy of a relationship with a white female.

A second standard theme involving Asians is the subjugation of Euroamerican society by Asians. We see this theme in allegorical form in many international spy thrillers. The evil mastermind is often an Asian male. In the past it was the threat of the importation of crime to the US that played as a standard theme. Then the threat of world domination by Asian Communists provided a convenient theme. The threat of the flooding of American streets with drugs from Asia has become a metaphor for the Asian domination of America. Marchetti refers to this as "the threat of rape" by the yellow peril (1993,p.3).

A variation on the domination theme is the theme of being overrun by immigrants. This is a past and current threat to the American psyche and we see countless stories of illegal Asian immigrants and hear comments from non-Asian Americans that those # * ! Asians own everything!

The last theme, cases of mistaken identity, has to do with a white person who has fallen in love with the forbidden Asian only to find that the person is really white. Marchetti (1993) lists three movies, *Broken Fetters* (1916), *Sons of the Gods* (1929) and *East is West* (1922,1930), that used this theme.

Standard Contexts

TV series and movies involving Asians often have similar contexts in which the stories take place. Broad contexts include an Asian country or city; Chinatown in a European or American city; or an Asian theater of war. Specific locales consist of the work place such as herbal shops, Chinese restaurants or bars, the laundry and high-tech businesses.

Other locations include the martial arts studio, the temple or monastery, a drug/crime infested area, or a place shrouded in the mystery of the occult. TV programs or movies involving Asians will often include a combination of these locales. They are the cinematic equivalents of "in walked the Asians".

What this discussion has provided is a conceptual framework for understanding the absence or presence of Asian characters and story lines in popular culture. The framework provides a taxonomy of characters, standard themes and standard contexts. Furthermore the motives that shape the images of Asians on screen has been explored. Now, let's take a look at Asian images in Star Trek.

Sulu

In TOS Sulu was the only permanent Asian character. His first name, authorized by Roddenberry, was Hikaru, but has only been used in STVI: *The Undiscovered Country.* He was born in San Francisco in 2237 and first appeared in TOS in the episode *Where No Man Has Gone Before* (Okuda, Okuda & Mirek, 1994). In that episode he was assigned as a physicist, but by the episode Corbomite Maneuver he had assumed the role of helmsman. I believe Sulu was much more visible at the helm than he would have been as a physicist.

At the helm Sulu served as a tactical officer. The line most frequently spoken to him was "Fire now, Mr. Sulu". His most frequent lines were to the effect of "Yes sir". In the episode *The Omega Glory* Sulu was in temporary command of the ship.

During TOS, Sulu was never seen practicing martial arts on the ship, but in one episode he was seen wielding a fencing foil (Okuda, Okuda & Mirek, 1994). This was in keeping with his hobbies, which were botany, fencing and gun collecting (Okuda, Okuda & Mirek, 1994).

Sulu is the only supporting character of TOS to serve as captain of a ship (Takei, 1997). In *The Undiscovered Country* he commanded the Excelsior. He deceived Starfleet command about the location of the Enterprise and showed up just in the nick of time to help save the Enterprise from a rogue Klingon commander. In the movie ST: *Generations* the audience met Sulu's daughter, Demora (Nemecek, 1995). She handled the helm as her father did. I, like Kirk, wondered, when did Sulu have time to have a family? A book about Demora titled The Captain's Daughter has already been published.

The character of Sulu did not fit any of the mythic Asian stereotypes. He was not a martial arts expert nor was he an evil mastermind. I would think he fit the professional Asian person image. This image would consist of an Asian person working in an integrated environment holding an autonomous position within the organization. The professional Asian person would not serve anyone, nor act as the sidekick.

The person would have little if any contact with other people of colour and would display no ethnic markers. The professional Asian person would speak General American English. The character of Sam Fujiyama on *Quincy, M. E.*, would be a good example of the professional Asian male. However, Fujiyama did not appear until the late 70's. Sulu was a professional Asian male in 1966. He fit all of the criteria. His English was much better than General English. George Takei has a stage trained, full baritone voice and sounds as though he would be right at home on the Shakespearean stage.

Though Sulu was not often part of the action his face at the helm was historic in episodic television. At the time when ST first aired, 1966, there were four other episodic shows featuring Asians, *Hawaii Five-O* (1968-1980), *Bonanza* (1959-1972), *The Courtship of Eddie's Father* (1969-1972) and *The Green Hornet* (Wilson and Gutiérrez, 1985, 1995).

There was the evil mastermind, Wo Fat, on *Five-O*, but there were also three Asian actors who were regular cast members. They played professional Asians as detectives. In *Five-O* the stereotypical treatment of Asians was evident, not in the roles Asians played, but in the McGarrett role. He was a white man in charge in an Asian cultural context (Wilson and Gutiérrez, 1985).

In *Bonanza and Courtship...* the roles played by Asians were housekeeper and cook respectively. On *The Green Hornet* the Asian Kato (Bruce Lee) was a chauffeur and martial arts expert. It appears that the Sulu character took Asian images where none had gone before, to the professional ranks. And Trek beat *Hawaii Five-O* by two years. Not only was the Sulu character not stereotypical, but he also was not placed in any standard contexts. His presence signaled a period of racial harmony in the Alpha quadrant.

Khan Noonien Singh

Khan was the only South Asian character to appear in TOS. He was Asian Indian and identified as a Sikh warrior. Ricardo Montalban, a Latino in dark make-up, played the Khan character (*Space Seed:* TOS). Khan was a genetically engineered "superior" human bred during Earth's Eugenic Wars. He ruled one-fourth of Earth during his tyrannical reign before he was overthrown. He and some of his people escaped Earth in 1996. They traveled in cryogenic sleep until Kirk and the Enterprise crew found and awakened them.

The Enterprise crew took the frozen bodies on board and

revived them. Once revived Khan immediately began to plot a take-over of the Enterprise. While in sick bay he studied the schematics of the ship: armament and guidance. He then seduced, Lieutenant Marla McGivers, a member of the Enterprise crew (Okuda, et al, 1994).

McGivers was a white female assigned as a historian. Khan fascinated McGivers because of his personal charisma and her attraction to bold men of the past. When she realized that Khan would actually hurt the crew she helped Kirk regain control of the ship. Rather than send her to trial Kirk allowed McGivers to go into exile with Khan on the planet Ceti Alpha V.

While Khan and a few of his men survived life in exile McGivers, who became his wife, did not. Revenge for his wife's demise was the premise for the movie STII: *The Wrath of Khan*. In *The Wrath...*Khan and his men were rediscovered 18 years after their deposit on Ceti Alpha V. Khan took over a ship and set into motion his plan of revenge for James Kirk. The Enterprise was on a mission to conduct an experiment with the Genesis Project. The Genesis Project was a prototype machine that could generate life out of inanimate material, therefore it was perfect for turning dead planets into livable ones. Khan stole the device, but in the end he died. Spock also died in this film.

The role of Khan fit many of the stereotypical Asian images, though at the time this character would not have been thought of as Asian. It was not until 1984 that Indians from the subcontinent were officially listed in the Census as Asians. Before that they were listed as white. In fact it was not until I began this project that I thought of Khan as an Asian. I only knew him as a Sikh warrior.

The application of the taxonomy of Asian images reveals Khan to be an evil mastermind, the perfect villain. The standard theme was galactic domination. After all he had already ruled a large portion of Earth. Not only was Khan presented as an evil mastermind, but he was also an oppressor of women. Well, actually he wanted to oppress everyone who was not genetically engineered. Khan's relationship with McGivers was tyrannical.

As soon as he could, he put McGivers in her place as a sex object. He took her hair down and told her to keep it that way. She seemed to be sexually aroused by his attention and his masterfulness. In a later scene when McGivers first hinted that she questioned Khan's plan to take over the Enterprise he pushed her aside. He then said to her, "Go...or stay. But do it because it is what you wish to do!"

As soon as McGivers was in the presence of Khan she was made to feel like a sex object and her self-esteem was lowered. Then, when Khan pushed her away from him, she quivered at the thought of him not wanting her. She relented and agreed to do his dirty work. So here we have in the relationship between Khan and McGivers an Asian male-white female relationship. She seemed to be caught in it because Khan mesmerized her, she lost all free will.

What was the impetuous for this story? What were the motives informing the shaping of this Asian image? Well, America was heavily invested in the Vietnam war in 1967. Perhaps this story played into the American fears that the yellow peril, represented by the Asian Communists in North Vietnam, would win the war and the dreaded domino effect would take place. If the Communist won the war in Vietnam they would take over all of Asia, then on to world domination. At last that was the war propaganda American citizens were fed to persuade them to support the "police action" in South Vietnam.

The story might also have been a warning to war protesters. They were already making their voices heard in the mid 60's and Martin Luther King Jr. had dubbed the Vietnam war an "immoral war". Of course the seduction and oppression of McGivers could have been an allegorical reference to the war protesters that spoke against the war. The message was, "don't be seduced by the North Vietnamese claim of the illegitimacy of the war. If you are seduced by them then you are making the U.S. and the entire free world vulnerable to a Communist take over".

An alternate interpretation of this story is that it was a

warning against the genetic engineering of humans. It could have been an allegorical reference to the experimentation conducted on Jews in Nazi concentration camps and Hitler's notion of the master race. Hitler's idea of the master race was based on the Aryans. These people were originally from Northern India, the Punjab region where the Sikhs are from.

Gene L. Coon and Carey Wilbur, the authors of the *Space Seed* episode, used the original Aryans, Hitler's master race, to exemplify the dangers of breeding to superiority. The moral was that attempts to produce superior humans by genetic engineering would wreck havoc on human civilizations. It would produce power hungry tyrants with the capability of dominating and enslaving others.

The framework for understanding Asian screen images provides a motive for the shaping of the Khan character and it also aids in the identification of the theme and the analysis of the Khan-McGivers liaison.

Elaan: Dohlman of Elas

Elaan (France Nuyen) came aboard the Enterprise in 2268 (Okuda, et al, 1994). She was being transported to the planet Troyius for an arranged marriage (*Elaan of Troyius* TOS). The Dohlman, her official, title, was said to come from a line of women who were reported to have "a subtle, mystical power that drives men wild"(Dr. McCoy). Her marriage to the leader of Troyius was to seal a political alliance between two worlds that were warring. Elaan did not like the idea of the arranged marriage. The leaders of Troyius hoped that during the voyage to her new home Elaan would learn more of the Troyius culture.

The Dohlman was a spit- fire. She did not answer to anyone. She wounded Ambassador Petri who was sent from Troyius to teach her the ways of his people. After she wounded Petri it was up to Kirk to teach her the ways of a mature leader.

Of course the Dohlman had eyes for Kirk and she spent much of the voyage to Troyius trying to seduce him. She was attracted to him for two reasons: he could destroy Troyius and save her from a marriage that she did not want; and Kirk was not afraid of her.

The women of Elaan's planet had the ability to shed tears that bonded a man to them. The Ambassador from Troyius described the tears as a biochemical poison for which there was no known antidote. The men of Elas had searched for one for centuries.

Well of course, Elaan managed to get a tear on Kirk's hand and he was hooked! Kirk could think only of the Dohlman. They ended up in bed, signified by Kirk sitting on the bed with her, his hair tussled.

Unfortunately a Klingon battle cruiser was chasing the Enterprise, just at the time when Jim was consumed with desire and not thinking well. Bones worked feverishly in the lab to find a cure. Dr. McCoy found one, but in the end it was Kirk's love and the responsibility he felt for the Enterprise that proved to be the antidote for his addiction to Elaan. The Dohlman finally accepted her responsibility to her world and the peace process. She was "tamed" and regretfully went to perform her duty.

France Nuyen, the actress who played Elaan, was a beautiful Asian woman. I believe the spelling of her name is an Americanization of the Vietnamese "Nguyen". According to Robert Greenberg in the *25th Anniversary Star Trek* magazine, Nuyen and Shatner (Kirk) had worked together previously in *The World of Suzie Wong* on Broadway. Perhaps France played the Suzie Wong role herself.

The Dohlman was a symbolic image in the broadest sense. She represented all of the women throughout history whose lives and bodies have been used like pawns in the political arena to bring nations together. She and Kirk also represented that white male, Asian female combination that could not last. Though they did consummate their relationship in the end they had to give it up.

The Dohlman, Elaan, was Cleopatra, Helen of Troy, Madam Butterfly (Cio Cio San), Suzie Wong, even Pocahontas all rolled into one. What a woman!

Elaan wore the elaborate braids of African origin. Her make-up was in the fashion of Hollywood's Egypt hence my reference to Cleopatra VII. The planet Troyius may have been a metaphor for the city of Troy with the Dohlman representing Helen of Troy. Helen was said to have been the most beautiful woman in the world. The myth was that "she had the face that launched a thousand ships". France Nuyen certainly had such a face.

The Dohlman may also have been modeled on Pocahontas, the daughter of a Powhatan (Wa-hun-sen-a-cawh) chief (Stedman, 1982). She is said to have saved the life of John Smith. More importantly, Pocahontas was kidnapped to bring her father to the peace table. While in captivity she was converted to Christianity by Rev. Alexander Whitaker and was indoctrinated to the lifestyle of the British court. She then married John Rolfe and moved to England with him where she became the darling of the European courts (Feest, 1990).

Kirk constantly referred to Elaan as "savage and uncivilized". He pointed out the need for her to be civilized and taught civilized manners in order that she might marry the leader of Troyius. This was in effect what happened to Pocahontas during her captivity with whites.

Elaan was also compared to Madame Butterfly and they were similar in that they both experienced an ill-fated romantic liaison with a white male. Madame Butterfly is a character from a play of this same name by Giacomo Puccini (1904). The central character, Cio Cio San (Madam Butterfly), met and married an American GI, Pinkerton, in Nagasaki. Shortly after the marriage her white American husband left for a tour in the U.S. He was gone three years. During that time Cio Cio was shunned by her family and had only her servant Suzuki to rely on as she waited for her husband to return. During that time she gave birth to Pinkerton's child, a son (Robert, 1992).

When Madame's husband returned he was married to an American white woman. The American woman demanded custody of Cio Cio's son. She consented only if her husband would come to get the child. She prepared her son to go with his father, then killed herself moments before Pinkerton arrived (Robert, 1992). Madame Butterfly was originally written in the early 1900's and was demonstrating that the Asian female, white male liaison would never work. In the Trek episode Elaan of Troyius the message was repeated.

Throughout the episode the Dohlman was scantily clad as one might expect of a prostitute (a suzie wong). Then too, many of the Europeans of the 1500's imagined that Amerindian women ran around the forest with breasts bared (Indian maiden).

The Dohlman had a great deal of sexual appeal in her physical presence and the script gave her the power to emotionally and physically bind a man to her with her tears. This presentation of an Asian woman was built on the long held myth of "the power of the lascivious Asian woman to seduce the white male" (Marchetti, 1993, p.3)."Asian females are often depicted as sexually available to the white hero" (Marchetti, 1993, p.2). This image of Asian women is prevalent and it is also a persistent image of Amerindian women.

Near the end of the episode the Enterprise was in trouble because the dilithium crystals had been damaged. Onto the bridge walks Elaan with a beautiful necklace made of dilithium, common stones on her planet used to make costume jewelry. She gladly gave the necklace to Kirk so that the ship could run.

The resolution of the plot was predictable. Elaan couldn't stay with the Captain because there was only one woman in his life, the Enterprise. But she also could not stay with Kirk because it would signify that this miscegenation was acceptable.

Lastly, the giving of the dilithium necklace to Kirk was very symbolic. This could have been a justification for the continued exploitation of natural resources in third world countries. Elaan, giving her jewels to Kirk, could have symbolized the need for Euro-Western nations to maintain control of third world resources because "they do not know the value of what they have".

Based on the Asian image taxonomy I would suggest that the Dohlman was a dragon lady. She was willful and dangerous: she was difficult to handle and very powerful at both the political and interpersonal levels. In that sense she was a dragon lady. However, she was also being treated as property, like a slave. Her life and body were to be sacrificed for the needs of her people. And it was through her romantic and sexual liaison with Kirk that she became resigned to her duty. As she left the ship Elaan said to Kirk, "You men are all alike. All you talk about is duty and responsibility."

Though the Elaan of Troyius exhibited certain characteristics of the dragon lady she was a much broader character than that. She represented the countless women throughout time who were forced to ignore their personal needs for the good of the people.

Governor Cory

The governor appeared in only one episode of TOS, *Whom Gods Destroy*. Donald Cory (Keye Luke) was the administrator of a Federation penal colony on Elba II. This facility housed the criminally insane. Captain Garth, a former Federation Starship captain, was housed at the facility.

Kirk met who he thought was Cory when he beamed down to the planet. Actually Cory was being impersonated by Garth because Garth had acquired the powers of shape shifting. The real Cory was locked up in a cell. Eventually Kirk learned the truth of his situation and was able to keep Garth from boarding the Enterprise. Kirk then freed the real Cory.

Governor Cory was an Asian professional. He was an administrator holding an autonomous position in the Federation. He spoke General American English and displayed no ethnic markers. Cory did not fit any of the traditional Asian mythic types.

The Omega Glory

Gene Roddenberry himself penned this episode of TOS. The *Omega Glory* was aired in the 1969 season, but was written in 1965. It was originally considered as a pilot for a second Trek series (Okuda, et al, 1994). Omega is pregnant with symbolism and a difficult story to understand. It is not considered one of the best episodes of the series. Unfortunately, in this episode Asians were used as set pieces and plot devices for the story line. The Asian characters themselves were not developed.

Kirk and the crew received a distress signal from another Federation ship, the U.S. Exeter. The residue from bacteriological warfare on the planet Omega IV had killed the crew of the Exeter. The only survivor was the captain of the Exeter, Ronald Tracy. When Kirk and his crew arrived at the planet they found a war in progress. The two sides were the Yangs and the Kohms. It was apparent that Tracy had ignored the prime directive and provided weapons for the Kohms.

Omega IV was a parallel world of Earth. On this planet the Asians won the most recent world war: they were the Kohms. The Yangs, whites, were described as savages who do not value human life. It was thought that they were "too savage" to be communicated or reasoned with. The Yangs had been driven out of the cities into the country sides and had begun to live as the Indians, "Even coming to look like the American Indian", Kirk said. Whenever the Yangs were near there were drums playing, like Amerindian war drums and there were war cries like those that are heard on TV programs when the "Indians" are on the war path. Throughout the episode the Yangs were described as an infinite horde..."They kept coming and coming...we emptied four phasers on them and they still kept coming" said Captain Tracy.

Even though this story included an Asian presence, it was virtually muted. Captain Tracy, who had only recently arrived there and who looked like the enemy, spoke for the Kohms. The Asians were dressed in Mongolian type fur hats with brown quilted uniforms. They all carried rifles. Because Tracy was speaking for them we only heard one or two of the Kohms talk. Wu, a man who was guarding Kirk, was called in to tell Kirk that he had lived 42 cycles of the Red Bird, the equivalent of 462 earth years. Before Wu could finish Tracy had interrupted and before Wu could say anything else he was told to leave the room.

Tracy intended to isolate the immunizing factor in the planet that he reasoned allowed the inhabitants to live even more than a thousand years. Once the immunizing factor was isolated Tracy intended to sell it to the highest bidder, thinking that he had found the fountain of youth.

Eventually the Yangs won the war, despite the superior fire power of the Kohms using Federation phasers, because they had so many lives to sacrifice towards the war effort. It was then that Kirk, Spock, McCoy and Tracy realized that in this parallel world the Yangs had come to worship the Constitution. They cited it as the holiest of holy words. However, they had come to worship a blurred version of it because they no longer knew what the words meant. Kirk set them right by telling them how to interpret the Constitution and reminded them that these words were meant for everyone regardless of class or race. He said that the words of the Constitution were meant even for the Kohms. Then he and the Enterprise crew flew off to new worlds and left the Yangs to discover their history and acquire a new understanding of their Constitution.

Of course *The Omega Glory* was an allegory for the state of world affairs in the early 60's. In 1965, when this episode was written, America was escalating the "police action" in Vietnam. Europeans and Americans were afraid that the Chinese Communist and the Southeast Asian Communist would take over the world. Again Trek was dealing with the fear of the yellow peril, but with the players reversed. The Yangs, Yankees, represented Western society: the Kohms represented the Communist.

The Kohms were muted, we heard their side only through Tracy. In 1965 the Vietnamese and Chinese communists appeared to the American public to be muted and mysterious. We heard their side from the Russian Communists. The Asian presence in the episode simply represented the enemy. The viewers were not allowed to see them as humans, though we were allowed to gain a great deal of insight into the Yangs.

Roddenberry had subplot after subplot in this story and it was burdened with so much symbolism that it was difficult to decipher what his message was. It was clear that Roddenberry felt Americans had lost sight of the true meaning of the Constitution, but his use of the Asian soldiers was muddled. They were described as decent, friendly people. Did this mean that he thought Americans were misjudging the Asian Communists? Though they were decent friendly people, Spock theorized that the Kohms had driven the Yangs out into the country side causing the Yangs to turn to savagery (become like Amerindians).

What is central to this discussion is the presentation of the Asian characters, which was one dimensional. They were mysterious and muted providing little more than a backdrop for the Kirk/Tracy conflict over issues of the Prime Directive. This was hardly an illuminating use of Asian characters.

The Next Generation
Chang & Lian

Chang (Robert Ito) was the "officer in charge of Starfleet Academy entrance examinations at the Starfleet facility on planet Relva VII" (Okuda, et al, 1994). He appeared only in the episode *Coming of Age*. Chang spoke General American English and held an autonomous position in Starfleet. He was a professional Asian. Ensign Lian T'Su appeared in the 20th episode of ST: TNG. In *The Arsenal of Freedom* T'Su was at the navigation panel when Geordi had the saucer separate from the ship to save it from danger.

Alyssa Ogawa

Alyssa Ogawa (Patti Yasutake) was a nurse. She appeared in over ten TNG episodes including *Genesis* and *All Good Things*. In *Lower Deck* the viewing audience found out that Nurse Ogawa married fellow crew member Andrew Powell and in *Genesis* she was pregnant. This was very fortunate for the crew.

Lt. Barclay was given a synthetic T-cell for the flu. It mutated and created a virus that caused the entire crew to de-evolve to earlier stages of development. Barclay de-evolved to a spider, Riker to a cave man, Troi to an amphibious creature, Worf to a violent exo-skeleton covered Klingon, and Ogawa to a figure resembling "Lucy". Lucy refers to the remains of a forerunner of modern humans found in Hadar, Ethiopia. The remains were dubbed "Lucy"(Mann & Minugh, 1992; Tierney, Wright & Springen, 1988). So Ogawa looked like a prehistoric woman.

During the *Genesis* episode Ogawa was in sick bay either in a coma or asleep. She stayed there on the treatment table and the audience watched her de-evolve to a pre-historic woman. The saving grace of Ogawa's pregnancy was that Data discovered that the fluid or tissue in the amniotic sac could be used to reverse the de-evolving process. A serum was made from biogenetic materials taken from Ogawa's womb and was administered to the crew. Therefore, this Asian woman and her baby saved the crew from extinction.

In effect, the biological mother of the Enterprise crew is Nurse Ogawa. This is not far from the belief of Emory University biogeneticists who hypothesized that the genetic mother of modern humans was Asian (Tierney, Wright & Springen, 1988). Unfortunately, in the last episode of *All Good Things...*, Ogawa lost her baby.

Ogawa appeared in several episodes treating patients in the medical facilities and assisting in surgery. She was a professional Asian, married to a non-Asian. She spoke General English and was devoid of ethnic markers.

Jim Shimoda

Shimoda (Benjamin Lum) was an assistant engineer who appeared in *The Naked Time*. He became infected with the Psi 2000 virus and unfortunately disabled the ship by removing the isolinear optical chips (Okuda, et al, 1994). Shimoda fit the Asian professional stereotype.

Cross overs from* The Next Generation to *Deep Space Nine

Keiko O'Brien

Keiko O'Brien (Rosalind Chao) was originally Keiko Ishikawa before she married Chief O'Brien (Okuda, et al, 1994). She worked on the Enterprise-D and was a botanist. Keiko married Miles in a ceremony using Japanese and Irish traditions (*Data's Day*:TNG). Captain Picard performed the ceremony and Data walked Keiko down the aisle. Keiko married in a traditional Japanese wedding dress. A year after the wedding Keiko gave birth to Molly, with Worf in attendance at the birth.

Keiko transferred to Deep Space Nine with O'Brien. She was not happy there because there was very little work for her to do. She did start a school for the children on the station, but it was later shut down because the Bajorans did not like the fact that Keiko was not that the entities in the wormhole were divine.

In the second season of *Deep Space Nine,* Miles encouraged Keiko to leave the station to work on a botanical expedition on Bajor. She agreed and took Molly (Caroline Junko King/TNG ;Hanna Hatae/DS9) to Bajor with her. Keiko visited the station regularly.

During the third season on DS9 Keiko informed Miles that she was pregnant. It appeared that Miles was a bit suspicious of the pregnancy because Keiko had a close relationship with a man who worked on the expedition. Since that point there has been no reference to this suspicion.

At the end of the third season, Spring 1996, Keiko, Dr. Bashir and Major Kira were on a short mission together on a shuttlecraft. A meteor fragment hit the shuttlecraft and. Keiko was severely injured. Dr. Bashir was able to save Keiko, but the baby was surgically removed from Keiko. Bashir then implanted the fetus into Major Kira in order to save the baby's life. Keiko's baby had to be brought to term by Kira because Bajoran woman develop a complex blood vessel system with the embryo that could not be broken. In other words, the baby could not be removed from Kira, she had to give birth.

Keiko was naturally concerned about the baby and missed it. She told Miles, "It doesn't feel right having to make an appointment to see my own baby." Keiko and Miles invited Major Kira to move in. Keiko and Kira developed a close bond. Miles said they would stop talking when he came into the room. He threatened to invite Dr. Bashir to move in just to even things a bit. Eventually, Major Kira gave birth to Keiko's baby boy, Yoshi.

Keiko is a professional Asian woman. She was a member of Starfleet and held an autonomous position within that organization. However, as with the other characters of colour on DS9, Keiko has proven to be much more than the stereotypical Asian female character.

Keiko chose the traditional option of moving with her husband even though she did not like the assignment. Keiko is the only professional woman to have done such a thing on DS9. None of the women who had intimate relationships with Kirk did it, not even the mother of his son. None of Picard's great loves did it. And, Troi moved on with her career when Riker wanted to break-up. Keiko was the only professional woman on Star Trek to put family needs before professional goals.

In many ways Keiko is different from the stereotypical Asian woman. Even though she made the traditional choice of moving with her husband she was willing to voice her discomfort with her lack of professional opportunities on DS9. Secondly, she was willing to carry on a long distance relationship in order to pursue her professional goals (like the anchor woman, Connie Chung in real life). Thirdly, the character of Keiko has been given texture and depth with the addition of ethnic traits. In *Dax* (DS9) Keiko visited Earth for her grandmother's 100th birthday. She remembered helping her grandmother, Obachan, with her Japanese brush painting. It was her job to fill the cups with water so that her grandmother could clean the brushes (Okuda, et al, 1994).

I believe the marriage of O'Brien and Keiko was a plot point used to reemphasize the colour blind world envisioned by Roddenberry. The race and ethnicity of the characters were not a factor in their marriage. However, it has not been established that this union will last. With O'Brien's continued assignment to DS9 and the lack of professional opportunity for Keiko there it may be difficult for them to stay together. Though there is yet much to be revealed about the Keiko character, we already know that she is a multidimensional Asian woman.

Molly O'Brien

Molly has been simply growing up as the child of Miles and Keiko. It was through her birth that the viewing audience saw the stoic Worf pushed into a very human event, the birth of a child. Molly may also have some religious significance in the unfolding of the DS9 story. In the episode *Battle Lines* Kai Opaka of Bajor, left DS9 on a trip to the Gamma quadrant. While leaving the station she passed Miles O'Brien carrying Molly. The Kai took off her earring and gave it to Molly. This gesture may have implications for Molly's future.

Voyager
Harry Kim

Ensign Harry Kim (Garrett Wang) is the Asian character on

Voyager, the fourth Star Trek TV series. Kim is a member of Starfleet and is a bridge crew member. On the bridge Kim manages the Operations and Communications consoles. Kim carried a lead role in *Emanations* when he woke up dead on another planet. In *Non Sequitur* he woke up back on Earth with his white fiancée. He was also central to the episode titled *The Thaw* where the crew met the incarnation of fear. Kim has appeared in almost every episode of the new *Voyager* (*Star Trek: Voyager*, 1996, p.6).

The character of Kim has been likened to a cross between Sulu (Asian) and Wesley Crusher(young). However Wang says that Kim is neither. While he is young (just out of Starfleet) he is not the helmsman nor is he a boy genius (Swallow, 1996). Kim is perhaps the voice of inexperience in the crew. He is a recent graduate of Starfleet and while there he studied journalism and served as editor of the school newspaper (*Investigations:* STV)

Kim is a professional Asian character, a member of the organization. His character follows in the footsteps of Robert Ito. Ito played Sam Fujiyama, a lab technician on *Quincy, M.E* during the 80's. We have only seen a small portion of Kim's personal life. That was in *Non Sequitur* where we met his fiancée (a non-Asian woman). Kim, like Keiko and Alyssa has been paired with a white person. He, like the other Asian characters, is being used to indicate a Federation devoid of racial strife. However, it would be good to see an Asian character involved with another Asian. It seems as though the only way Trek can be comfortable with an Asian character is when he/she is paired with someone white. Does this perhaps mitigate the yellow peril?

Conclusion

Sulu, Keiko and Kim are all Asian professionals. Sulu fits the professional Asian stereotype. He was one dimensional, working as an assimilated Asian and speaking General American English. However, Keiko and Kim have broken those stereotypes. Keiko is a multidimensional Asian woman and hopefully Kim will be a multidimensional Asian man. To date, the Kim character has not been pushed into samurai, gangster or immigrant roles and he probably will not be.

The major permanent Asian characters of ST including Sulu, Keiko, Ogawa and Kim have been professional Asians. Sulu was a new Asian image. His character was new because of the time at which he appeared, the mid 60's. The other Asian roles on television at that time were servants and martial arts experts. Keiko and Ogawa are Asian women who do not fit traditional images of Asian women. They are multidimensional and professional women.

Kahn and Elaan were characters that appeared only once in TOS. Kahn was the traditional Asian enemy, the mastermind. Though at the time the Kahn episode appeared Asian Indians were listed as white on the U.S. Census, Kahn was an Asian character, a Sikh Indian.

While the physical presentation of the Dohlman was Asian the character development revealed her to be a woman of the world. Her character evoked images of Cleopatra, Suzie Wong, Madame Butterfly and even Pocahontas: certainly an international cast of women.

While, for the most part, Asians in ST were not presented in traditional or stereotypical ways, Kahn was and so were the Asians cast in The Omega Glory. In Omega the presentation was stereotypical in the sense that the Asian characters were simply set pieces and plot devices used to provide a backdrop for Kirk and Tracy. What I hope to see in the future on ST is the presentation of Asian characters in primary relationships with other Asians and Asians in more leadership roles.

References

Brislin, T. (1996). Exotics, erotics, and coco-nuts: Stereotypes of Pacific Islanders. In Paul Lester (Ed.) *Images that Injure.* Westport, CT: Praeger Publishers.

Burning Zone, Universal City Studios, Inc.: @WWW.MAC.Com/TV/

Greenberg, R. (1991). *Star Trek 25th Anniversary Special.* New York: Starlog Communications International.

Hien, D. (Spring 1997). Faculty member of the Social Science Department of San Jose State University.

Hoppenstand, G.(1983). Yellow devil doctors and opium dens: A survey of the yellow peril stereotypes in mass entertainment. In Christopher Geist and Jack Nachbar (Eds.) (3rd. ed.) *The Popular Culture Reader*. Bowling Green: Bowling Green University Popular Press.

Honolulu Police Department Museum (1997). 801 S. Beretania Street. Honolulu, HI. 96813

Hynson, J. (1997). Trial Lawyer. *Charlie Chan and the Oklahoma Trial Lawyer and Poetry.* @ www.autopen.com/charlie.chan.shtml/

Marchetti, G.(1993). *Romance and the "yellow peril": Race, sex, and discursive strategies in Hollywood fiction.*

Berkeley: University of California Press.

Nemecek, L. (1995)(2nd ed.) *The Star Trek Next Generation companion.* New York: Pocket Books.

Okuda, Okuda & Mirek(1994). *The Star Trek Encyclopedia.* New York: Pocket Books.

Swallow, J. (1996). Garrett Wang: Ensign Harry Kim, *Star Trek: Voyager*. New York: Starlog Group, Inc.

Takei, G. (August 1997). Lecture, Creation Science Fiction Convention, San Francisco, CA., Masonic Hall.

UltimateTV@www.Ultimatetv.com/utvl/

Wilson II, C. & Gutiérrez, F.(1985). *Minorities and media: Diversity and the end of mass communication.* Beverly Hills: Sage Publications.

Wilson II,C. & Gutierrez,F. (1995). *Race, multiculturalism and the media: From mass to class communication.* Thousand Oaks, CA: Sage Publications.

Yang, J., Gan, D., Hong, T. and the staff of *A. Magazine* (1997). *Eastern standard time: A guide to Asian influence on American culture from Astro Boy to Zen Buddhism.* Boston: A Mariner Original Houghton Mifflin, Co.

Watanabe, J. (March 1996). Kaimuki on the rise. *Star Bulletin.* @www.autopen.com/charlie.chan.shtm/

Chapter 8
Native American Images

> And when the last Red Man shall have perished, and the memory of my tribes shall have become a myth among the white men, these shores will swarm with the invisible dead of my tribe…(Chief Seattle, 1971, pg. 121).

The most important word in the above quote is 'myth' because the images of Native Americans among Euroamerican societies have always been mythical; merely thumb nail sketches drawn by observers with no understanding. The first images of Native Americans in the Old World were provided by Columbus (Stedman, 1982). Even at that early date of tribal and European contact the "American Indian" was a myth. There are several labels, which can be used to refer to the original citizens of this country. They include Indian, Amerindian, Native Americans, tribal people, and indigenes (the original inhabitants of a region). I use all of these terms through this chapter depending on the manner in which the term fits the sentence. I also use one of the above labels for variety and to enhance the poetics of a passage.

Native Americans are actually the people originally inhabiting the Americas, Alaska, and Canada who maintain cultural identification through tribal affiliation or community recognition. Indian was not a term that the indigenous people of North America called themselves. Columbus referred to the indigenes of America in his accounts of the first visit as "in dios", "in God" in Italian. Upon this utterance has been built the notion of tribal Americans as innocents in paradise. Therefore, from the first instant of contact between European explorers and the Amerindian these people were a myth.

In his first accounts of the peoples of the New World Columbus reported them to be docile and genteel, perfect material for servants (Clifton, 1990 and Stedman, 1983). Each explorer and trader who came to the shores of the U.S. created and circulated images of the Amerindian that fit the political or economic motives of the period.

The Myth

"A myth is an unverifiable and typically fantastic story that is nonetheless felt to be true and that deals with a theme of some importance to the believer"(Bierhorst, 1976,p.3). While a great portion of mythologies may not be verifiable through empirical means most often there are kernels of truth in them. Myths are frequently woven from fact and fiction. The myth may be designed to fit the current political, social or economic needs of a people.

James Clifton, in his work *Invented Indian* (1990, pp. 32-38), gives a full accounting of the cultural myth of the Indian. This myth contains facts that are true and facts that are false. This is so because a fact is simply an item of information that can be proven true of false through empirical investigation. It includes both verifiable information and opinions. Furthermore this myth incorporates elements that provoke guilt and shame. There are many other elements of the Indian myth, more than can be included in this work. Therefore I have included just the basics.

Once upon a time in North America lived millions of indigenes living in what could be described as paradise (Clifton, 1990).

The original inhabitants were incorrectly called Indians by the first wave of the European invasion. While these people were tribal in nature they had certain undeniable commonalties among them i.e. the tradition of living in harmony with nature and man. Every aspect of their lives was permeated with spirituality (Clifton, 1990, p.33).

The life of the average Indian was marked by tolerance for diversity, humaneness, self-lessness and high positive regard for others. The government was perfect because all decisions were shared.

The people were virtually free of disease because of the use of natural foods for living and natural herbs and traditional medicine for healing. The Indians lived very long lives. Native Americans lived in this virtual paradise until white invaders showed up.

Even though badly treated the Indians gave whites many things including a set of infallible ideals & values and the model for the federal government (Clifton, 1990, p.35).

The white man gave the Indian a few trinkets, enslaved them, and killed them off with infectious diseases (Clifton, 1990, p.35).

Even after generations of intermarriage Indian blood is so strong that it will dominate in the descendent empowering them to know, understand and behave in distinctly Indian ways even without exposure to tribal life (Clifton, 1990, p.37). Indian blood and black blood are strong in that way.

The Amerindians were promised that they could live out their lives on remnants of the land they once occupied, but many of these promises have been broken(Clifton, 1990, p.38).

In recent times, due to court cases and laws, Native Americans have taken their rightful place in American history (Clifton, 1990, p.38). They no longer exist so they have no role in America's future.

This accounting of the Indian story reveals only the bare bones of it. It is much more involved and can be read in its entirety in Clifton's "The Indian Story: A Cultural Fiction". Of course like any fiction there are variations of the story depending on who is telling it and for what purpose.

Exigencies

The first stereotypical images of Native Americans were used to justify the exploitation of the people and the natural resources.

> The first colonials wanted to subdue the new world and to bring order to what they perceived as chaos. One of the impediments to this goal was the American Indian. (Bataille and Silet, 1985, xvii)

Enslavement and genocide followed in the footsteps of Columbus. Then Amerindians were identified as the barrier to manifest destiny, the European belief that it was the white man's inalienable right to rule the continental U.S. The indigenes were considered a barrier that had to be removed by whatever means necessary.

A second notion that influenced the images of Amerindians was that the west was empty, the land just lay there for the taking. The people who were already on the land were equivalent to nothing. Once these myths were in place Euroamericans could move as they chose across the land.

The 40's through the 70's the Amerindians were cast as the enemy in hundreds of western movies and TV serials. They were considered the major obstruction to settling the west. Use of the Indian provided a quick way to sketch the bad guys.

In the 60's and 70's things began to change as Native

Americans joined the civil rights movement. They began to sue the federal and state governments to force them to honor treaties or pay for stolen lands The public became more aware of the issues and the 70's became the pro-Indian decade.

The most recent major events to shape images of Native Americans were the 500th anniversary of the landing of Columbus and the revisionist movement among historians. The 500th anniversary of the landing of Columbus invited a reexamination of that event. Rather than seeing Columbus as a great explorer many denounced the celebrations of Columbus Day. Russell Means argued that the celebration of Columbus Day promoted "racist images of Indians" and thus encouraged the genocidal practices begun by Columbus (Means, 1995, pg. 520).

The revisionist movement is the trend among a segment of scholars to reinterpret American history. As more women and people of colour become scholars they are rewriting history in the light of their experiences. There is also the work of extremists who write actual events out of history. This is the case with the Christian Identity movement. Their proponents claim that the holocaust never took place. And lastly, there is a revisionist movement in Hollywood. Movies relevant to tribal Americans tend to romanticize them.

Myths That Bind

There are several myths about Native Americans that contribute to the society's stereotypical images of them. The first is that Native people live only in the past. Hollywood has not yet determined how to depict Native Americans of the present without falling back to the stereotypical images. Thus when they show up in the present or in the future they are living fossils (Ganje, 1996).

A second myth is that Native people can be used as objects or symbols. Due to this myth we see things like tribal names used for cars and sports teams and logos using the imagery of Native people (Arizona Teas). Furthermore, often when photos

Amerindians in native dress are used the caption reads " Native Man", while other pictures use the person's name (Ganje, 1996).

The third myth is that Native Americans are one homogeneous group and that they speak "Injun". "To say someone speaks 'Indian' would be the same as saying someone speaks 'European' (Ganje, 1996, pg. 45). This myth allows people outside of the tribes to lump tribal people together and pay no attention to distinct and unique groups and individuals.

Taxonomy of Mythic "Indian" Characters

Images of the "Average Indian"

The average Indian is a misnomer if there ever was one. It is a fabricated image designed to answer the needs of the dominant society. While statistically one might be able to find the "average" Indian, the reality is that Native Americans are not a homogeneous group. However, for story telling purposes, many composite images of Native Americans have been concocted for use in popular culture. For the most part Indian characters have been portrayed as "two-dimensional stereotypes, cardboard figures of marauding savages circling the wagons, or red Step'n Fetchits like Tonto playing second banana to the white Lone Ranger" (Means, 1995, pg. 513).

The Savage and the Noble Savage

Here is one of the more popular stereotypes of tribal American men (Clifton, 1990; Stedman, 1983; Vanderwerth, 1971). The savage is one who is uncivilized (does not act like white people). He is blood thirsty and violent, displaying little regard for human life. The savage does not work and has strange religious practices. The savage lusts after white women and will rape one every time he has an opportunity to do so

(Clifton, 1990; Stedman, 1983; Vanderwerth, 1971). Euro-westerners have attributed the so called Indian savagery to madness in a warrior, the lack of appropriate morals and the need to exact revenge.

The "noble savage" is a Native American male who is considered uncivilized, but is deemed worthy because he exhibits traits that Europeans think are like them (Ganje, 1996). Most often the noble savage is one who sacrifices for the white man or accepts Eurowestern imagery of himself.

The Chief

No Indian story would be worth its weight in salt if it did not feature a chief. Chiefs lead the tribes. They are shown as strong warriors or wise old men. Very often they have a daughter. The chiefs meet in council, negotiate with the white people, plot to kill white people, lead their people into oblivion on reservations or they are blood thirsty and bent on revenge. Usually the chief role is ceremonial or very limited. Leland Donald, in his essay on "Liberty, Equality Fraternity" and the Indian suggests that centralized leadership among Native Americans on the Northwest Coast was weak (p.163). He writes that the chiefs, a European designation, more likely should have been called Titleholders. Even in fiction "actors playing such roles had little authority over people outside their own kin group, even among non-kin within their own community (Donald, 1990,p.163). Many screen chiefs are based on the mythology surrounding real life historical figures such as Sitting Bull (Sioux), Geronimo (Apache), Crazy Horse (Sioux), Blackfoot (Crow), Cochise (Apache), and Seattle (Suquamish) (Vanderwerth, 1971, pp.xi-xv)

The Man Servant

Apparently even though tribal males were stereotyped as

savages, they could also be gentle and good-natured. This made them excellent man servants or sidekicks. Jay Silverheels perfected this image in The Lone Ranger. Silverheels played Tonto, a man whose whole life was devoted to helping the Lone Ranger root out evil in the wild west. The character Friday, in Daniel Defoe's Robinson Crusoe, was also a man servant. Crusoe "rescued" Friday from a life of "savagery and cannibalism".

James Fenimore Cooper embellished the image of the manservant in his books. Hawkeye, a white male and Chingachgook, a Mohican were the perfect example. Russell Means played this role in the 1992 film, *The Last of the Mohicans* (Means, 1995, pg. 511). The trade mark characteristics of the Indian man servant are his willingness to give his life to protect Kemo Sabe, to leave family and friends behind and to live only for the purposes of his master (Stedman, 1982). They sound much like Christian disciples don't they? Most often the tribal male as man servant to a white male is a binary relationship at the center of white male, Native male bonding.

A variation of the man servant relationship is the side kick relationship. The sidekick is different from the man servant in that the side kick has a bit more social status and independence than the man servant. As recently as 1994-1995 a TV series titled Hawkeye aired where the Hawkeye-Chingachgook binary relationship was prominent. Matt Houston played the title role. I will call the white-tribal male binary relationship the crusoe-friday formula.

Renegade is a series currently on the air that showcases the white-male, tribal male relationship. Lorenzo Lamas plays Reno, a police officer wrongly accused of a murder. Now he is an outlaw and his life dominates the work of his friend, Bobby Sixkiller.

Bobby is a Native American who owns a bounty hunting business. He has a blonde foster sister, Cheyenne, who works in the business with him. Bobby speaks General American English, has shoulder length hair and wears dangling silver earrings. He is most often dressed in a very loud colored sports coat, bright yellow or turquoise blue. Actually the coats are beautiful, but off the beaten track for the average American male. While Bobby owns the bounty hunting agency it is Reno, the Renegade, who leads the action.

The Shaman

In many cultures where traditional medicine is practiced there exist shamans. Traditional medicine is the art of healing using the natural flora, fauna and wild life of an area coupled with spiritual channeling. The shaman is a doctor-priest that heals through the use of spirits channeling through his/her body and traditional medicines. The medicine man/woman may attribute an illness to a physical problem or a spiritual problem. The medicine man is often cast as an enemy who inflames the tribe against white people or a traditional doctor who can heal everything while spouting lines of wisdom.

The character of Ed in *Northern Exposure* has been in training to be a Shaman. During his training Ed diagnosed a young woman who later fell in love with him. On a second occasion Ed advised a young married woman to find her own path.

Ed (Darren Burrows) is a young Amerindian in his twenties. He lives in one room where he spends most of his time watching old movies. He does odd jobs around town. Ed once took care of a bear cub in his room until the task became too much for him. When Ed is unsure of himself he is visited by a demon called the Green Man. When he needs guidance Ed's spirit guide appears, an elderly tribal man in white buckskins. The spirit guide is a popular stereotype of Native American males (Ganje, 1996). The creators of *Northern Exposure*, Falsely and Brand, say that Ed is a Friday character as in Robinson Crusoe.

Native American Women

There are basically two images of Native American women: the princess/maiden (Feest, 1990; Stedman,1982; Hilger, 1986) and the squaw. Native women images are often patterned after the Pocahontas myth. The princess maiden is a young, nubile girl of dynastic lineage. She falls in love with the white visitor or stranger. She is earthy and innocent. The most important thing about her is that she is willing to risk her own life to save that of her white lover (Stedman, 1982). Very often the maiden princess dies. The enemies kill her, she dies in childbirth or a disease takes her. According to the myth a true Indian princess will always chose an available white man over a man of her tribe.

> The cinematic Indian woman, usually a dark beautiful young maiden or 'princess' has a special ability to recognize the superiority of the white man and will often fall in love with one rather than an Indian. (Hilger, 1986, p.2)

The princess image alternates with the squaw. Squaw is a word for wife in only one tribal language (Stedman,1982). Whites used it to describe most Indian women. The squaw is usually a silent mother, wife or daughter going about her duties with an humble air. She does not speak much and is obedient. Most often the squaw is overweight and does not have the sex appeal of the Indian maiden character.

Images of Native American women have been seen in the movies more often than on television. No television images have been cited in the references I have used and the only one that comes to mind in current TV programming is the Native woman on *Northern Exposure.* Her name is Marilyn Whirlwind and she is Dr. Joel's receptionist. Most often she is doing some sort of needlework and she says very little. In fact on one episode this Native woman character dated a circus mime that never talked in or out of the circus. She took him home to meet her parents and they really liked him. Marilyn, at times, gives cryptic advice to Dr. Joel. She takes piano lessons and once made 1,000 origami cranes to hang in the church for a wedding of her neighbors.

The Tortured Half-Breed

Half-breeds would be people of white and Native descent. This image is akin to the tragic mulatto among black stereotypes. According to the myth, the tortured half breed would be a male who would be an excellent person if not tainted with Indian blood. Or the half-breed is a male who is self tormented by his mixed heritage. The half-breed woman is one that could marry a white man if it were not for her Indian blood. Half-breed women fulfill the femme fatale role: she drives men to dangerous passions. Due to her excessive influence she is a bad Indian and therefore must be killed before the end of the story (Hilger, 1986).

Half-breeds frequently trace their ancestry to an Indian woman rather than male. The woman ancestor could be thought of as a princess who gave herself to a white man. Unfortunately the male ancestor would be a savage who violently raped a white woman (Stedman,1982).

Protester

Just as African Americans have been labeled the problem people, the protester, the trouble makers, so have the tribal people of America. The difficulty with this stereotype is that viewers get the notion that Native Americans are just "making trouble for the heck of it". The stereotype denies the historical and cultural factors that demand that Native Americans be revolutionary in order to survive in this country (Ganje, 1996).

The Savior or the Enemy of Western Society

As a group, Native Americans either represent the edenic people or the enemy. "Edenic" is an adjective describing a utopian society or paradise. The edenic setting is a place where everything is alright, people are still innocent and all they have to worry about is living. The edenic people are humble, harmonious, wise, spiritual and long lived. They have no need for thinking and reasoning because they work with emotions and intuition.

On the other hand Amerindians frequently represent the enemy; the savage, the uncontrolled element in an unprotected environment (Cawelti, 1983). With the Indian character the writer can unleash a great deal of violence and anger. The tribal people of the U.S. make perfect villains or edenic characters depending on the politics of the day and the message of the story. This is so because "stereotypes continue[d] to change in order to reflect the current political viewpoints, racial attitudes, and moods of the White majority audience"(Wilson and Gutiérrez, 1985, p.91).

Standard Themes

More often than not, when Native Americans appear in a story the purpose is to identify the context, time or issues rather than explore a character. Stories set in colonial America, the west during the 1700's and 1800's or present day wilderness will frequently feature Native Americans. Furthermore, conflicts between Native Americans and whites are often used as allegorical references to current issues.

> For example, Arrowhead (1953) was seen by critics as an ultra-right-wing allegory of the McCarthy era, while Cheyenne Autumn(1964) spoke against German extermination camps as well, as Indian persecution.(Wilson and Gutiérrez, 1985,p.91)

During the 70's a group of movies were produced to purge the guilt of white America over the mistreatment of tribal Americans (Wilson et al, 1985). During that time a few independent filmmakers broke from the stereotypes and portrayed American Indians as significant characters in their own right. *The House Made of Dawn* (1972), *Three Warriors* (1977), and *Spirit of the Wind* (1979) were three such films. Just as the 70's were considered pro-Indians so were the 90's, a period when America geared up to celebrate the 500th anniversary of Columbus coming to America.

Clifton (1990) provides an excellent list of standard Indian myth themes. They include the paradise people and context, authentic spirituality, harmony with nature, collective guilt and redemption, egalitarianism, health and long life, genocide, struggle and survival, dominance and freedom, selfhood and identity, racial harmony, and the advantages and disadvantages of interracial love (p.386).

The advantages of interracial love are frequently explored through the story of a white-male/tribal woman relationship. Of course the tribal woman would have to give up her Indian ways and her people (just as in the Asian woman/white male relationship) in order for this liaison to work. This would be the Pocahontas-smith pattern.

The tribal male/white woman relationship does not sell much copy so audiences are not shown this pattern very often. After all, a white woman would have to be mesmerized, beaten into submission, unable to escape or unable to kill herself before she would be involved with a tribal man or at least so the myth goes.

Standard Contexts

As with black and Asian characters Amerindian characters are found in standard contexts. Those contexts include the West and Southwest, reservations, the frontier and in nature. Native American characters tend to be confined more by time periods and themes than by environments or contexts.

The Original Series
The Paradise Syndrome

Margaret Armen wrote the episode titled *The Paradise Syndrome* (1968). Kirk and the crew were on their way to an unnamed planet because it was in the path of an asteroid that would destroy it. Kirk's mission was to stop the asteroid before it reached the planet. When the triumvirate; Kirk, McCoy and Spock beamed down they found that the planet was very much like Earth. Kirk said he wished he could stay for awhile because it was so restful and idyllic. McCoy told him he was suffering from the Tahiti Syndrome. This was a "21st century term for a human longing for a peaceful, idyllic natural setting when suffering from the stresses of modern life"(Okuda et al, 1994, p.332).

Kirk and his compañeros finally spotted the inhabitants of the planet. They were startled to find that the inhabitants were Amerindians. Spock said they were "a combination of Navajo, Mohican and Delaware, three of the more advanced groups." Kirk went to investigate an obelisk in a clearing. He accidentally opened it, fell through, hit his head and lost his memory. Spock and McCoy could find no way to open the obelisk so Spock decided to leave to try to stop the asteroid before it reached the planet.

Miramanee, a young Indian princess, and another maiden came to the obelisk to put flowers on it when up popped Kirk. Since he was coming out of the obelisk she thought he was God. She took him to her father, the chief. The chief told about the prophecy that a god would come to save them when the skies were dark (asteroid got too close).

Miramanee was betrothed to the medicine chief. The medicine chief challenged Kirk to prove he was a god. Just at that moment a child was brought in who had fallen in the pond. The people thought the child was dead. Kirk performed CPR and voilà---the people were convinced that he was a god! However, the medicine chief was still skeptical of Kirk as god. Miramanee was instructed to take the medicine chief headdress from the medicine man and place it on the head of Kirk.

Of course Miramanee now would wed Kirok (as her people called Kirk). I mean, who would expect her to go ahead and marry the medicine man when god was in town? Needless to say, the medicine chief was very upset. Kirk and Miramanee wed and she became pregnant. Then the asteroid came nearer because Spock and the crew could not figure out how to stop it. The sky darkened, the winds blew and all of the people ran to the obelisk. They waited for Kirk to save them, but of course he didn't know how to work the obelisk. The people realized that he was not a god and they stoned him (how quickly the masses can turn). Miramanee covered his body with hers. The stones hurt her and she fell to the ground.

Spock and McCoy arrived in time to restore Kirk's memory so that he was able to open the obelisk. Spock activated the device so that it would deflect the asteroid from the planet. Unfortunately, Miramanee was so badly hurt that even McCoy couldn't save her. Jim mourned her death.

McCoy and Spock hypothesized that Miramanee's people had been brought to the planet by a race called the Preservers. Spock said that the Preservers removed primitive cultures on the verge of extinction from Earth and placed them on other planets. Kirk, McCoy and Spock beamed back up to the ship and went on to another mission.

Now that you have read the plot the story hardly requires analysis. *The Paradise Syndrome* was plain and simply a retelling of the Pocahontas story. All of the familiar stereotypes were there: the Indian maiden, the chief, the medicine man and the white man. Miramanee chose the white man over a man of her own people and she gave her life to save him.

The setting of the story was a standard for Native Americans, an environment where everything was available, edenic, where the people wanted for nothing. In fact, when Kirk first saw them he sighed, "They're just living." That is one of the standard images of Native Americans, that they do not engage in intellectual endeavors, they just live. Furthermore, both McCoy and Spock referred to Miramanee's people as "primitive".

Lastly, these tribal people were stuck in time. Jim Charles (1993) suggested that there are four basic stereotypes of Native Americans: the noble savage, the savage, the generic Indian and the living fossil. *The Paradise Syndrome* showed us a perfect example of "the living fossil". Let's say the ancestors of Miramanee's people were taken from Earth around the late 1760's. Kirk found them in 2268. Five hundred years later they were still living in teepees and leading a pastoral life. There appeared to be no changes in technology, medicine or even architecture! Their society was basically a petrified culture.

The *Paradise...* episode used every convention in the book. Standard themes, standard setting, fabricated images, the entire structure of one of America's favorite "Indian" myths. Here was one instance where Star Trek not only failed to go where no man had gone before. The writer simply used traditional fare in the retelling of the Indian tale.

The Next Generation
Time's Arrow: Part 1

In the fifth year of ST: TNG one Native American character appeared in the episode titled *Time's Arrow: Part 1.* The character Joe Falling Hawk had only one line. He was in San Francisco in the mid 1800's. Data was transported to San Francisco where he met Mark Twain. When he first got there a young bell hop named Jack London took Data to play in a poker game. One of the players was Joe Falling Hawk. When Joe saw Data he said, "Paiiille face". Of course Joe was included to indicate the period, the 1800's, and the place, the West.

Journey's End

Like TOS, TNG had one big "Indian" episode. It was titled *Journey's End* and was written by Ronald D. Moore (1994). In this episode Picard and the crew were called upon to evacuate Federation colonies outside of a newly reconfigured Federation/Cardassian border. One group that was to be evacuated were Amerindians on Dorvan V. They had "settled there after a decades-long search" in order "to avoid the cultural assimilation of Earth" (Nemecek, 1995, p.289). Of course the Amerindians resisted the move. Furthermore they insisted that it was the duty of Picard to help thwart this order as a method of redemption. One of Picard's ancestors took part in a savage massacre of a tribal village in the late 1800's.

A subplot in this episode involved Cadet Wesley Crusher, Beverly Crusher's son. He was on leave from Starfleet Academy and was out of sorts. He became concerned for the welfare of the Native Americans and warned them of Picard's plan to beam them onto the ship without their permission.

When the Amerindians and the Cardassians first came aboard the Enterprise to negotiate Wesley met a young Native named Lakanta. Lakanta took Wesley to a habak (a ceremonial building) to seek some answers concerning his restless, irritable attitude. While there Wesley's father came to him in a dream and told him that it was time for him to follow his own path. After the dream Wesley understood that he did not truly want to be a Starfleet officer. He was simply doing what he thought was expected of him. At that point Lakanta revealed himself to be the Traveler. The Traveler was a being from another dimension who could travel through space and time with the aid of thought. He felt that it was Wesley's destiny to learn to be a Traveler. Wesley and the Traveler left to begin Wesley's training.

At the end of the episode the Cardassians were firing on the Amerindians. At first Wesley wanted to change time in order to rearrange things, but then he realized with the help of the Traveler that he was not to go in and save them: they were to save themselves.

Once again Native Americans on Star Trek were used to exemplify standard themes rather than particular characters and they were played in a standard context. Those themes were displacement, redemption and resistance to oppression. The context was the wilderness of hostile territory in the boundaries of Cardassian space.

When the Federation and Cardassia reconfigured their boundary lines several planets were politically displaced. Dorvan V had been in an alliance with the Federation. Because of the peace treaty the Native Americans were occupying Cardassian space. They refused to move to another planet in the Federation. The Cardassians were ruthless landlords. They sought to colonize the planets that had formerly been in the Federation. The Amerindians on Dorvan V resisted yet another displacement.

Redemption was the theme played out through the actions of Picard. He was told that his ancestor had participated in a brutal massacre. He did not want to exacerbate the atrocities of his forefather through any response he made in his encounter with the Native Americans. At the end he helped the Native Americans negotiate an uneasy peace with the Cardassians so that they could stay on the planet.

Resistance to oppression was the third standard theme interwoven into this story. As so many Amerindians did in the past, these Natives in the future chose to stand their ground rather than face relocation. Not only did they stand their ground in refusing to be moved, but when the time came they fought the Cardassians. Their actions were meant to underscore the rightness of resisting oppression.

It is important to note that the writers and producers of this episode used generic Indian costumes and set pieces out of deference to actual Native Americans.

> At first, reference was made to the Hopi Indians and Tribes...but even with the series' use of advisers the tribes involved asked not to be depicted for fear of misrepresentation, so the terms were generalized: kachina dolls becoming mansaras, the ceremonial kiva now a habak...(Nemecek, 1995, p.290)

The need to create a "very visual culture from scratch" had to be scraped (Nemecek, 1995, p.290)."Nothing could have any [real-life] Indian indicators" (Meese, 1995, p.290). So what we saw in this episode were average Indians and average Indian artifacts.

The creative forces driving Star Trek, to this point, have failed to explore a Native American character. Native Americans have been very stereotypical. They have been used to explore standard themes and placed in the standard contexts of paradise or the frontier.

Voyager

The most recent addition to the Trek universe is *Voyager*. The show first aired in the Spring of 1995. Though another TV show has already used this title, "lost in space" is a subtitle that would fit nicely for this series. The basic premise is that Voyager was sent to bring back a group of people fighting for the Maquis. While chasing the Maquis ship in the bad lands Voyager was transported to the Delta quadrant by an alien referred to as the Caretaker. Unfortunately, the Delta quadrant of the Milky Way has not been charted by the Federation and for a very good reason. It is 75 light years from Alpha quadrant, which is a very long way. A light year is the distance light can travel in a year's time. No wormhole has been found to connect the Alpha and Delta quadrants.

Chakotay was the leader of a Maquis group including B'lanna Torres, Seska (a Cardassian disguised as a Bajoran), and Tuvok (a Starfleet infiltrator). While Janeway was chasing

Chakotay and his crew in the bad lands Chakotay's ship was damaged and his crew had to be beamed aboard Voyager. Since both crews, Federation and Maquis, were lost a long way from home they decided to come together in their effort to reach home. All of the Maquis became part of Starfleet with Chakotay becoming the First Officer (second in command). B'lanna Torres was chosen to be chief engineer over the Starfleet engineer on the mission. It is a struggle for the two crews to work together.

The combined crews, under the leadership of Captain Janeway, are trying to make it home. They hope to find a wormhole to make a swift transit back to Alpha quadrant or find the Caretaker's mate and get it to send them back. If the crew does not find a wormhole or get the second Caretaker to send them back, this particular Voyager crew may never see home again. The present crew could live another seventy-five years with the medical technology available to them, but they would be at the end of their lives and would have spent their middle years in transit. There is a possibility that Voyager will reach Alpha quadrant with crew members that are the descendants of this crew. That would be called intergenerational space travel.

Voyager is very different from any other Trek series. The ship is cut off from the Federation and both the Captain and the chief engineer are women. The tactical officer and aide to the captain is a black Vulcan, the first ever seen on Star Trek and the doctor is not a real person. Lastly, this series can boast the first Native American permanent character in Star Trek history.

Character Sketches

Kathryn Janeway: White female, Captain of the U.S.S. Voyager. Strong and decisive.

Tuvok: Black male, Vulcan. Commander, Tactical and Security officer. Infiltrated the Maquis cell led by Chakotay. Around 100 years old. Is married and has children.

Harry Kim: Asian male, Ensign. Communications and Operations. Recent graduate from Starfleet.

Tom Paris: White male, Lt., helmsman. Was not able to fit into Starfleet. Was imprisoned. Released to go on the mission to capture the Maquis.

Neelix: Talaxian male, guide, chef, and morale officer. Native of the Delta quadrant.

Kes: White female, Occampa. Life span nine years. She is now three. Assistant to the doctor. Neelix's significant other.

The Doctor: White male, computer generated. The human doctor on the mission was killed in the first episode. The Doctor is a holographic image designed to take care of medical problems in an emergency. He is now a permanent member of the crew because no other doctor is available. Programmed with the medical knowledge of several hundred worlds.

B'lanna Torres: Half human, half Klingon female. Chief engineer. Excels in temporal mechanics. Does not like her Klingon side. Part of the Maquis. Attended Starfleet Academy, but could not fit in.

Chakotay: Native American male, first officer. Was leader of the Maquis cell Janeway was in pursuit of. Has a face tattoo.

Chakotay

Robert Beltran plays Chakotay. Because he is the First

Officer, he has appeared in virtually all of the episodes, but he was the central figure in four: *Cathexis, Tattoo, Initiations* and *Resolutions*. I do not believe that Chakotay's tribe has been named, but it is possible that he is from Dorvan V, the planet that was negotiated into Cardassian space by the Federation in TNG. It is possible that Chakotay was a Maquis because his planet was being ravaged by Cardassian rule. Chakotay was trained as a Starfleet officer, but as a member of the Maquis he was fighting guerrilla warfare against the Cardassians.

In *Cathexis* an alien entity was aboard the ship and Chakotay lapsed into a coma. While he was in the coma the doctor and B'lanna were trying to heal him with various types of therapies including the medicine wheel. Chakotay had tried to teach B'lanna something of its use and she was attempting to use that knowledge to bring his lost spirit back to the living.

While on a mission to a planet Chakotay encountered the ancient people who visited Native Americans on Earth (*Tattoo*: STV). He found that the people on the planet wore a tattoo similar to his. While on this away mission Chakotay remembered a trip he took with his father. The ancient people on the planet recognized the tattoo that Chakotay was wearing. They told him of their visit to Earth where they encountered the tribal people of the Americas who "had no culture." The ancient sky people gave Chakotay's people culture.

Chakotay encountered a Kazon youth in Initiations. The Kazons are one of the bad groups in Delta quadrant. Chakotay was on a shuttlecraft alone when he rescued the boy. He found out that the lad was on a ritual coming of age hunt. The fact that Chakotay rescued the boy made the youth a failure in his coming of age trial. Chakotay found a way to escape from the Kazons and also allow the young teen his victory in the coming of age ceremony.

Janeway and Chakotay contracted a deadly virus in Resolutions. The doctor could find no cure for the disease and the Captain and Chakotay did not want to infect the rest of the crew. They ordered the crew to set them down on an inhabitable planet.

The two were left with everything that colonists would need to survive and in addition to that they brought a lab with them so that Janeway could continue looking for a cure.

Very early on, Chakotay resigned himself to living out his life on the planet and he set about making life comfortable for Janeway and himself. On the other hand Janeway refused to give up hope and spent most of her time researching their disease. Since Janeway and Chakotay were the only ones on the planet the inevitable arose: the nature of their relationship would have to change from captain and first officer to a more personal level. Janeway let Chakotay know that she was not ready for that kind of change. Chakotay reassured her by telling her a story of his people. The story Chakotay told basically assured Janeway that any change in their relationship would happen in her own time. Chakotay said he would wait until she was ready for such a change and until that time he would simply devote his life to making her happy.

Fortunately, the doctor was able to develop a cure for the disease with the help of a doctor from the Delta quadrant. Tuvok took the crew back to get Chakotay and Janeway. As soon as they were aboard the ship Janeway assumed her role as Chakotay's captain. This was evidenced when Janeway ordered Chakotay to check all systems.

Chakotay is a professional Native American working as an assimilated novel character. He carries himself as a well trained military man. In some ways Chakotay is also a warrior or freedom fighter. After all he was leading a Maquis cell when he came aboard Voyager. He was resisting oppression by the Cardassians.

Even though Chakotay speaks General American English he is not devoid of ethnicity. The writers have utilized many characteristics of the "average Indian" mythic culture. The spirit of his father visits Chakotay when he is troubled. He taught Janeway how to find her animal guide. And, all of the flashbacks of his people identify them as Native Americans. Chakotay also wears a face tattoo, which I believe is used as an ethnic marker, but in this day and time (the mid 90's) tattoos are very popular. The face tattoo may not indicate anything to the general public about Chakotay's ethnicity.

For the most part, the presentation of Native American images on Voyager has been effective. However, I feel that the writers and producers have made two serious blunders; one was in the episode Tattoo, the other in the first episode of the third season (Fall 1996). The sky people who visited Earth said that the Native people had "no culture." In this day and age the creative minds that drive Voyager should realize that all people have culture--all of them! And, if the sky people were so advanced, they would have recognized that the Native Americans did indeed have a culture. The writer of Tattoo propagated the notion that people whose lives are not dominated or maintained by technology have no culture. The second faux pas committed was in the first episode of the third season. The Kazons trapped the crew on a dangerous planet. They needed to start a fire to keep warm. Chakotay said, " I would be the only Indian in the universe who cannot start a fire by rubbing two sticks together". In that same episode, Tuvok devised a bow and arrow from sticks and strings. Chakotay looked at it and said, "I can't shoot that". Tuvok assured Chakotay that the bow and arrow were not for him. Tuvok intended to use them his self.

Other than those problems it appears that Trek has finally presented a Native American character that is new in many ways. Chakotay is not a servant, nor is he a savage. He does not wear buckskins, his hair in not in long braids and he sports no turquoise or silver. He does not exhibit stoic silence nor does he speak in cryptic one liners. Most importantly, Chakotay has not been shown as a person who deals only with intuition. He has been shown to be a thinker. He is an able leader and has good personnel management skills. These capabilities have been evidenced by his ability to help his crew work alongside Federation personnel.

There has been one instance in the series when Chakotay was not treated with the respect due him and that was in the episode titled *Investigations*. In this outing, Janeway and Tuvok were searching for a traitor aboard Voyager, someone who had been giving information to the Kazons. Janeway and Tuvok developed a ruse to help find the traitor. They had Lt. Paris behave in an insubordinate manner, finally hitting Chakotay. Then Paris asked to be let off the ship and the Kazons captured him. While a prisoner of the Kazons Paris discovered who the traitor was. Chakotay was not informed of this ploy until it was almost over. Naturally he wanted to know why he was not informed. Janeway and Tuvok said they did not want him, Chakotay, to be put in an awkward position because they suspected that the traitor might have been a person formerly under his command. In other words, they used Chakotay as a dupe. This could have only served to undermine his authority with the crew.

In *Resolutions* the writers played on the tribal male-white female liaison. Janeway and Chakotay were the only two people on the planet, in effect, Adam and Eve all over again. Although the two were in an edenic context Janeway resisted any sexual attraction. She said it would signal that she had lost hope of ever getting off the planet. Chakotay did not respond in a savage fashion. He told her he would wait. Janeway had difficulty stepping out of her role as Captain and she also still held on to her memories of her significant other left behind in the Alpha quadrant. In a fashion typical of the treatment of tribal male-white female relationships it was unthinkable to Janeway that she would allow herself to be attracted to Chakotay.

The inclusion of the Native American character, Chakotay, does more than signal particular issues or contexts. Although *Voyager* does deal with resisting oppression and being lost in the wilderness, the viewing audience is being allowed to come to understand Chakotay as a person, a human being.

In the history of television Chakotay is unique. He is unique even in today's TV market as a tribal character. On *Northern Exposure* Marilyn is a guised squaw and Ed is a shaman in training who serves everybody on the show (Crusoe's Friday). On *Renegade* Bobby Sixkiller has been given a traditional job for Amerindians on the screen, bounty hunter (tracker). He has long hair and wears silver & turquoise jewelry. He has even donned his buckskins.

On *Walker: Texas Ranger*, a Native American setting is often used to show why Walker can be so intuitive as he tracks down criminals. It is a further indication of why he does not fit with middle-class white America: he was raised on a reservation. Furthermore the use of Native American settings on *Walker* indicates the wild nature of the open expanse of the Texas range. It is possible that the Native presence on Walker is a reference to the real life experiences of Chuck Norris. His father was Cherokee and his given name was Carlos Ray (*TV Guide*, July 22, 1996).

Chakotay is unique among present day Native characters in that he does not display the expected trappings of the average Indian, except in the area of spirituality. He is also unique in that he is a professional Native American, but not devoid of his cultural heritage. And lastly, Chakotay is unique in that he does interact with other people of colour: Tuvok, a black Vulcan; Harry Kim, an Asian male; and Torres, a Klingon/human woman. So while he is novel, as the only Native in the story, he is not isolated from other people of colour.

Conclusion

Images of Native Americans on Star Trek have been quite standard until the Voyager series. There was the *Paradise* episode in TOS, which was a retelling of the Pocahontas story. Then there was *Journey's End* (TNG) where Native Americans were used in the standard themes of resisting oppression and displacement. They were set in the standard context of the wilderness. Only on *Voyager* have we seen an Amerindian character as an individual that we can come to know. He is a professional and a freedom fighter. Chakotay is a skillful blend of the conventional Indian myth and the inventiveness of a unique individual. *Voyager* has taken the Native American image where none has gone before.

References

Bataille, G. & Silet, C. (1985). *Images of American Indians on film: An annotated bibliography.* New York: Garland Publishing Inc.

Bataille, G. and Silet, C. (Eds.) (1980). *The pretend Indians: Images of Native Americans in the movies*. Ames, Iowa: Iowa State University Press.

Casey, C. (Summer 1994). Distorted images. *Tribal College*,6,(1), pgs.12-15.

Charles, J. (November 1993). Of mascots and tomahawk chops: Stereotypes of American Indians and the English teacher's response. Paper presented at the Annual Meeting of the National Council of Teachers of English (82nd, Louisville, KY). ED 355 535

Clifton, J.(Ed.)(1990). *The invented Indian: Cultural fictions and government policies.* New Brunswick, NJ: Transaction Publishers.

Ganje, L. (1996). Native American stereotypes. In Paul Lester (Ed.) *Images that Injure*. Westport, CT: Praeger Publishers

Greer, S., (Spring 1993). The noble savage. *Winds of Change*,8, (2), pgs.89-92.

Hilger, M. (1995). *From savage to nobleman: Images of Native Americans in film.* Lanham, Maryland: Scarecrow Press Inc.

Hilger, M. (1986). *The American Indian in films.* Metuchen, N.J. The Scarecrow Press Inc.

Means, R. with Wolf, M. (1995). *Where white men fear to tread: The autobiography of Russell Means.* New York: St. Martin's Griffin.

Nemecek, L.(1995)(2nd ed.).*The Star Trek Next Generation companion.* New York: Pocket Book.

Okuda, M., Okuda, D. & Mirek, D.(1994). *The Star Trek encyclopedia.* New York: Pocket Books.

Seattle, Chief.(1971). The Indians' night promises to be dark. In *Indian Oratory: Famous Speeches by Noted Indian Chieftains.* by WIC. Vanderwerth. Norman, OK: University of Oklahoma Press.

Star Trek Voyager #8(September 1996). New York: Starlog Group.

Stedman, R.(1982). *Shadows of the Indian: Stereotypes in American culture.* Norman, OK :University of Oklahoma Press.

Svenningsen, K. (1990). <u>Stereotypes of the Latin Image in American Films: Silent Period to 1945</u>. ED 365 313

Weatherford, E. & Seubert, E. (1988). *Native Americans on film & video, Vol. II.* New York : Museum of the American Indian.

Wilson, II, C. & Gutiérrez, C. (1985). *Minorities and media: Diversity and the end of mass communication.* Beverly Hills: Sage Publications.

Wilson, II, C. & Gutiérrez, F. (1995). *Race, multiculturalism, and the media: From mass to class communication.* Beverly Hills: Sage Publications.

Zerzan, J. & Carnes, A.(Eds.)(1991). *Questioning technology: Tool, toy or tyrant?* Santa Cruz, CA: New Society Publishers.

Chapter 9
Images of Latinos on Screen

> Mexican Americans in the Southwest still find themselves labeled as "the invisible minority," "the forgotten people," or "the minority nobody knows. (Pettit, 1980, p.157)

Of all of the ethno-racial categories described in the first chapter Latino was the longest. Latino refers to: (1) Spanish people from the Old World that settled in the New World (Castilians); (2) those indigenes of the New World who were conquered by Spain (including inhabitants of Mexico, Puerto Rica, Cuba and Costa Rico); (3) those who do not identify themselves by tribal or community affiliation ; (4) people who speak Spanish as a first language or; (5) have a Spanish surname. This definition excludes Native Americans and people who live in Spain. The latter consider themselves European. Latinos include racial groups ranging from dark to fair skin.

It is difficult to determine what is the most appropriate label to use when discussing people of Spanish heritage in the New World. It depends upon the region of the country, the self-definition of specific communities, and the political consciousness of a group or individual. Presently the term “Latino” seems to be enjoying high popularity on the west-coast. However, Mexican Americans who honor their Amerindian heritage frequently refer to themselves as Chicano. It seems that people with Spanish heritage who are at the diffuse stage of identity development, have not done much thinking or searching in terms of their identity, have no problem with Hispanic. However, I have heard several of my Mexican American students voice resentment at being called Latino. No matter which term is used, Hispanic, Latino, Chicano, even Mesoamericans, there will be those who are pleased and those who are offended. One thing is for sure, people of Spanish descent in the New World use all of the above: there is no consensus. Therefore, throughout this section when I refer to people of Spanish descent in general I will use the terms Hispanic or Latino. If an individual or group has a publicly stated preference I will use the preferred term. When I know the specific group a person belongs to I will use that term, such as Cuban, Mexican or Puerto Rican.

Because Latino is more of an ethnic than racial designation it is difficult to identify a person of Latino heritage "just by looking at them". There are Asian Latinos in the Philippines and there are black Latinos in Panama, Cuba, Puerto Rica and South America. Furthermore, there are white Latinos who are descendants of the Castilians who settled in the Southwest and Mexico.

Primarily Latinos are a mixture of indigenes and Spanish people. In Mexico this mixture of people is divided into three groups: Indians, Mestizos, and Castilians. Castilians consider themselves pure Spanish. Mestizos are a Spanish and Indian mix. And, Indians are of the original people of the region not mixed with Spaniards. The social structure of the society revolves around these three designations.

When I began this book I could not think of any Latino characters on Star Trek. Outside of the stereotypical markers there are few indicators of Latino heritage. In a study of minority images in magazine advertising it was ascertained that, "Hispanic Americans were the most underrepresented among the three groups, indicating low levels of social acceptance (Taylor, 1995, pg. 608). The three groups in the study were African, Hispanic and Asian Americans.

The National Council of La Raza conducted a study titled “Don't Blink: Hispanics in Television Entertainment”. The data from that study indicated that "Latinos accounted for 2 percent of all characters depicted in prime-time series during the 1994-95 season" (Garcia, 1996, pg. E1). That number was up from 1% in the previous year. These numbers indicate a low rate of Latino screen characters in view of the fact that they make-up 10% of the American population (Garcia, 1996). Hispanics are underrepresented on TV in general and specifically in Star Trek.

If a character is not speaking Spanish, does not have a Spanish last name and does not have physical characteristics or a costume that a viewer might associate with Mexicans, Cubans, or Puerto Ricans a Latino character might be "invisible" in a popular culture medium. I almost made the mistake of not including this chapter because I could not think of any Latino characters in Star Trek. The omission of this chapter would have been a travesty given the area of the country in which I teach.

So, I decided to search the *Star Trek Encyclopedia* entries one by one in order to identify characters or actors with Spanish last names. Lo and behold, I came up with thirteen such characters! Federico Varona, a faculty member in my department, verified the list for me. The list of names included Flores, Juarez, Lopez, Mendez, Mendoza, Saviola, Quinteros, Rodriguez, Sanchez, Orfil, and Torres. This chapter is based on an examination of these characters.

Art Pettit wrote the classic critical work on Latino images in popular culture. It is titled *Images of The Mexican American in Fiction and Film* (1980). The work is a classic because of the historical information it provides, the in-depth critique of Latino images it contains, and the almost encyclopedic nature of its scope. There are no recent editions of Art's work because he died of cancer in 1976 before he could finish the book. A colleague of his, Dennis Showalter, finished his work. Most of the subsequent works on Latino images in popular culture refer to this seminal work by Pettit. Because there have been few critical works about

Latino images, particularly of the magnitude of Images, I have based much of my discussion relevant to themes and images of Latinos on Pettit's treatise.

Exigencies

The significant situations, among Euroamericans, that demanded the deliberate shaping of Latino images in popular culture have been many. One of the first was the need to justify the occupation of the Southwest territory. It was necessary for the Latinos there to be portrayed as less than human. Furthermore, historically there has been economic and political competition between the U.S. and Mexico (Hadley-Garcia, 1990, p.32). This competition has been for the natural resources of land and elements to run the industrial complex such as oil. And, there has been competition between the U.S. and Mexico for control of the human resource, the people themselves. When the U.S. had a need for ready labor or market share for product distribution Mexicans and other Latinos have been shown in a favorable light. Unfortunately there have been more instances of the shaping of negative rather than positive images.

In the late 1800's the popular press was used extensively to support the settlement of lands west of Texas by white Protestants. Newspaper articles and dime novels were used at the forefront of the campaign. There were many novels written about the Southwest and it was in these novels that the negative images of Latinos became crystallized. “Perhaps the most persistent early exploiter of these images in popular fiction was Ned Buntline" (Pettit, 1980 p. 26). His books were filled with negative stereotyped Mexicans to serve in contrast to the "enterprising Protestants who came south to conquer..."(Pettit, 1980, p.26)

From Buntline, Beadle and Adams publishers, and Frank Tousey Publications came hundreds of novels and short stories to entertain the American reading public. These writers had a need for a villain who would offer maximum contrast to the heroes. The actual presence of some skin colour between the two ethnic groups was used to support the racial bigotry that characterized the U.S. (Pettit, 1980, p.23)

After World War II a significant change in the images of Latinos took place. There was an increased need for agricultural labor since so many American men were fighting in the war. This generated a flood of immigrants from Mexico. They were sorely needed. Not only that, but after World War II business and government sought to open up Latin markets for American culture and products in order to help the economy (Hadley-Garcia 1990, p.81). During these periods the images of Mexican/Latinos improved. Readers and movie-goers were often treated to redemption stories; tales of Mexicans who became worthy of inclusion in white society because they were light, Castilians, and they sacrificed themselves for whites.

A second influence on improving Latino images was the emergence of U.S. and Latin American studios (Hadley-Garcia, 1990, p. 89). These studios wanted to cash in on the entertainment dollars of people south of the border. They started to make movies that guised the traditional stereotypes of Latinos.

Lastly, Latino images were improved during World War II so that the U.S. could emphasize unity among the Americas. The U.S. wanted to insure that their borders at the south were safe from attack while they fought the war in Europe (Hadley-Garcia, 1990, p.91).

Standard Themes

The recurring themes in stories that have Latino characters are similar to those used in popular culture works featuring African and Asian Americans. Miscegenation and racial pollution stories were popular. The basic theme was that Castilian Spaniards who settled in the southwest had degraded their racial stock by intermixing with the indigenes (Pettit, 1980, p.23). This intermarriage or racial mixing was blamed for the degeneration of the great Castilian houses of the era. The repeated theme was that "the Spaniards and their polluted descendants have committed racial and national self-genocide by mixing voluntarily with inferior dark-skinned races" and were therefore fated to become extinct (Pettit, 1980, p.24).

Catholic tyranny was another theme that was persistent in the presentation of Latinos. Since the US was and is dominated by Protestants much of the popular fiction work in the late 1800's and early 1900's was propaganda against the Catholic church. These works presented many corrupt priests and other church official who were out to dominate the lives of the people and take their property for the church (Pettit, 1980).

One other popular theme was the inability of Latinos to run their own countries. Because of high corruption and incompetence these countries needed the steady moral hand of US whites (Pettit, 1980, p. 24).

There were several stock formulas in these early novels, short stories and movies. Here are four of them. The Anglo heroes beating Mexican bandits was a favorite along with blonde heroines beating out Castilian and Mestizo women for the marriage bed of white men. Because of their supposed cowardice, Mexican helplessness in the face of white domination was a frequent formula and redemption of the Mexican by their joining the conquering race was too (Pettit, 1980, p.24).

Latino men and women characters were to be killed, mocked, seduced or redeemed by whites (p.132). They have been used primarily to add color or flavor to a story, to serve as the entertainment, to provide moral lessons about the evils of race mixing, and to indicate diversity in a community or organization. Latinos have also very nicely filled the role of villain.

Standard Contexts

Latinos appear in several standard contexts. White washed characters with Latino names are often placed as the man or woman in the crowd, to indicate diversity. Their names are called in passing, but they do nothing. Latinos also often appear in barrio/ghettos to indicate a poverty-ridden area. That area would also be riddled with crime.

The gang is a frequent place to find young Latino males, most often Mexican and Puerto Rican. Many are in stories about jail, once again to emphasize the myth of the criminal element of Hispanic people.

In order to indicate that a setting is in Texas, the southwest, or south of the US border Mexican characters and locales are often used. Of course, Latinos are a favorite in vacation spots as entertainers, servants or criminals. And, we cannot forget the anti-Catholic sentiment. Latinos are a great people to use to explore that religious bigotry.

Taxonomy of Mythic Characters

As with the stereotypes of other people of colour "general media advertising depicts Latinos as tokens and stereotypes while those in the Latino media portray them as unbelievably successful and wealthy (Penaloza, 1994). Most often we see extreme images of Latinos.

In early fiction there were several images of the Mexican including the bandit, the clown or buffoon, the dark lady and the caballero or cowboy. From the dime store novels there were the arrogant hidalgos (aristocratic Spaniards), lazy peons (peasants), sexy senoritas, and loose-principled priest (Pettit, 1980, p.26)

Greasers

The greaser can be added to the list of Latino stereotypes. He was the enemy Mexican male described as "... oily and ugly, crude and overdressed..." (Pettit, 1980, p. 143). The greaser was a violent male Hispanic

(Hadley-Garcia, 1990, p.36). Jeremiah Clemens, a

romance writer of the 1800's posited the notion that the term greaser originated in western descriptions of Mexicans. He wrote this passage:

> The people look greasy, their clothes are greasy, their dogs are greasy--everywhere grease and filth hold divided dominion, and the singular appropriateness of the name bestowed by the western settlers, soon caused it to be universally adopted by the American army. (Wilson, II and Gutiérrez, 1995, p 66)

Bandidos

Among the bandidos there were the bad and the not-so-bad. The bad bandidos were targets that stood against white men only to be killed. White actors usually played the not-so-bad bandidos. They provided "morally ambiguous roles that add[ed] a pleasant note of uncertainty to here-to-fore predictable patterns of villainy" (Pettit, 1980, p. 214).

"If they are light enough, they sometimes try to join the favored race, or to give honorable battle to it. If they are too dark to pass, they resort to villainy to vent their frustration and cover their failure". (Pettit, 1980, p. 26) These characters blurred the former moral lines between white and Mexican. They also were the beginnings of the humanization of Latino characters.

Clerics and Peons

Other stereotypes included the clerical rogues. They were a threat to the moral fabric of Protestant life. Corrupt priest characters were used to voice anti-Catholic sentiments. Then there were the Peon servants. The "fawning peons bear startling resemblance to the shuffling Sambos of the era." (Pettit, 1980, p.28). They were used for comic relief. Fawning servility to inept villainy was the range of the peon.

The servile peon evolved into the sympathetic sidekick clown who was there to entertain the white man and/or sacrifice his life for the white man.

During the late 40's and early 50's the images of Latino men were humanized in the persona of the manly Mexican. He was a superior light-skinned mestizo with a particular gift: looks, physical prowess, or managerial capacity (Pettit, 1980, p.183). This man was most often not even visibly Mexican, unlike the Asian and African American professional characters that were white washed.

Latin Lovers

This section would not be complete without mentioning the Latin lover. The Latin lover is a character that is of Spanish descent and very romantic. He has dark eyes and dark hair, and is portrayed as having fiery, smoldering passion (Svenningsen, 1990, pg. 28).

Latina Women

Huaco-Nuzum maintains the Latina, Chicana, or Hispanic woman has been granted little space to develop their authentic selves in real life. The cultural specificity of Latinas, Mexicanas, and Chicanas has been absent or overshadowed by racism and sexism (Huaco-Nuzum 1996, pg.263). "Minority status has been instrumental in bringing the various Hispanic peoples together, but it has also perpetuated many stereotypes" of Hispanic women (Garza, 1994, pg. 5). While most of us have heard the term machismo we have not heard the counterpart for it. Hembrismo is the concept of docile femininity and many apply that stereotype to Latina women (Garza, 1994). And yet, while that stereotype is perpetuated so is that of the "sexually provacative, generic Latinas. They are shown as an exotic commodity

(Huaco-Nuzum, 1996, 263).

> Mestiza images are bound by white feminism and Chicano patriarchal ideology...They are marginalized between ideologies. Chicanas speak with a multiplicity of voices and experiences. (1996, pg. 263).

Hershfield, in her book *Mexican Cinema/Mexican Woman...* suggested that there are basically three stereotypes of Mexican women: virgin, whore, or temptress (LaMalinche). The virgin image is revered as an outgrowth of the worship of the Virgin Mary and the patron saint of Mexico, the Virgin of Guadalupe.

If the Mexican woman was not a virgin then she was a whore. The term whore is used to describe not only women who sell their bodies for money, but also those who are considered promiscuous. Mexican, Cuban and Puerto Rican women characters were used for sexual exploitation. They could do all the thrilling, sinful things that good white girls couldn't do. The Latina could have a lasting affair with an Anglo male character, but not with one of her own kind (Hadley-Garcia, 1990, p. 35). La Malinche will be discussed in the section on "dark ladies".

Half-Breed

The half-breed harlot provided sexual titillation. She was a product of tainted racial heritage and the antithesis of the Spanish or white woman. She was fit for sex, but not marriage for she was the counterpoint to the white virgin (Hadley-Garcia, 1990, p.61)

Half-breed flirts may appeal to the American male's baser instincts, but they must be rejected because their religion, their complexion, and their pasts are shadowed. (Pettit, 1980, p.63).

Temptress/ The Dark Lady

The temptress among Latinas were intemperate and hyperemotional. They were often shown behaving like pampered children. Unfortunately the woman of the Castilian conquers were the counterparts of the Amerindian squaw. They were stereotyped as women who aged badly. They might look good while young, but they matured into fat, dumpy, lazy, pampered, grown up babies. The writers used this stereotype as another example of why Euroamerican women were preferable to Latino women.

Young Mestiza women were frequently used as a plot device to give away the family deeds and titles to her white lover or to betray her people in some way. Hence she was a "dark lady". Hershfield refers to the “dark lady” as La Malinche, the traitor of Mexico. The prototype of Hispanic woman as traitor could very well be the wife of Hernando Cortez. According to folk rumor in the Mexican community La Malinche was the mistress/wife of Hernandez Cortez the conqueror. In March 1519 he arrived in Tabasco, Mexico with 600 men, fewer than 20 horses and only 10 fieldpieces. La Malinche (christened Marina) was an Aztec woman who was the wife/mistress of Cortez. Cortez conquered the Aztecs and other tribes with the very limited number of resources that he brought with him. Community folklore/rumor suggests that the only way Cortez could have conquered so many with so few and on foreign soil was with inside help. It is believed in the Mexican American community that Marina was a traitor to the community because she allegedly reported military information to Cortez. They maintain that this supposed treachery by a woman was the only way Cortez could have been so victorious in central and South America. So a Latina character in fiction who is a La Malinche is a person who sells out her family, community, or country to whites.

This discussion would not be complete without addressing the fact that tribes such as the Tlascaluns joined forces with Cortez to help him defeat the Aztecs. The Tlascaluns were already enemies of the Aztec before Cortez arrived. They saw his arrival as an opportunity to defeat their long time foe. And they were not the only tribe to join forces with Cortez, though they were the most loyal to him. This blaming of Marina for the fall of the Aztecs is a typical ploy of patriarchal societies. They blame some of the major downfalls or faults of a society on one woman. For example, it was Eve who was responsible for man's fall from grace. It was Pandora who loosened the major evils of society from the box. And it was Marina who caused the fall of the Aztecs. Of course the fact that the Tlascaluns and other tribes joined forced with Cortez to defeat the Aztecs is ignored. Who would have thought that one woman was so powerful that she could destroy an entire society all by herself?

Modern Images

Several scholars have maintained that there are a few basic stereotypes of Latinos males that have persisted over the past 150 years (Pettit, 1980; Hadley-Garcia, 1990; Woll, 1980; Alfred, 1996). These stereotypes include harassed victims, light-skinned-Americanized Mexicans, dark avengers and jolly loafers.

Victims, Americanized, Avengers, Loafers

Harassed victims are those who retreat passively from the American enemy. Their response to oppression is to accept it in silence (Pettit, 1980). "The passive dark skinned victim invariably goes down to defeat or death." (Pettit, 1980, p. 177)

The light skinned, Americanized Latinos were those who made it in American society. They tried so hard to abandon their brown brothers and sisters to join the white race that they usually won a permanent position within the ranks of the favored society (Pettit, 1980, p.178).

Dark Avengers are those who set out to cripple and wound the American oppressor. He "punishes the white man for his sins...

he is a genuine threat and somehow must be punished (Pettit,p.178). Lastly, there is the jolly loafer who accepts his miserable lot with little bitterness or recrimination. The jolly loafer is harmless, therefore he may be ignored, subjected to humor, affection, or harassment. Freddie Prince in *Chico and the Man* was a 1970's version of the jolly loafer. The character Hector on *Malcolm and Eddie* is a 1990's version.

The archetypal image of Latinas was "the dark lady" as identified by Pettit. The lady was "dark" not necessarily in skin colour, but as a plot device. The dark lady character was used to explore the sexual elements in a story or to betray the family, town, or country to the whites. The older Castilian woman was the counterpart to the Ma Squaw, a woman who did not age well. And, the half-breed like, the tragic mulatto, was used as a place to "sow wild oats", but not to settle down with.

In the 40's Latinos often appeared as entertainers. The entertainer was a Latino that had been rendered harmless because s/he was only interested in his/her craft. The musicalization of the Latino and African American renders them devoid of political and social ambitions.

Latinos on Television

The history of Latinos on television is relatively short. The first Mexican characters to emerge as stars were Cisco Kid, and his sidekick, Panache. They appeared in the 1950's (Wilson, II and Gutiérrez, 1995, p. 100).

Desi Arnaz, a Cuban entertainer, was one of the biggest Latin personalities in TV history. He was the husband of Lucille Ball and appeared on the *I Love Lucy Show.* The show ran 10 yrs. from 1951-1961 (Wilson, II and Gutiérrez, 1995, p. 100). The DesiLu production company deserves special recognition from Trekkers because it brought *Star Trek: The Original Series* to television. Arnaz and Ball owned the company.

Zorro has been an enduring story appearing as a movie and television series. The show debuted in 1957 on TV. It was set in early California and had all of the stock stereotypes of Latinos (Wilson, II and Gutiérrez, 1995, p. 101).

In the 60's there were three serials with Latino characters. The first was *The Real McCoys* with Tony Martinez as Pepino Garcia. The second was *The Bill Dana Show* in 1963 with a hotel bellhop named, Jose Jimenez (Wilson, II and Gutiérrez, 1995, p. 101). Lastly, there was *The High Chaparral*, which ran from 1967-1971. The show featured an interracial marriage between the daughter of a Mexican cattle rancher and a rich white rancher (Wilson, II and Gutiérrez, 1995, p. 101).

Only three shows in the 70's featured Latino characters. These included *Chico and the Man,* with Freddie Prince and *CHIPS* with Erick Estrada. The character of Chico was highly stereotypical. He was always trying to escape work. That image was toned down after Mexican American activists pressured Prince and his producers. Erick Estrada was a highway patrolman and therefore fit the professional Latino character. The third show was *Fantasy Island* starring Ricardo Montalban in 1978. Montalban was the Latin lover type character (Wilson, II and Gutiérrez, 1995, p. 101).

The 90's can boast the shows *Everybody Loves Raymond* and *Nash Bridges.* In the first show, the lead is a Latino man. He is married and has a set of twins. In *Nash* Cheech Martin plays the sidekick of detective Bridges.

Current Latino Actors and Entertainers

I felt that this section would be helpful because so many Latino(a) actors and entertainers are not readily identifiable by appearance, and many have Americanized or changed their names. This list is by no means exhaustive.

Ana Alicia, Desi Arnaz,
Antonio Banderas, Robert Beltran,
Dolores Del Rio,
Rene Enriquez, Gloria Estefan,
Emilio Estevez, Erick Estrada, Andy Garcia,
Rita Hayworth (Rita Cansino),
Julio Iglesias, Wanda de Jesus,
Raul Julia, Kathy Jurado,
Fernando Lamas, Lorenzo Lamas,
A. Martinez, Carmen Miranda,
Ricardo Montalban, Rita Moreno,
Edward James Olmos, Freddie Prince,
Anthony Quinn,
Duncan Renaldo, Gilbert Roland,
Cesar Romero, Linda Ronstadt,
Charlie Sheen, Martin Sheen, Jimmy Smits,
Ritchie Valens (Richie Valensuela), and
Raquel Welch (Raquel Tejada).(Hadley-Garcia, 1990)

Latinos on Star Trek

The Original Series
Commodore Mendez

The first Latino character to appear on ST was Commodore Jose Mendez, played by Malachi Throne. Mendez was the commanding officer of Starbase 11. In two episodes, *The Menagerie, Parts I and II*, the audience was introduced to characters from the pilot of TOS, *The Cage,* and the permanent characters of the subsequent episodes. In the *Menagerie* Spock abducted Fleet Captain Christopher Pike to take him to Talos IV. Spock had to face court martial proceedings to determine what should be done about him breaking the Starfleet rule that no one from the Federation should ever go to Talos IV. Commodore Jose

Mendez was the senior officer in those hearings and in that position was in charge of them.

When the court martial tribunal was over and Spock was cleared of all charges Commodore Mendez disappeared, that's right, he disappeared. You see, he was only a projection of the Talosians, the people that Spock was taking Captain Pike to. You might remember them: they were the aliens with the big heads, veins pulsating on them, and they used mental telepathy to communicate. The Talosians projected the image of Commodore Mendez onto the Enterprise so that Spock could explain his reasons for taking over the ship.

So in fact there was a Latino on the very first episode of Trek. Commodore Mendez was a professional Latino, unidentifiable as Latino, working as a novel person of colour, totally assimilated. Wasn't it a pity though: the first Latino to appear on Star Trek really wasn't there at all. And though Latinos were present and their names were called in subsequent episodes and series they still "were not there". There were three other Latinos on TOS: Rodriguez, Rodriguez and Sanchez.

Lt. Esteban Rodriguez (Perry Lopez) was part of the landing party to an amusement park planet. He explored to see if the planet was safe for a visit (*Shore Leave* :TOS). Another Rodriguez was found in the genetically engineered humans of Khan's group. He was trained in communication technologies and survived the Eugenics Wars on Earth. (*Space Seed*: TOS). Dr. Sanchez, a physician, performed an autopsy on one episode of the TOS (*That Which Survives)*. There were four Latino characters in TOS, but none had a recurring or permanent role. All of the Latino characters were professionals, working as the only person of colour with their ethnicity erased. Most often their names were mentioned in order to indicate diversity among characters.

The Next Generation

Latino characters fared a little better on TNG. There were

seven of them including Lt. Torres, Miss Flores, Lt. Juarez, Ensign Lopez, Mendez, Dr. Mendoza, Solis and Commander Quinteros. Let's take a look at the Latino characters in TNG.

Lt. Torres (Jimmy Ortega) was a flight control officer when the Enterprise D first encountered Q. Q is an antagonist who periodically appears on the series. He belongs to a communal community where individuality is discouraged. The powers of the Q make them appear omnipotent in comparison to other humanoids. Torres was frozen by Q, but later recovered (*Encounter at Farpoint*, Part 1: TNG).

George de la Pena played the character of Orfil Solis. He took the navigational console when LaForge assumed command of the Enterprise while Picard was absent. This was in the episode *The Arsenal of Freedom*.

Marissa Flores was the winner of a primary school science fair on the Enterprise. She, along with two other winners, came to see Captain Picard when the ship experienced a disaster. Flores, her companions and Captain Picard were cut off from the other decks when they became stuck in the turbo lift (elevator). Picard decided that the best way to keep the children safe and in good morale was to treat them like Starfleet personnel. Flores was named his Number One, the second in command, as the four journeyed through the bowels of the ship to reach safety. (*Disaster*: TNG)

Lieutenant Juarez was a Starfleet officer. She gave birth to a boy on the day that Miles and Keiko O'Brien were married (*Data's Day*: TNG). Ensign Lopez was a division crew member responsible for preparing the duty roster on Enterprise D during the episode *Birthright Part 1*: TNG. And, Mendez was an officer on the U.S.S. Victory. The character was only mentioned by last name during the *Identity Crisis*: TNG episode.

Dr. Mendoza (played by Castulo Guerra) was a Federation representative in the negotiations for rights to the Barzan wormhole. Members of the Ferengi delegation poisoned him in order to improve their negotiating position (*The Price:* TNG). In in charge of the Starfleet team that assembled the ship (Okuda, Okuda and Mirek, 1994).

Nothing new happened with Latino characters on ST:TNG. They were professionals, members of Starfleet, with ethnic markers erased, very fair, not working with other people of colour, and speaking General American English.

Deep Space Nine

Camille Saviola played Kai Opaka. The Kai (her official title) was a spiritual and political leader of the Bajoran people. She appeared early in the DS9 series and was a member of the religious caste on Bajor. The Kai visited the Gamma Quadrant with Commander Sisko and Major Kira in a runabout. While there they crashed and the Kai was killed.

Sisko and Kira found that two factions of warring prisoners inhabited the planet. They were kept alive by special microbes on the planet. They fought, wounded and killed each other on a regular basis. Unfortunately, no one on the planet ever died, so the factions were in a perpetual hell, doomed to live with constant conflict, pain, and recurring death experiences.

The Kai was resurrected on the planet. She realized that she would die if she left, but the Prophets had also told her that she would have a new mission. Opaka recognized that her new mission was to stay on the planet to help the warring factions learn to live in peace and so she remained there (*Battle Lines:* DS9). The Kai is not a Latina character, but a Latina actress plays her. Her ethnicity is not part of the character.

Munez

Enrique Muñez, was the break out role for Latinos on ST to date. He was played by F. J. Rio and appeared in the episode *The Ship*: DS9 (Fall 1996). Enrique appeared to be Mexican and spoke Spanish while delirious.

Munez

Enrique Muñez, was the break out role for Latinos on ST to date. He was played by F. J. Rio and appeared in the episode *The Ship*: DS9 (Fall 1996). Enrique appeared to be Mexican and spoke Spanish while delirious.

Enrique was part of a mission with Sisko, Dax, O'Brien and Worf. While on a mission away from DS9 Sisko and his crew witnessed a ship crash. It was a Jem'Hadar ship and Sisko wanted to take it back to Federation space. A woman from the Vorta and a contingency of Jem'Hadar arrived to take the ship back. This was the central conflict of the story.

The episode opened with Enrique and O'Brien bantering back and forth about climbing hills and mountains. It was apparent that O'Brien liked Enrique very much and had taken him under his wing in a sort of paternal-big brother way. O'Brien called Enrique, Qui Que. I don't believe O'Brien had this type of relationship with any other Starfleet personnel; he had certainly not called any of them by a nick name, which implied intimacy, paternalism, or superiority.

Early in the episode, *The Ship,* Qui Que was wounded. Throughout the rest of the story O'Brien was so paternalistic about Qui Que that he could not keep his mind on the work he needed to do. Furthermore, he was in denial about Qui Que's impending death, unlike Worf ,who announced in true Klingon fashion that being wounded in battle was an honorable way to die. What was so different about this paternalistic behavior from O'Brien was that he had never shown such behavior before. It would have been appropriate if Qui Que and O'Brien had been related, like Sisko and his son Jake. But, there was no familial relationship between the two. Perhaps the paternalistic behavior of O'Brien stemmed from the fact that Enrique was young enough to be his son or that he was an ethnic minority among humans.

Latinos are often used in a story to indicate foreignness, alieness or expendability. Frequently the very fact that a character is of colour, foreign or alien is the kiss of death. The viewer realizes early on that that character will be killed off because he/she is expendable. Such was the case with Enrique. He was one of five people to die on the mission including Hoya, a Benzite who was flying the runabout; T'Lor, probably a Vulcan female based on her name, Rooney; and Bertram. Sisko recited their names in remorse after the mission. Muñez was included in this group of expendable characters and he was ethnically identifiable. Could there be a connection?

O'Brien and Worf sat with the body of Enrique while they awaited his burial, a jettison of his casket into space. Alas, dear Enrique, he was just too ethnic to survive the story.

Enrique was a character that was more than a cardboard cutout Latino. We came to know a little of him. He was a professional, working as the only Latino in the situation, and for the most part he spoke General English.

Voyager

B'lanna Torres, played by Roxann Biggs-Dawson, is the chief engineer aboard Voyager. She did attend Starfleet, but left due to her inability to fit into that organizational culture. B'lanna subsequently joined the Maquis and was part of Chakotay's crew. Since Chakotay's Maquis crew has joined forces with the Voyager crew to find their way home from the Delta quadrant B'lanna was chosen to serve as chief engineer over a Starfleet trained officer.

B'lanna is a brilliant engineer and especially abled in the area of temporal mechanics. She is included in this section because the character is half human and half Klingon and her last name is a Latino name. Furthermore, a Latina actress plays the character. The viewing audience has not yet been informed of B'lanna's family heritage, but since she is half human and carries a Latino last name it might very well be that one of her parents was Latino.

Conclusion

It appears that the Latino characters on ST could primarily be categorized as professionals. They have been white washed to the point of being unrecognizable in terms of ethnicity, they are novel in a white work setting, and speak only General English. Furthermore, the Latino characters have been members of the organization based on their skills and education rather than their relationships with white characters. Enrique was the only one that had any ethnic markers and he was killed.

What we haven't seen on ST in the way of Latino roles is characters that are identifiable as Latino who are in recurring or permanent roles. While Robert Beltran is Mexican American he plays a Native American on *Voyager*. The creator, writers, and directors of ST have not used any of the older derogatory stereotypes of Hispanics, but neither have they been inventive with them.

References

Alfred, J., R. (1996). *Censorship and Hollywood's Hispanic image: An interpretive filmography 1936-1995*. Westport Communication: Greewnwood Press.

Alicea, I.P. (1995). Sex, lies, & stereotypes: The true facts about Hispanic infidelity. *Hispanic*, 8(1), p4.

Fitzgerald, M. (1994). State of Hispanic America. *Editor & Publisher*,127(32), p.11

Garcia, E. (December 28, 1996). Honoring positive television portrayals of Latinos. *San Jose Mercury News*, pg. E1, E4.

Garcia, H. (1994). *Latinas: Hispanic women in the United States: The Hispanic experience in America*. New York: Franklin Watts.

Hadley-Garcia, G.(1990). *Hispanic Hollywood: The Latins in motion pictures*. A Citadel Press Book. New York: Carol Publishing Group.

Hershfield, J. (1996). *Mexican cinema/Mexican woman*, 1940-1950. Tucson: University of Arizona Press.

Huaco-Nuzum, C. (1996). (Re) Constructing Chicana, Mestiza representation: Frances Salome Espana's 'Spitfire'. In C. Noriega and A. Lopez (Eds.) *The Ethnic Eye: Latino Media Arts*. Minneapolis : University of Minnesota Press.

Penaloza, L. (1994). 'Ya Viene Atzlan! Latinos in US advertising. *Media Studies Journal*, 8(3), p 133.

Pettit, A. (1980). *Images of the Mexican American in fiction and film.* College Station: Texas A & M University Press.

Richard, Jr. A. (1996). *Censorship and Hollywoods's Hispanic image: An interpretive filmography.* Westport, Conn.: Greenwood Press.

Stein, M.L. (August 1994). Racial stereotyping and the media. *Editor & Publisher*, 127(32), p.12.

Taylor, C.(1995). Portrayals of African, Hispanic, and Asian Americans in magazine advertising. *American Behavioral Scientist*, 38(4), p. 608.

Woll, A. (1977). *The Latin image in American film.* Los Angeles: UCLA Latin American Center Publications.

Wilson, C.,II. and Gutiérrez, F. (1985). *Minorities and media: Diversity and the end of mass communication.* Beverly Hills: Sage Publications

Wilson, C. II and Gutiérrez, F. (1995) (2nd ed.) *Race, Multiculturalism and the Media: From Mass to Class*. Thousand Oaks, CA: Sage

Woll, A. (1980). Bandits and lovers :Hispanic images in American film. In Randall M. Miller, *The Kaleidoscopic Lens: How Hollywood Views Ethnic Groups.* US: Jerome S. Ozer

Zuzana, P. (1993). *The new American cinema: A continental project.* Austin, TX: University of Austin Press.

Chapter 10
Racial and Ethnic Images On Screen

In general an historical overview of popular culture:

> reveals stereotyping of non-whites to be contextual to the social, political, and economic realities of the moment and changes accordingly. At any given historical period the nature of a specific group's portrayal may be much more positive than the portrayal of another's. Basic negative traits, however, have never been totally abandoned, although specific instances of mass guilt purging periodically appear in entertainment media. (Wilson, II and Gutiérrez, 1995, p. 105)

So far, the four Star Trek series have been explored to determine how images of people of colour have been treated in the Star Trek universe. These images were examined in terms of the race/ethnicity of the actors and/or characters they played. Chapter 1 introduced the concepts of multicultural communication, stereotypes, and popular culture in order that the relationship(s) among them might be established. In Chapter 2 a framework for analyzing black images on screen was developed. Blacks in *The Original Series* was the topic of the 3rd chapter while Blacks in *The Next Generation* was the central topic of Chapter 4. Images of Blacks in *Deep Space Nine* and *Voyager* were the focal points of

Chapter 5 and in Chapter 6 Blacks as aliens and the slavery motif in *Deep Space Nine* were investigated. Asian images were analyzed in Chapter 7, Native American images in Chapter 8 and Latino images in Chapter 9.

In the first nine chapters some common ground for the discussion of images of people of colour was established. Furthermore the screen images of people of colour have been described and analyzed in general and specifically in Star Trek. The purpose of this exercise was to develop a framework from which to engage in critical analytical thinking about screen images, thus enabling viewers to be better consumers. Furthermore, with the appropriate descriptive and analytical tools we can begin to take stock of how the images we see on screen impact on self-concepts and multicultural relationships.

Based on the critical work completed in the previous chapters one can begin to speculate on the nature of racial and ethnic images on screen. There are several factors that influence those images and the relationships among them. Since these tasks have been accomplished you can begin the work of influencing the images we see on TV and in film.

The Nature of Theory

What I have been writing about here is the development of a theory.

> A theory is a set of interrelated constructs (concepts) definitions and propositions that present a systematic view of phenomena by specifying relations among variables, with the purpose of explaining and predicting the phenomena. (Kerlinger, 1973, p.9)

This definition says three things. One, a theory is a set of factual statements consisting of a set of ideas, which are connected and have been defined. These ideas are relevant to an object, person, or event. Two, a theory helps one to understand the relationships among the ideas, and in doing so, presents a systematic way of talking about and analyzing the object, person or, event described by the ideas. Finally, a theory explains objects, people or events by specifying which ideas are related and how they are related. This enables an observer to predict from one idea to another. Ultimately a good theory will allow one to exert control or influence over an object, person or event in order to achieve certain goals (Stacks and Hocking, 1992,p.28-30; Best, 1970,p.5-6)

The theory I have developed here based on the description and analysis of minority images on screen is called the **Theory of Racial and Ethnic Images on Screen** (TREIS). This theory provides several critical tools that will facilitate the analysis and evaluation of minority screen images. Those tools are as follows: (1) a taxonomy of mythic characters or stereotypes; (2) a method for identifying the exigencies (motives) for shaping African, Asian, Native American and Latino images in a particular manner; (3) a list of standard themes and contexts; (4) definitions of specific binary relationships prevalent in the themes; and (6) categories for the relationships between people of colour and whites.

The first basic premise of TREIS is that the images of people of colour on the screen are a function of the needs or demands of the dominant society; current stereotypes; marketability of the images; formula of the story; social and political trends; and pressure from activist groups. A second premise of the theory is that the racial and ethnic images on screen vary little from the mythic stereotypes developed in the late 1800's and early 1900's. The images are simply dressed-up or recycled for the current time periods. The third premise is that the racial and ethnic images on screen influence individual self-concepts, group identities, and multicultural relationships within a society.

The cultural objects that are under consideration here are the screen images of racial and ethnic groups in the US. The ideas that are related to these screen images include:

exigencies, mythic stereotypes, standard themes, standard contexts, binary interpersonal relationships, assimilated or non-assimilated into the larger community, and the impact of these images

The most difficult part of this analytical process would be to actually predict what images will occur on screen because often scripts are written years before they appear on TV or film. However, viewers can influence the images that are presented in the future by joining activists groups and fan clubs, and through letter writing campaigns to networks and production companies.

Exigencies

The term 'exigency' has been used in several previous chapters. In general it has been defined as a motive, the reason for doing something. Actually, the word exigency is more complex than that. Synonyms for exigency include needs, demands, crisis, difficulty, emergency, or predicament. As you know a crisis, emergency or predicament is a situation, which calls for an immediate response. It is something that must be taken care of or solved. Here are the exigencies shaping racial and ethnic images on screen.

War Efforts

When nations are at war several needs arise. They include the need to:

1. Populate the military forces
2. Raise public support for the war
3. Solidify potential allies
4. Increase the work force to fill in for those who are at war

At one time or another all of these needs have informed the shaping of racial and ethnic images on screen.

Activist Groups

Protests by activist groups such as the National Association for the Advancement of Colored People, the Anti-Defamation League, the American Indian Movement and La Raza have served to reduce some stereotyping of minority images.

Social Forces and Government Policy

Images are shaped to fit the consciousness of the dominant culture. Social and legal forces such as the civil rights movement, separatist movements, the Good Neighbor Policy and Affirmative Action have served to lessen the stereotyping of minority characters. They have encouraged new directions in race relations in the country (Bogle, 1995; Guerrero,1993; & Kern-Foxworth, 1994).

The Exploitation of Resources

When a power dominant group wishes to exploit the resources of another group it must generate support for such actions. Casting the group it wishes to exploit as animal-like, without social order, child-like, unclean, evil, etc does this. The people in danger of being exploited will also be cast as a threat to the continued biological, social, cultural and economic existence and well being of the power dominant. The less powerful are then referred to as the mongrel hordes, waves of illegal immigrants, baby factories and welfare seekers, savage and incompetent. These images are established so that the power dominant can take the natural resources that they want.

When there is a wish to exploit the human resources of a society, the actual people themselves, the images on screen will reflect the roles the dominant society wishes them to play. These can include farm laborers, railroad workers, house servants, entertainers, construction workers, house keepers, laundry people, engineers, computer experts, engineers and so forth and so on.

There are those who would suggest that there is a conspiracy to incarcerate more and more people of colour to exploit them for cheap labor (Davis, 1996). The wholesale incarceration of a people also keeps a major segment of the population out of the labor market leaving more jobs for the haves. Hence the proliferation of movies and television programs about criminals.

Japanese Americans were cast in a bad light during World War II and thrown into internment camps as a response to the bombing of Pearl Harbor. But there also were people who may have thought the Japanese had become too prosperous. Incarcerating them for national security reasons was a good excuse to seize properties.

Group Identification through Polarization

Racial and ethnic images on screen are often used to aid in the self-identification of whites. The fabricated impropriety of men and women of colour underscores the fabricated appropriateness of white men and women. People of colour provide a model of wrong in order that the correlation between white and right is strengthened. Stereotypes allow a method of self and group identification by projecting manufactured images onto another group. Screen images help to do this.

Revisionist History

A last force that shapes the images of racial and ethnic groups on screen is revisionist history. The revisionist movement is the trend among scholars to reinterpret American history. As more women and people of colour become scholars they are rewriting history in the light of their group experiences. Extremist also rewrite history to remove certain events such as the Holocaust.

These revisions of history make their way to the screen.

Taxonomy of Characters

On the screen, stereotypes serve as short cuts to character and story development. There are stereotypes of all racial and ethnic groups. The following are basic categories of stereotypes of people of colour. Each racial- ethnic group fits a particular niche. The setting of the story or the occupation of the character usually limits Black images. Asian characters are also most often shaped to fit a context or specific occupation. Native American characters tend to be fixed by time and place. And Latino characters are shaped to fit specific contexts. All of the racial and ethnic images fit a particular story theme and most are placed in subordinate positions to whites. In the upcoming sections stereotypes are categorized not by race or ethnicity, but by types.

The Humble Servants

Tom

The good Negro is content with his lot. A tom never turns against the white 'mass'. He remains hearty, submissive, stoic, generous, selfless and kind. One of the reasons the tom character has been around so long is that he never shows anger. (Boggle, 1995; Kern-Foxworth, 1994; and Van DeBurg, 1984).

Coolie

This character in its traditional configuration is comparable to the black house slave or servant character. The coolie was used for his cheap labor to build the railroad. He would frequently be seen in movies of the early west wearing the cone shaped hat. Coolie is efficient, quiet and ready to sacrifice for the master/employer.

The Man Servant

The Amerindian male was stereotyped as excellent man servants or sidekicks. The trade mark characteristics of the Indian man servant are his willingness to give his life to protect Kemo Sabe, to leave family and friends behind and to live only for the purposes of his master (Stedman, 1982).

Mammy

Mammy is a female coon. She is highly independent, very dark, fat, cantankerous with no sex appeal. This character has also been called a "handkerchief head". A variation on mammy is aunt jemima. She is a female tom blessed with religion (Bogle, 1995). She is sweet, jolly, good tempered, more polite than mammy, and never head strong.

Comics Buffoons

Buffoons come in all colours, black, Asians, Latinos, and Native Americans. S/he is included in the story as an amusement object and comic diversion. A buffoon can be no count, unreliable, crazy and lazy and is often characterized by his/her antics.

Mulattos, Half-Breeds, and the Almost White Asian

Any character that is a product of racial intermixing with whites can only be a symbol or caricature in a storyline. He/she is either likable and sympathetic, no doubt due to white blood or the victim of racial inheritance because s/he has been tainted with black, yellow, or red blood. Racially mixed characters bring moral ambiguity to a role. They present themselves as redeemable and fit companions for whites to explore the more sensual side of life with. If they are not redeemable then they become a moral lesson in the dangers of race mixing.

The racially mixed male would be a fine fellow if not for tainted blood. The racially mixed woman would be fit to marry a white man if not for her racially tainted blood. They are candidates for honorary "whitehood" or they are tormented souls due to their mixed racial heritage.

Worf of TNG and DS9 is a culturally mixed character. Molly and Yoshi O'Brien, the children of Miles and Keiko, are racially mixed. Dianna Troi of TNG is half human and half Betazoid. B'lanna Torres of DS9 is half Klingon and half human. And, our Mr. Spock of TOS was half human and half Vulcan. If Worf and Jadzia of DS9 have children their children will be the first interracial children not of human biological lineage.

Women of Colour Stereotypes
The Seductress/Dark Lady/Traitor

The seductress is often a black, Asian or Latino woman who woos men into dangerous or fatal situations. The seductress could also be a woman who men fall for because of her neediness, but the love causes the man to put himself in jeopardy. Kassidy Yates on DS9 began as a seductress. Her character has now been redeemed with a jail sentence. Marta, a consort of Garth at the Elba II penal colony was a green Orion woman, appeared in *Whom Gods Destroy*: TOS, She sought to seduce Kirk.

A subcategory of the seductress is "the dark lady". Originally used as a descriptor of Latino women this label could be applied to any woman of colour who betrays her relatives or people because of her love for a white male or her need to be identified with the white community.

Dragon Lady

The dragon lady is a derivative of the Asian mastermind. The dragon lady is deadly, ruthless and frequently is involved with drug smuggling, spying and plots to destroy the West. She is interested in power. She is a combination villain and seductress. Martia, the shape shifter in ST: *The Undiscovered Country* was such a woman. Uhnari was believed to be such a woman in TNG episode *Aquiel.* And Nona, the wife of Tyree in *A Private Little War* :TOS fit this category (A white actress in dark make-up played Nona). And, last but not least, the Klingon sisters B'etor and Lursa are certainly dragon ladies. They have appeared in TNG (*Redemption)* and DS9 (*Past Prologue*).

The Geisha

The Geisha is a female Asian entertainer and companion. She is trained in many of the arts including music, painting and theatre. One of her most sought after talents is the art of conversation. The Geisha is often portrayed as the ideal woman, the one every man would want. She is intelligent, yet does not upstage the male.

Whores and Prostitutes

Black, Asian and Latino women as prostitutes is a widespread image. If a woman in the sex industry is Asian she is called a suzie wong mythic type. If the character is black she is referred to as a whore. These women use their bodies to seduce men, to divert them from the narrow path. She implements his sexual fantasies and does not bother him again until he wants her.

The Princess and the Squaw

There are basically two images of Native American

women: the princess/maiden and the squaw. The princess is often patterned after the Pocahontas myth. She is earthy and innocent. The most important thing about her is that she is willing to risk her own life to save that of her white lover. Miramanee in *The Paradise Syndrome:* TOS fulfilled this mythic role.

The princess image alternates with the squaw. The squaw is usually a silent mother, wife or daughter going about her duties with an humble air. She does not speak much and is obedient. Most often the squaw is over weight and does not have the sex appeal of the Indian maiden.

Earthmother, Sage, Spiritual Wellspring

Women of colour can often be found in nurturing roles. They could be the earth mother, the sage or spiritualist. Kai Opaka of DS9 and Guinan of TNG could be labeled as such.

Stereotypes of Men of Colour

Destroyers of Western Culture and Ravagers of White Women

Black Bucks

The black buck is a big, bad man, oversexed, savage, violent and frenzied with great lust for white women. The black brute is barbaric and out to raise havoc. He dominates with physical violence and is depicted as suffering from sexual repression; he occupies the status of subhuman or feral. The major differences between the black buck and the black brute are intensity & duration of emotions and extremism in behavior. Early images of Klingons fit this classification.

The Mastermind Villain

The mastermind is an astute, strong character who plots the destruction of Western civilization (Hoppenstand, 1983). The destruction of Western civilization (Hoppenstand, 1983). The person understands and utilizes Western science and Eastern magic. An army of assassins are always at his service. Khan of *The Wrath of Khan* was an evil mastermind.

A variation on the mastermind stereotype of the Asian male is the Chinatown gangster. They frequently appear in martial arts and drug stories.

The Savage and Bandidos

The savage is one who is uncivilized (does not act like white people). He is blood thirsty and violent, displaying little regard for human life. The savage does not work and has strange religious practices. The savage lusts after white women and will rape one every time he has an opportunity to do so.

Immigrants

The immigrant stereotype is often associated with Asians and Hispanics. Americans still do not view these groups of people as "Americans". They are the interlopers, the ones threatening to overrun American society. Immigrants are viewed as potential destroyers of Western culture, or more accurately immigrants of colour. This is ironic in view of the fact that all of the people of European descent here came as immigrants.

The Inscrutable Detective

Charlie Chan exemplified the inscrutable detective, an Oriental version of Sherlock Holmes. He has exceptional powers of deduction and often spouts what passes for Chinese philosophy along the way of the investigation. The detective is always self-effacing and at the service of whites.

The Fighters/Gladiators/Athletes

Asian, black and Latino males often appear as people especially good at physical endeavors such as martial arts experts, boxers, and bullfighters and those modern day gladiators, the athletes. They can fight for the good or evil. They are able to take on huge groups of enemies and never be defeated. As they fight the enemy the experts deliver words of wisdom.

Ceremonial Leaders

Ceremonial leaders are those people throughout the minority communities who act as gatekeepers of information and can be used as enemies of the white community or people to manage the minority community. They usually have very little real power. These include the chief, preacher, monk, priests.

The Preacher/Priests

In stories involving black, Asian and Latino communities the preacher/priest is a frequent character. He is the leader of the church and is frequently a shaper of community opinion. He can be cast as a manipulator of the community to the advantage of whites or hey can be cast as a revolutionary.

The Chief

Chiefs lead the tribes. They are shown as strong warriors or wise old men. Very often they have a daughter. The chiefs meet in council, negotiate with the white people, plot to kill white people, lead their people into oblivion on reservations or they are blood thirsty and bent on revenge.

The Shaman/Medicine Man/Witch Doctor

In many cultures where traditional medicine is practiced there exists shamans. The medicine man is often cast as an enemy who inflames the tribe against white people or a traditional doctor who can heal everything while spouting lines of wisdom.

The Victims

At the bottom, being a victim is a standard character for people of colour. Blacks, Asians, Hispanics and Native Americans are frequently characters that are in hopeless situations and must be rescued by a white avenger.

The New Mythic Type

Professional People of Colour

The professional person of colour stereotype grows out of the persistent appearance of professional men and women identifiable by race and ethnicity. What we see first are people of colour who do not fit the traditional stereotypes: the untyped or colorless black, Asian, Latino or Native American. The characters are so enmeshed in white culture that except for physical features s/he can not be distinguished from whites. These are characters for which all ethnic edges have been sanded down so that while they look like a person of colour everything about them is expressed in a white cultural context.

Then the "untyped" and "colorless" race/ethnic identified character appears frequently enough to form a new category, the "professional person of colour". These characters have been prevalent since the 60's and 70's. Both men and women fit this category. They are intelligent, educated, career people, functioning in integrated work settings and existing in isolation from other people of colour. They speak General American English and work by the book. Frequently the professional person of colour is devoid of ethnic markers. Unlike the faithful sidekick the professional person of colour either holds an autonomous position within an organization or s/he is a member of a team.

What makes the professional person of colour mythic character new and different is his/her autonomy in the organization and the amount of power wielded in the work environment. The professional person of colour will have a measure of formal power inherent in the position s/he holds within the organization rather than power derived from association with a white person. The professional person of colour is also different from other mythic characters in that s/he works as a member of a cohesive team, rather than as a servant to the team. One of the functions of the professional person of colour is to act as a conservatising force in the organization. They most often spout the party line, support the status quo and insist on playing by the book.

Most of the people of colour on Star Trek have been professional mythic types all the way from Uhura, Sulu, Geordi, Worf, Sisko, Bashir, and Kim, to Chakotay & Tuvok.

The Guises

As the decades passed variations of the mythic characters appeared in several guises and created the illusion that the screen representation of people of colour had moved beyond the stereotypes. Guises are variations on mythic characters designed to fit current images. There is a bit more flexibility in the role boundaries, with traits that coincide with dominant culture behaviors. Often guises are difficult to recognize and may appear to be new. They include villains, court jesters, servants, entertainers, troubled people, angry militants (Bogle, 1995) and care taker administrators.

The villain is often used to camouflage black bucks, bandidos, dragon ladies, and evil masterminds. Drug dealers and pimps are popular 90's versions of the black buck. Court jesters camouflage the coon and servants are thinly disguised house slaves.

The caretaker administrator has been a popular guise in the 90's. It is a variation on the tom and coolie characters and the faithful servant guise. The caretaker administrator is a person of colour in a position of responsibility without authority. The role could be that of captain of a police precinct, mayor, or manager in a company. Caretakers are considered such because, while they are in visible roles of responsibility, they have no real decision-making power: he or she is there simply to facilitate the matriculation of paper work. Caretaker administrators usually serve as foils for the white main characters that work outside of the system.

In the 80's and 90's the guises have broadened to include the secretary, nurse, teacher, school principal and barkeep. These are all societal roles that involve nurturing and looking after the needs of others to the exclusion of self.

Standard Themes

Several themes emerged that dominated stories with minority characters. For blacks the list included slavery and the old south, blacks as a social problem, integration and separatism, as well as the themes of the changing south, the new south, and colour blind society.

Wong and Jones identified themes involving Asians as miscegenation (interracial love affairs), tragic love affairs and cases of mistaken identity (Marchetti, 1993, p.2). The dangers of race mixing are also frequently explored among Asian male-white female liaisons. The subjugation of Euroamerican society by Asians is a popular theme. We see this theme in allegorical form in many international spy thrillers.

Clifton (1990) provides an excellent list of standard Indian myth themes. They include the edenic people and context, authentic spirituality, harmony with nature, collective guilt and redemption, egalitarianism, health and long life, genocide, struggle and survival, dominance and freedom, selfhood and identity, racial harmony, and the advantages and disadvantages of interracial love (p.386). The advantages of interracial love are frequently explored through the story of a white-male tribal woman relationship.

When Latino characters are used standard themes to be explored include white men sowing their "wild oats", miscegenation, racial pollution, Catholic tyranny, government corruption, and government ineptitude.

Standard Contexts

Just as there are standard themes that feature people of colour there are also standard contexts in which they appear. Each racial or ethnic group will be placed in stereotypical places.

Blacks

For black characters the standard contexts are the south, churches, prisons, ghettos, inner cities, crime ridden & drug infested areas, the sex industry and entertainment. Now that blacks have moved into the professional ranks they will be shown in educational settings, judicial arenas, and police precincts.

Asians

TV series and movies involving Asians often have similar contexts in which the stories take place. Broad contexts include an Asian country or city; Chinatown in a European or American city; or an Asian theater of war. Specific locales consist of the work place such as herbal shops, Chinese restaurants or bars, the laundry and high-tech businesses. Other locations include the martial arts studio, the temple or monastery, a drug/crime infested area, or a place shrouded in the mystery of the occult.

Native Americans

Standard contexts for Native Americans are an unprotected environment and the frontier. Colonial America and the west during the 1700's and 1800's are settings for Amerindians since according to the myth they are caught in the past. The Southwest territory and Texas are other contexts in which Native Americans will be found. Lastly, pastoral environments or edenic settings often feature Native Americans.

Latinos/Hispanics/Chicanos

Latino characters or faces are used to indicate diversity in the crowd through the use of Hispanic surnames. They can be found in stories of the barrio/ghetto, poverty and crime ridden areas. In order to indicate that a setting is in Texas, the southwest, or south of the US border Mexican characters and locales are often used. Of course, Latinos are a favorite in vacation spots and the Catholic church is also a favored setting.

Binary Relationships

Imbedded in the standard themes incorporating whites and people of colour in close associations are certain formulaic binary interpersonal relationships. There are two characters orbiting together, like two stars. They are the huckfinn fixation (Bogle, 1995) and the miss daisy syndrome, the crusoe-friday scenario, the tonto-kemo sabe script, the lethal weapon pattern, and the green hornet-kato model. At the center of most of these relationships is the issue of white male-man of colour bonding.

Whites Playing Ethnic Roles

In every area of film, TV, or theater it has been unusual to have an actor of colour play a character of colour, at least not a lead character. The first African American lead characters on stage were played by white actors in "blackface". In fact blackness as a symbol was so important to white producers that when African American actors started actually playing black characters in what were called "race films" their skin was darkened (Snead, 1997, pg. 25). This was the case with Lena Horne and Dorthy Danderidge.

When playing Asian characters white actors worked in "yellowface" (Ray, 1994). Film maker and critic Satyajit Ray, in his book *Our Films, Their Films,* spoke about this practice in the 40's and 50's Hollywood. In fact, two of the most famous Asian characters, Charlie Chan and Kwai Chang Caine of Kung-Fu, were played by white actors.

Brislin, in *Images that Injure* (1996), complained of the same phenomena for Pacific Islanders. He refers to white actors playing Pacific Islanders as acting in "brownface". The same can be said about white actors playing Mexicans, they are doing it in brownface. Whites playing Native Americans could be said to be working in "redface".

Relationships to Larger Community

People of colour are usually shown in one of two relationships with the larger society. They are either novel characters, totally assimilated into the dominant culture, or they are in segregated situations dealing primarily with people of colour. There are few, if any TV programs or films, that successfully show integrated settings. There is either a lone person of colour in a white setting, a lone white person in a minority community, all white communities, or all minority communities.

The Impact of the Images

I would hardly say that screen images shape the American experience. I would say that screen images simultaneously reflect and create stereotypical images in society. For the past 20 years I have been using an activity in class to help students come to understand who shaped their self-concepts, their values, their attitudes. I ask them to list ten groups that influenced them. They need not be formally organized groups with membership cards. I was looking for any group that an individual saw him/herself as a member of. By analyzing these groups an individual can gain insights into who he or she is. In the late 70's to mid 80's students could list on the average about 8 groups. They included sports groups, civic organizations, youth groups, religious institutions, communities, friendship circles, family groupings, school communities, hobby groups, etc. I began to notice a change in the late 80's, they were able to name fewer and fewer groups.

As a youngster and teen-ager I belonged to several groups. I was a member of the church choir, church youth fellowship, school choir, debate team, 4-H Club, the African American community, the Rowe family, the Byrd family, and I was the third member of a trio of girls who went from junior high to college together. My twelve-year-old son is limited to his school classmates, his work crew, and a few young men in the community. My college students usually name their families, the college population, perhaps their occupational group and that's about it as far as whom they relate to. More often when they talk about identity they talk about a state identity or a regional identity. So how do they find out who they are? Not from direct life experiences with groups of people, but from highly individualized, segmented experiences or popular culture. Racial and ethnic images in popular culture therefore, are very important. Screen images can confirm or disconfirm a self-concept. Story lines can validate or invalidate life choices and experiences.

In 1996 my 12-year-old was astonished to see Mali Vai Washington playing tennis on TV. He said, "Wow, I didn't know black people played tennis". The fact that blacks played tennis as a profession was brought home only because he saw it on television. In 1995 I invited a white female to my home. This woman had had extremely limited dealings with African Americans. She hesitated at the invitation and finally asked, “What will your neighbors think about a white woman coming to your house? What will your children think about seeing a white woman there?” She had only her images from popular culture to guide her.

A young student of mine who is Filipino wishes to disown his ethnic heritage because he only knows Filipinos as a poverty stricken people. He “knows’ this from what he has seen in the media. He has not been to the Philippines.

A Chinese American student taking a speech course with me was completing the assignment of giving a 5-8 minute speech about his ethnic heritage. His entire speech was built around debunking popular cultural myths about Asians, not about his ethnic heritage. To him, the popular myths shaped who he was or was not, his identity was not grounded in any teaching from his family or search of his own.

The Cherokee nation was only something that he had heard about in cowboy flicks until a young Chicano student of mine conducted his research project to fulfill requirements for his ethnic heritage assignment.

The faces that people see in popular culture, the stories they tell that bind the society together, the environments in which they see people like themselves are very powerful. These images, these myths can serve to reinforce the status quo or move viewers toward new visions of who they are and what they can do.

Conclusion

Visual and verbal messages play a profound role in social memory as news reel footage of dogs and fire hoses being used to control civil rights marchers clearly indicates. In addition to influencing group memories visual and verbal messages in popular culture also impact on general audiences, individual audience members and segments of audiences as well.

As with all things man made Star Trek is not perfect. I’ve mentioned several points during the previous chapters. There is a need to see more women have significant friendships on the series and we definitely need to see more fat people. We need to see an Asian character in a relationship with another Asian character and it would be good to have permanent Latino characters with their ethnicity in tact. I would like to see black characters in relation to black characters and some in positions that are semi-skilled. And of course they have got to do more with Native Americans characters. In other words the creative stall driving Trek still has new territory to cover. Even so they have already taken us across the galaxy and into the future.

As popular culture continues to provide the public with rhetorical visions and fantasies that bind us together several steps must be taken. Characters of colour must be shown in less stereotypical story lines and contexts. Audiences must see more Asian, Latino, and Native American characters outside of the stereotypical roles. Writers, directors and producers must find new ways to be inclusive in their works. And lastly audiences must become critical consumers. Informed consumers force products to change and be improved. This must be done so that film and television can reach audiences, cover news, and provide entertainment to a multicultural, multiracial society in a manner that not only generates profit, but also enhances human potential.

References

Best, J. (1970) (2nd ed.). *Research in education.* Englewoods Cliffs, NJ: Prentice-Hall, Inc.

Bogle, D. (1995) (3rd ed.). *Toms, coons, mulattos, mammies, & bucks: An interpretive history of blacks in blacks in film.* New York: Continuum.

Guerrero, E. (1993). *Framing blackness: The African American image in film.* Philadelphia: Temple University Press.

Kerlinger, F. (1973). (2nd ed.) *Foundations of behavioral research.* New York: Holt, Rinehart and Winston, Inc.

Littlejohn, S. (1995)(5th ed.). *Theories of speech communication.* Belmont,CA: Wadsworth Publishing Company.

Stacks, D. and Hocking, J. (1992). *Essentials of communication research.* Harper Collins, Publishers.

Stedman, R. (1982). *Shadows of the Indian: Stereotypes in American culture.* Norman, OK: University of Oklahoma Press.

Van DeBurg, W. (1984). *Slavery and race in American popular culture.* Madison: University of Wisconsin Press.

Movie Review: *Independence Day*

While *Independence Day* was released in 1996 it is still a family favorite with high video sales and rentals. The basic premise of the movie: an alien space-craft sought to destroy the major cities of the Earth. The short title of the movie was ID4 because Earth forces beat the aliens on the 4th of July. I was very excited about this movie because it had all of the mythic characters, but not racially coded characters.

The hero of the film was a young African American, Captain Steven Hiller (Will Smith). Beside him flew his sidekick Jimmy (Harry Connick Jr.). The hero had a significant other, Jasmine (Vivica Fox). Then there was US President Whitemore (Bill Pullman) and the First Lady, Marilyn, played by Mary McDonnell. Randy Quaid played a fallen Vietnam pilot named Russell. And, last but not least, Jeff Goldblum played the 90's obligatory computer hero. This movie was excellent because the roles were counter-cast in terms of race/ethnicity. In other words, the characters were not cast according to the stereotypical status roles for people of colour. Even so the movie was not preachy, nor did it appear contrived.

The writers and directors of *Independence Day* showed us characters that we had not seen before. Captain Hiller, the young black pilot was not white washed. He actually spoke black dialect at a level that would be appropriate for a college educated black man. It was quite refreshing. And, unlike the few movies that show black heroes, like *Bad Boys*, another Will Smith movie, the hero in this movie was paired with a black woman. Too often the black hero is paired with a white woman as an apologia for the hero's blackness.

Jimmy, Hiller's sidekick, was the supporter. He died early in the film and in two or three scenes he spoke black dialect. In fact at one point he imitated Jessie Jackson. Usually it is the black sidekick who speaks just like the hero. Here it was the white sidekick speaking like the black hero. This was a small, but nice touch.

Jasmine, Hiller's girlfriend, had a significant role in the storyline. I was glad to see the black hero have a black woman in his life. For some reason her job was a strip teaser. Many black women viewers criticized that "diminishment" of the character. However, I could identify because my own biological mother was a stripper, so Jamine was alright with me. Jamine, saved her child, found and took care of the President's wife, and drove a heavy equipment truck picking up the wounded. She was a heroine in her own right.

The Presidential and First Lady roles were atypical. The President actually went into battle and in pure fictional style he was not killed. Unfortunately the First Lady was not so lucky, she died of her wounds.

Normally the Commander in Chief would have stayed in the bunker and the black female lead, not the President's wife would have been killed.

Russell, an alcoholic Vietnam veteran, was the pilot that delivered the final blow to the aliens. He flew his plane right into the mothership's core reactor. The black hero did not have to sacrifice his life!

Lastly, Jeff Goldblum played the computer nerd/expert. In these days and times computer experts must be in the picture. Twenty years ago they were the nerds, now they are the heroes. In addition to that David, the Goldblum character, was identifiably Jewish. No-no-no, not by looks (there is no such thing), but by cultural traits revealed in the story. His father spoke of their Jewish faith, his father prayed during the final battle.

Of course, there were problems with the film as there are with any film. However, I think those problems were far outweighed by the boldness of the non-traditional casting.

My score****

Movie Review: ***Cinderella***

This ambitious made for TV movie aired in the Fall of 1997. It was a Disney film with Whitney Houston as the executive producer. What was so ambitious about making the Cinderella movie? First, the damsel in distress saved by the handsome prince is not a story told in the African American community. It is not part of our mythology. Secondly, the story as produced by Whitney Houston, used non-traditional casting. In this case the casting was colour-blind. These two things made the production ambitious.

Brandy played Cinderella. She is a young black singer and actress with her own show, *Moesha.* With an African American actress in the lead role, the story had to be modified in some sense. The fairy god-mother, played by Houston, encouraged Cinderella to take charge of her life and that was great. However, Cinderella did have to remind the fairy god-mother that she couldn't get to the ball without a carriage, nor could she go without a gown. (Gosh darn, it's hard to pull yourself up by your bootstraps when you don't have any boots!).

Cinderella's family was a typical one for California and many other multiethnic cities in the US. It was a multiethnic and blended family. Cinderella's father (who was dead) was married to her white stepmother played by actress, Bernadette Peters. The stepmother had two daughters, one black and one white. The benefit of that was that we could dismiss the idea that Cinderella was being treated like the stepchild that she was because of her colour.

Now, let's get to the Prince and his family. Whoopi Goldberg played the Queen Mother, while Victor Garber, a white actor, played the King. An Asian Filipino actor, Paolo Montalban, played the Prince and he did an excellent job. Montalban (no kin to Ricardo) is very photogenic and obviously staged trained and experienced. I predict that he is a face we will be seeing much more of in the future.

Anyway, both Disney and Houston stepped out from the crowd. I don't know of a major production where the romantic male lead was Asian. Unfortunately here is where Whitney and Disney fell down on the job: they did nothing to promote the Asian Prince. Traditionally an Asian male would never be seen as a romantic male, but in fairy-tale land he was. To see a black Cinderella and an Asian Prince was electrifying!

On the real life social scene interracial dating and marriages are increasing. However the traditional pairings among interracial couples are black men/white women and white men and Asian or Latina women. Numerically the people who are left out of these equations are black women, Asian men, and Mexican men.

Seeing a black female/Asian male pairing on the screen was very new. The only other place I've seen it was in Jackie Chan's *Rumble in the Bronx.*

And, while we are more likely to see black men with Asian women than vice versa, NBC's *Today Show* nixed the idea of pairing Brian Gumble with Connie Chung for fear that the show would have a "Third World look". Apparently that was not the case with this Disney production.

There were a few problems with the production itself. The scene when the Prince's valet, played by Jason Alexander, announced to the village that there was going to be a ball was boring. After the first song in that scene the dancing went on forever; much longer than we needed to get the idea that the village was happy and the valet had a lot to do.

The other seriously problematic scene was the ball dance itself. There were two problems here; no black male dancers in the crowd and all of the girls were wearing virtually the same dress. The lack of black male dancers implied that black men don't do ballroom dancing. The problem with the dresses was that they were all in the blue to violet range. They seemed to be only variations on a theme and we all know that when young ladies go to the ball they want their dress to stand out! This variation on a theme ball dress then muted the impact of Cinderella's garment. Actually her gown was an excellent creation for a young girl. However, Cinderella's dress seemed to be the original while everyone else's was a bad copy. Having all of the dresses in the same colour range made for a dark, almost monochromatic scene. Fortunately, even these problems did not mitigate the move on the part of Houston and Disney to film a Cinderella story that was both bold and inclusive.

I myself had never watched the story because it was the tale of a helpless white girl being rescued by a prince, something outside of my experiential possibilities and wildest dreams. With the colour-blind casting I actually watch the movie. I could hone in on the stepdaughter experience and the destructive, defeating influence of verbal abuse. When the stepmother said to Cinderella something to the effect of "even if you clean yourself up and put on a clean dress you would still be common because your mother was common" I was there!
My score ***

About the Author

Marquita L. Byrd is an Associate Professor of Communication Studies at San Jose State University. She teaches courses in interpersonal, intercultural, and multicultural communication at both the undergraduate and graduate levels. As if you didn't already know, Dr. Byrd is an avid Star Trek fan and plans to write additional works on women and the disabled in Star Trek. She's hoping that her next assignment will be ambassador to Ligon II.

Marquita L. Byrd
1997